JUST ANOTHER JUDGEMENT DAY

JUST ANOTHER JUDGEMENT DAY

SIMON R. GREEN

ACE BOOKS, NEW YORK

THE BERKLEY PUBLISHING GROUP
Published by the Penguin Group
Penguin Group (USA) Inc.
375 Hudson Street, New York, New York 10014, USA
Penguin Group (Canada), 90 Eglinton Avenue East, Suite 700, Toronto, Ontario M4P 2Y3, Canada
(a division of Pearson Penguin Canada Inc.)
Penguin Books Ltd., 80 Strand, London WC2R 0RL, England
Penguin Group Ireland, 25 St. Stephen's Green, Dublin 2, Ireland (a division of Penguin Books Ltd.)
Penguin Group (Australia), 250 Camberwell Road, Camberwell, Victoria 3124, Australia
(a division of Pearson Australia Group Pty. Ltd.)
Penguin Books India Pvt. Ltd., 11 Community Centre, Panchsheel Park, New Delhi—110 017, India
Penguin Group (NZ), 67 Apollo Drive, Rosedale, North Shore 0632, New Zealand
(a division of Pearson New Zealand Ltd.)
Penguin Books (South Africa) (Pty.) Ltd., 24 Sturdee Avenue, Rosebank, Johannesburg 2196,
South Africa

Penguin Books Ltd., Registered Offices: 80 Strand, London WC2R 0RL, England

This is an original publication of The Berkley Publishing Group.

This is a work of fiction. Names, characters, places, and incidents either are the product of the author's imagination or are used fictitiously, and any resemblance to actual persons, living or dead, business establishments, events, or locales is entirely coincidental. The publisher does not have any control over and does not assume any responsibility for author or third-party websites or their content.

First edition: January 2009

Library of Congress Cataloging-in-Publication Data

Green, Simon R., 1955–
    Just another judgement day / Simon R. Green.—1st ed.
        p. cm.—(Nightside ; 9)
    ISBN 978-0-441-01674-7
    1. Taylor, John (Fictitious character)—Fiction. 2. Private investigators—England—London—Fiction. 3. London (England)—Fiction. I. Title.

    PR6107.R44J87 2009
    823'.92—dc22

                                                                                    2008043274

PRINTED IN THE UNITED STATES OF AMERICA

10   9   8   7   6   5   4   3   2   1

JUST ANOTHER
JUDGEMENT DAY

In the Nightside, that sour secret hidden heart of London, it's always three o'clock in the morning and the dawn never comes. Streets full of sin and cellars full of suffering, magic in the air and mystery around every corner; hot neon, hotter music, and the hottest scenes anywhere. Good and bad and everything in between. Dreams come true in the Nightside, especially the bad ones. Everything's available, for the right price. So shop till you drop, dance till you bleed, and party like Judgement Day will never come.

I'm John Taylor, private eye. I have a gift for finding things, and people. I won't promise you justice, or revenge, or your heart's desire. But I will find the truth for you, every damned bit of it.

Welcome to the Nightside. Watch your back. Or someone will steal it.

ONE

Retro Voodoo and the Spirit of Dorian Gray

You don't go to Strangefellows for the good company. You don't go to the oldest bar in the world for open-mike contests, trivia quizzes, or theme nights. And certainly not for happy hour. You don't go there for the food, which is awful, or the atmosphere, which is worse. You go to Strangefellows to drink and brood and plan your revenges on an uncaring world. And you go there because no-one else will have you. The oldest bar in the world has few rules and fewer standards, except perhaps for *Mind your own damned business.*

I was sitting in a booth at the back of the bar that particular night, with my business partner and love, Suzie Shooter. I was nursing a glass of wormwood brandy, and Suzie was drinking Bombay Gin straight from the bottle. We were winding down, after a case that hadn't gone well for anyone. We didn't talk. We don't, much; we don't feel the need. We're easy in each other's company.

My long white trench coat was standing to attention beside our table. I've always believed in having a coat that can look after itself. People gave it plenty of room, especially after I happened to mention that I hadn't fed it recently. The trench coat is my one real affectation; I think a private eye should look the part. And while people are distracted by the cliché, they tend not to notice me running rings around them. I'm tall, dark, and handsome enough from a distance, and no matter how bad things get, I never do divorce work.

Suzie Shooter, also known as Shotgun Suzie, was wearing her usual black motorcycle leathers, complete with steel studs and chains and two bandoliers of bullets crossing over her impressive chest. She has long blonde hair, a striking face with a strong bone structure, and the coldest blue gaze you'll ever see. My very own black leather Valkyrie. She's a bounty hunter, in case you hadn't guessed.

We were young, we were in love, and we'd just killed a whole bunch of people. It happens.

Strangefellows was full that night . . . the night he came to the Nightside. We thought it was just another night, and the joint was jumping. Roger Miller's "King of the Road" was pumping out of hidden speakers, and thirteen members of the Tribe of Gay Barbarians were line-dancing to it, complete with sheathed broadswords, fringed leather chaps, and tall ostrich-feather head-dresses. Two wizened Asian conjurers in long, sweeping robes had set their tiny pet dragons to fighting, and already a crowd had gathered to place bets. (Though I had heard rumours that only the dragons were real; the conjurers were merely illusions generated by the tiny dragons so they could get around in public without being bothered.) Half a dozen female ghouls, out on a hen night, were getting happily loud and rowdy over a bottle of Mother's Ruination and demanding another bucket of lady-fingers. It probably helps to be a ghoul if you're going to eat the bar snacks at Strangefellows. And a young man was weeping into his beer because he'd given his heart to his one true love, and she'd put it in a bottle and sold it to a sorcerer in return for a pair of Manolo Blahnik shoes.

In a more private part of the bar, a small gathering of soft ghosts were flickering in and out around a table that wasn't always there. Soft ghosts—the hazy images of men and women who'd travelled too far from their home worlds and lost their way. Now they drifted through the dimensions, from world to world and reality to reality, trying desperately to find their way home, fading a little more with every failure. A lot of them find their way to Strangefellows, and stop off for a brief rest. Alex Morrisey keeps the memories of old wines stored in Klein bottles, just for them. Though what they pay him with is beyond me. The soft ghosts clustered together, whispering the names of lands and heroes and histories that no-one else had ever heard of and comforting each other as best they could.

Alex Morrisey is the owner and main bartender of Strangefellows, last of a long line of miserable bastards. He always wears black, right down to designer shades and a snazzy black beret pushed well back on his head to hide his spreading bald spot, because, he says, anything else would be hypocritical. Alex wakes up every evening pissed off at the entire world, and his mood only gets worse as the night wears on. He has a gift for short-changing people, doesn't wash the glasses nearly often enough, and mixes the worst martinis in the world. Wise men avoid his special offers.

Strangefellows attracts a varied crowd, even for the Nightside, and Alex has to be able to cater to all kinds of trade, with everything from Shoggoth's Old and Very Peculiar, Angel's Urine (not a trade name, unfortunately), and Delerium Treebeard (taste that chlorophyll!). Alex will never say where he obtained some of the rarer items on his shelves, but I knew for a fact he had contacts in other dimensions and realities, including a whole bunch of disreputable alchemists, tomb-robbers, and Time-travellers.

I poured myself another glass of the wormwood brandy, and Suzie tossed aside her empty gin bottle and reached for another. Both our hands were steady, despite everything we'd been through earlier. A Springheel Jack meme had entered the Nightside through a Timeslip, sneaking in from an alternate Victorian England. The meme had spread unnaturally quickly, infecting and transforming the minds of everyone it came into contact with. Soon there were hundreds of Springheel Jacks, raging through the streets, cutting a bloody path through unsuspecting revellers. Every bounty hunter in the Nightside got the call, and I went along with Suzie, to keep her company.

We killed the Jacks as fast as they manifested, but the

meme spread faster than we could stamp it out. Bounty hunters filled the Nightside streets with the sound of gunfire, and bodies piled up while blood ran thickly in the gutters. We couldn't save any of them. The meme had completely overwritten their personalities. In the end I had to use my gift to find the source of the infection, the Timeslip itself. I put in a call to the Temporal Engineers, they shut it down, and that was finally that. Except for all the bodies lying in the streets. The ones the Springheel Jacks killed, and the ones we killed. Sometimes you can't save everyone. Sometimes all you can do . . . is kill a whole bunch of people.

Business as usual, in the Nightside.

There was a sudden drop in the noise level as someone new entered the bar. People actually stopped what they were doing to follow the progress of the new arrival as he strode majestically through the packed bar. In a place noted for its eccentrics, extreme characters, and downright lunatics, he still stood out.

A tall and slender figure, with a gleaming black face and an air of aristocratic disdain, he wore a bright yellow frock coat over a powder-blue jerkin and green-and-white-striped trousers. Calfskin boots and white satin gloves completed the ensemble. He didn't look like he belonged in Strangefellows, but then, I would have been hard-pressed to name anywhere he might have looked at home. He stalked arrogantly through the speechless crowd, and they let him pass untouched, awed by the presence of so much fashion in one person. He was too weird even for us; an exotic butterfly in a dark place. And, of course, he was heading straight for my table.

He swayed to a halt right before me, looked down his nose at me, ignored Suzie completely, which is never wise, and struck a dramatic pose.

"I am Percy D'Arcy!" he said. "*The* Percy D'Arcy!" He looked at me as though that was supposed to mean something.

"Good for you," I said generously. "It's not everyone who could bear up under a name like that, but you it suits. Now what do you want, Percy? I have some important drinking and brooding to be getting on with."

"But...I'm Percy D'Arcy! Really! You must have seen me in the glossies, and on the news shows. It isn't a fabulous occasion unless I'm there to grace it with my presence!"

"You're not a celebrity, are you?" I said cautiously. "Only I should point out Suzie has a tendency to shoot celebrities on general principles. She says they have a tendency to get too loud."

Percy actually curled his lip, and made a real production out of it, too. "Please! A celebrity? Me? I...am a *personality*! Famous just for being me! I'm not some mere actor, or singer. I'm not functional; I'm decorative! I am a dashing man about town, a wastrel and a drone and proud of it. I add charm and glamour to any scene simply by being there!"

"You're getting loud, Percy," I said warningly. "What do you do, exactly?"

"Do? I'm rich, dear fellow, I don't have to *do* anything. I have made myself into a living work of art. It is enough that I exist, that people may adore me."

Suzie made a low, growling noise. We both looked at her nervously.

"Your existence as a work of art could come to an abrupt end any moment now," I said. "If you don't leave off fancying yourself long enough to explain what it is you want with me."

Percy D'Arcy pouted, in a wounded sort of way, and pulled over a chair so he could sit down facing me. He gave the seat a good polish with a monogrammed silk handkerchief first, though. He shot Suzie an uncertain glance, then concentrated on me. I didn't blame him. Suzie gets mean when she's on her second bottle.

"I have need of your services, Mr. Taylor," Percy said stiffly, as though such directness was below him. "I am told you find things. Secrets, hidden truths, and the like."

"Those are the kinds of things that usually need finding, yes," I said. "What do you want me to find, Percy?"

"It's not that simple." He looked round the bar, looking at everything except me while he gathered his courage. Then he turned back, took a deep breath, and made the plunge. It was a marvellous performance; you'd have paid good money to see it in the theatre. Percy fixed me with what he thought was a commanding gaze and leaned forward confidentially.

"Usually my whole existence is very simple, and I like it that way. I show up at all the right places and at all the right parties, mingle with my friends and my peers, dazzle everyone with my latest fashions and devastating bon mots, and thus ensure that the occasion will be covered by all the right media. I do so love to party, and make the scene, and generally brighten up this dull old world with my presence. There's a whole crowd of us, you see; known each other since we were so high, you know how it is ... There isn't a club in the Nightside that doesn't benefit regularly from the sheer spectacle of our presence ... But now it's all changed, Mr. Taylor! And it's not fair! How can I be expected to compete for my moment in the spotlight when all my friends are cheating? Cheating!"

"How are they cheating?" I said, honestly baffled.

Percy leaned in very close, his voice a hoarse whisper. "They're staying young and beautiful, while I'm not. I'm aging, and they're not. I mean; look at me. I've got a wrinkle!"

I couldn't actually see it, but I took his word for it. "How long has this been going on?" I said.

"Months! Almost a year now. Though I've had my suspicions ... Look, I know these people. Have known them all my life. I know their faces like I know my own, down to the smallest detail. I can always tell when someone's had a little work done, around the eyes or under the chin ... but this is different. They look *younger*, untouched by time or the stresses of our particular life-style.

"It started last autumn, when some of them began patronising this new health club, the Guaranteed New You Parlour. Very expensive, very elite. Now all my friends go there, and every time they appear in public, they're the absolute peak, the very flower of beauty. Not a detail that isn't perfect, no matter how dissolute their private lives may be. I mean, people like us, Mr. Taylor, we live ... extreme lives. We experience ... everything. It's expected of us, so the rest of you can live the wild life vicariously, through us. Drink, drugs, debauchery, every night and twice on Saturday. It all gets just a bit tiring, actually. But anyway, as a result, we've all been in and out of those very discreet clinics that provide treatments for the kind of diseases you only get by being very social, or help in getting over the kind of good cheer that comes in bottles and powders and needles. We all need a little help to be beautiful all the time. A little something to help us soldier on to the next party. We all need damage repair, on a regular basis.

"But that's all stopped! They don't need the clinics any more, just this Parlour. And they all look like teenagers! It's not fair!"

"Well," I said reasonably, "If this Parlour is doing such a good job, why don't you go there, too?"

"Because they won't have me!" Percy slumped in his chair, and suddenly looked ten years older, as though he could only maintain his air of glamour through sheer effort of will these days. "I have offered to pay anything they want. Double, even triple the going rate. I begged and pleaded, Mr. Taylor! And they turned me away, as though I were nobody. Me! Percy D'Arcy! And now my friends don't want me around any more. They say I don't . . . fit in.

"Please, Mr. Taylor, I need you to find out what's going on. Find out why the Parlour won't let me in. Find out what they're really doing behind those closed doors . . . and if they are cheating, shut them down! So I won't be left out any more."

"It's not really my usual kind of case," I said.

"I'll pay you half a million pounds."

"But clearly this is something that needs to be investigated. Leave it with me, Percy."

He stood up abruptly, pulling his dignity back about him. "Here's my card. Please inform me when you know something." He tossed a very expensive piece of engraved pasteboard on to the table before me, then stalked off back through the crowd with his head held high. A smattering of applause followed him. I picked up the card, tapped it thoughtfully against my chin a few times, and looked at Suzie.

"It's something to do," I said. "You interested?"

"I'll come along," said Suzie. "Just to keep you company. Will I get to kill anybody?"

"Probably not."

Suzie shrugged. "The things I do for love."

In the sane and normal world outside the Nightside, if you're getting older and starting to look your age, there's always cosmetic surgery and associated treatments. In the Nightside, the rich and the famous and the powerful have access to other options, some of them quite spectacularly nasty and extreme.

The Guaranteed New You Parlour was situated in Uptown, the very best part of the Nightside, offering only the very best services for the very best people. Suzie and I went there anyway. The rent-a-cops in their colourful private uniforms took one look at us and decided they were needed urgently somewhere else. The neon there was just as hot, but perhaps a little more restrained, and the clubs and restaurants and discreet establishments glowed in the night like burning jewels. And the lost souls filling the streets and squares were all pounding the pavements in search of a better class of damnation.

In Uptown, even the Devil wears a tie.

The Guaranteed New You Parlour occupied the site of what used to be a rather tacky place called The Cutting Edge, an S&M joint for people with a surgery fetish. It got closed down for cutting corners on the after-care services, and for being too damned tacky even for the Nightside. The new owner had pulled the old place down and started over, so the Parlour was a gleaming new edifice of steel and glass, style and class, with pale-veined marble for the entrance lobby. Someone had spent a lot of money pushing the place up-market, and it showed. But then, money attracts money.

Suzie and I studied the Parlour from the other side of the street. Very rich people came and went, in stretch limousines and private ambulances, but though a great many old people went in, only young people came out. Which was...odd. There are ways of turning back the clock to be found in the Nightside, but the price nearly always involves your soul, or someone else's. And there are any number of places that will sell you false youth, but nothing that lasts. What did the Guaranteed New You Parlour have that no-one else could provide?

I headed for the main door, Suzie right there at my side. Her steel chains jangled softly, and the butt of her pump-action shotgun stood up behind her head from its holster down her back. There were two very large gentlemen in well-fitting formal suits standing on either side of the door. Security, but discreet, so as not to frighten the nice ladies and gentlemen. They tensed visibly as they saw Suzie and me approaching but made no move to challenge us. We swept past them with our noses in the air and strolled into the lobby as though we were thinking of buying the place. We got various looks from various people, but no-one said anything. We walked right up to the huge state-of-the-art reception desk, and I smiled pleasantly at the coldly efficient young lady sitting behind it. She wore a simple white nurse's uniform with no markings on it, and her smile was completely professional while at the same time possessing not an ounce of any real warmth. She didn't bat an eye at my trench coat or Suzie's leathers. This was the Nightside, after all.

"Welcome to the Guaranteed New You Parlour, Mr. Taylor, Ms. Shooter," said the receptionist.

I considered her thoughtfully. "You know who we are?"

"Of course. Everyone knows who you are."

I nodded. She had a point. "We're here about Suzie's face," I said.

Suzie and I had already decided this was our best chance for getting a close look at the Parlour's inner workings. One side of Suzie's face had been terribly burned during an old case, leaving it a mess of scar tissue. Her left eye was gone, the eyelid sealed shut. It didn't affect her aim. The damage was my fault. She'd never have been hurt if she hadn't been helping me out. Suzie forgave me almost immediately. But I don't forgive me, and I never will.

She could have had her face healed or repaired in a dozen

different ways. She chose not to. She believed a monster should look like a monster. I never pushed her on it. We monsters have to stick together.

The receptionist's smile didn't waver one bit. "Of course, Mr. Taylor, Ms. Shooter. If you'll just fill out these forms for me..."

"No," I said. "We want to see what this place has to offer first."

The receptionist gathered her papers together again. "One of our interns is on his way here, to give you a guided tour," she said, still professionally cheerful. If I smiled like that on a regular basis, my cheeks would ache. "Ah, here he is. Dr. Dougan, this is..."

"Oh, I know who you are, Mr. Taylor, Ms. Shooter," the intern said cheerfully. "Doesn't everyone?"

"Our reputation precedes us," I said dryly, shaking his proffered hand. He had a firm, manly grip. Of course. He offered his hand to Suzie, but she just looked at it, and he quickly pulled it back out of range and stuck it in his coat pocket as though he'd meant to do that all along. He wore the traditional white coat, along with the traditional stethoscope hanging loosely around his neck.

"Every medico in the Nightside knows about you two," he said, still cheerful. "Most of us get our training in the emergency wards, patching up people who've come into contact with you."

I looked at Suzie. "If nothing else, it seems we provide employment."

Dr. Dougan babbled on for a while, telling us how marvellous the Parlour was, and how fantastic its new techniques were, while I looked him over. His coat was starched blindingly white and had clearly never seen a bloodstain in its life. And he was far too young and handsome for a real hands-on doctor, which meant he was a shill. He was just for show. He wouldn't know anything about the real inner workings of the Parlour. But we followed him through the rear doors into the show ward behind the lobby, because you've got to start somewhere. Dr. Dougan never stopped talking. He'd been given a script designed to sell the Parlour's services, he'd learned every word of it, and by God we were going to hear it.

The show ward turned out to be very impressive, and utterly artificial. Neat patients in neat beds, none of them suffering from anything unsightly or upsetting, attended to by very attractive young nurses in starched white uniforms. There were flowers everywhere, and even the antiseptic in the air had a trace of perfume in it. Lots of light, lots of space, and no-one in any pain at all. A complete dream of a hospital ward. We weren't actually allowed to talk to any of the patients or nurses, of course. The intern did his best to blind us with statistics about recovery rates, while I looked around for something, anything, out of place. The ward looked absolutely fine, but . . . something about it disturbed me.

It took me a while to realise that the whole ward was simply too normal for the Nightside. If this was all the rich and powerful patients wanted, they could get it in Harley Street. The clincher was that not one of the patients or the nurses so much as glanced at me, or Suzie. And that was very definitely not normal.

Dr. Dougan broke off from his speech when the doors burst open behind us and half a dozen security men moved quickly forward to surround us. Large men, with large bulges under their jackets where their guns were holstered. Suzie looked at them thoughtfully.

"We're not here to make any trouble," I said quickly. "We're just looking."

"Visiting hours are over," said the largest of the security men. "Your presence is disturbing the patients."

"Yeah," I said. "They do look disturbed, don't they? We'll come back another day, when they're feeling more talkative."

He didn't smile. "I don't think that would be wise, Mr. Taylor."

"Is he giving us the bum's rush, John?" said Suzie. Her voice was calm and lazy and very dangerous. The security men held themselves very still.

"I'm sure the nice gentleman didn't mean anything of the kind," I said carefully. "Let's go, Suzie."

Suzie fixed the man with her cold blue eye. "He has to say *please*, first."

You could feel the tension on the air. Everyone's hands were only an impulse away from their guns. Suzie was smiling, just a little. The main security man gave her his full attention.

"Please," he said.

"Let's get out of this dump," said Suzie.

The security men escorted us out, maintaining a respectful distance at all times. I was impressed at their professionalism. I'd known Suzie to reduce grown thugs to tears with only a look. Which begged the question—why would a supposedly straightforward operation like the Guaranteed New You Parlour need heavy-duty security like them? What kind of secret were they hiding, that needed this level of protection?

I couldn't wait to find out.

We gave it a few hours before we went back again. Long enough to make them think we were thinking it over and still planning our next move. We killed the time at a pleasant little tea-shop nearby, where I enjoyed a nice cup of Earl Grey while Suzie wolfed down a whole plate of tea-cakes, and amused herself by practising her menacing glare on the trembling uniformed maids and the steadily decreasing number of fellow customers. The place was pretty much empty by the time we left, and the maids were refusing to come out of the kitchen. I left a generous tip.

"Can't take you anywhere," I said to Suzie.

"You love it," said Suzie.

When we returned to the Guaranteed New You Parlour, the whole place had been locked down tight. Doors were firmly closed, windows were covered with reinforced steel shutters, and a dozen security men were making themselves very visible, politely informing anyone who approached the Parlour that it was currently closed to all visitors and new patients. Some very rich and famous people wanted to get inside very badly, but for once, shouting, bribes, and temper tantrums got them nowhere. The Parlour was closed. I felt quite flattered that I'd made such an impression. Though to be honest, a lot of it was probably due to Suzie. Quite a few places close early when they see her coming, which is why I usually end up doing the shopping.

The security men looked like they knew what they were doing, so Suzie and I wandered casually round the side of the building. Not to the back. That's an amateur's mistake. Any security force worth its wages knows enough to guard the back doors as closely as the front. But there's nearly always a side entrance, used by staff and maintenance, that most people don't even know exists or think to mention. There were still a few oversized gentlemen keeping an eye on things, but they were so widely spaced it was easy to sneak past them.

The side door was right where I expected it to be. Suzie dealt with the lock in a few seconds, and as easily as that, we were in. (Getting past locked doors is just one of the many skills necessary to the modern bounty hunter. Though it does help if you've got a set of skeleton keys made from real human bones. Personally, I've always attributed Suzie's skills with locks to the fact that they're as scared of her as everyone else is.) We found ourselves in a narrow corridor, whitely tiled and brightly lit, with not a shadow to hide in anywhere. There was no-one about, for the moment. Suzie and I moved quickly down the corridor, trying doors at random along the way, to see what there was to see. A few store-rooms, a few offices, and a toilet that could have used a few more air fresheners. It all seemed normal and innocuous enough.

A set of swing doors let us into the main building. The lights were bright, every surface had been polished and waxed to within an inch of its life, but still there was no-one about. It was as though the whole place had been evacuated in a hurry. The silence was absolute, not even the hum of an air-conditioner. I looked at Suzie. She shrugged. I'd seen that shrug before. It meant *You're the brains; I'm the muscle. Get on with it.* So I chose a corridor at random and started down it. Several corridors later, we still hadn't encountered anyone, not even a guard doing his rounds. Surely they couldn't have shut the whole place down just because Suzie and I had expressed an interest? Unless . . . there never had been anything going on there, and the whole place was only a front for something else . . .

I was starting to get a really bad feeling about this. When hospitals go bad, they go really bad.

It didn't take long to find the ward we'd been shown earlier. It was as still and silent as everywhere else. I quietly pushed the door open, and Suzie and I slipped inside. The lights had been turned down low, and the patients were shadowy shapes in their beds. There were half a dozen nurses, but they were all standing very still, in the central aisle between the two rows of beds. They didn't move a muscle as Suzie and I slowly advanced on them.

It was so quiet I could hear Suzie's steady breathing beside me.

Up close, the nurses seemed more like mannequins than people. Their faces were utterly empty, they didn't breathe, and their fixed eyes didn't blink. Suzie produced a penlight and briefly shined it in a nurse's face, but the eyes didn't react at all. Suzie put the light away, then punched the nurse in the shoulder; but she only rocked slightly on her feet. We checked the beds. The patients lay flat on their backs, staring sightlessly upwards. They weren't dead. It was more like they'd never really been alive. A show ward, with show nurses and show patients, not a bit of it real. I murmured as much to Suzie, and she nodded quickly.

"Window dressing. But if this is just a show for the visitors, where's the real deal? Where are the real wards and the real patients? Percy D'Arcy's celebrity chums?"

"Not here," I said. "I think we need to dip below the surface, see what's underneath all this."

"Underneath," said Suzie. "The real deal's always going on underneath, in the Nightside."

We made our way quickly through the ward, heading for the far doors. I kept expecting the nurses and patients to come suddenly alive, and raise the alarm, or even attack us. Instead, the nurses stood very still, and the patients lay unmoving in their beds, like toys that weren't currently being played with. A horrible suspicion came over me, that perhaps the whole world was like this, whenever I turned my back... By the time we got to the far doors, I was practically running.

We found a stairwell easily enough and descended a set of rough concrete steps to the next level. There were no signs on the walls, nothing to indicate where the stairs might lead. Clearly either you knew where you were going, or you weren't supposed to be there. The air was very still, and there wasn't a sound to be heard except for our feet on the rough concrete. The steps fell away before us for quite a while, taking us deep down into the bedrock under the streets. At the bottom of the steps we found another set of swing doors, perfectly ordinary, with no lock or alarm. Suzie and I pushed cautiously through them, and found ourselves in an entirely different kind of ward.

It was huge, with rows and rows of beds stretching away into the distance. And in these beds were hundreds and hundreds of very real patients served by more high-tech medical equipment than I'd ever seen in one place. Suzie and I moved slowly forward. There were no doctors, no nurses, just naked men and women lying flat on their backs, hooked up to intravenous drips, and respirators, and heart and lung and kidney monitors. Breathing tubes and catheters and more than one set of heavy leather restraints . . .

I found my first clue in the nurse's cubicle. There was a large book lying open on a table, next to a row of monitor screens. The old-fashioned printed pages were written in English, French, and Creole, and I understood enough of it to know what it was about. Voodoo. The gods of the loa, their powers and practices, and all the things you could do with their help.

"Look at this," said Suzie. She'd found a printout listing all the patients in the ward. No details, no instructions, only basic identities. Suzie and I flicked through the pages, and a whole bunch of familiar names jumped out at us. Not just Percy's friends, the beautiful people from the colour supplements; but the rich and the powerful, the real movers and shakers of the Nightside. I went back into the ward, moving quickly down the rows of beds, staring into faces. I recognised quite a few, but none of them recognised me. Even with their eyes open, they saw nothing, nothing at all.

At least they were breathing...

The next big clue was that they all looked so much older than they should—all wrinkled faces, sagging flesh, and shrivelled limbs. I'd seen many of them recently, and they'd all looked in their prime, as usual. Now their faces and bodies showed the clear ravages of time and much hard living, along with any number of destructive antisocial diseases. There were also clear signs of elective surgery, some of it quite extensive, on faces and body parts. Some of the patients were so heavily wrapped in blood-stained bandages they were practically mummified. It was like touring a hospital in a war zone, and many of the patients looked like they'd been through hell. Some were clearly barely hanging on, only kept alive by invasive medical technology.

It took me a while to get it. A very new twist on a very old practice. The voodoo book was the key. These patients on their beds of pain weren't the real rich and famous faces of the Nightside; they were living duplicates. The techniques in the book had been used to turn them into the equivalent of voodoo dolls, but in reverse. Instead of whatever happening to the doll happening to the victim, what happened to the original happened to the duplicate. Like Dorian Gray's painting, these poor bastards soaked up the excesses of the real people's lives, so they could go on being young and beautiful and untouched...The patients aged and suffered and underwent the elective surgeries, while the rich and powerful reaped all the benefits.

No wonder poor Percy D'Arcy couldn't compete.

I ran it through for Suzie, and she wrinkled her nose. "Now that...is tacky. Where are they getting all these duplicates from? I mean, they'd have to be exact doubles for this to work."

"Any number of options," I said. "Clones, homunculi, doppelgängers...It doesn't matter. The point is, I very much doubt any of these people are here by choice. The heavy restraints are a bit of a give-away there. This isn't a hospital ward; it's a torture chamber."

In the end, we found the answer behind a very ordinary-looking door. The sophisticated electronic lock aroused our suspicions, and Suzie opened it easily with her skeleton keys. (Magic still trumps science, usually by two falls and a sub-mission.) She pulled the door open, and we both stepped quickly back. There was nothing behind the door. Lots and lots of nothing. Space that wasn't space, filled with squirm-ing, shimmering lights you could only see with your mind, or your soul. There was a terrible appeal to it, an attraction, that made you want to throw yourself into it and fall forever...I carefully pushed the door shut again.

"A Timeslip," I said. "Someone's stabilised a Timeslip and held it in neutral; a ready-made door into another real-ity." That would take time and serious money. Timeslips are inherently unstable. The universe is self-correcting, and it hates anomalies. "The only people I know to have worked successfully with Timeslips are Mammon Emporium, that mall that specialises in providing goods and services from alternate time-lines. And they've never shared that knowledge with anyone."

"Could they be behind this?" said Suzie.

"No. I don't think so. They've already made themselves rich beyond the dreams of tax accountants by legitimate means. Why risk all that, for this? Still, at least now we know where the duplicates come from. Whoever owns this place goes fishing in some other world, for that place's equivalent of our important people. Exact physical duplicates... forcibly abducted and brought here, to suffer every conceivable illness, surgery, and self-inflicted injury, so their other selves don't have to and can remain young and pretty forever..."

We both looked round sharply. Someone was coming. A lot of people were coming. Suzie and I moved quickly to stand shoulder to shoulder, facing the main doors. There was something odd about the sound, though; the pounding feet sounded muffled, flat... And it took me a moment to realise that the sound was approaching from below, not above. Coming up the stairs, from some further, lower level. The main doors finally burst open, and a small army of heavily armed nurses stormed into the ward in perfect lock-step. Suzie and I stood very still. The guns were no surprise, but the nature of the nurses was.

They weren't alive. They were constructs, their bodies made entirely from bamboo woven and twisted into a human form. Their faces were blank bamboo ovals with neither mouths nor eyes, but every one of them orientated on Suzie and me. They all wore the same starched white nurse's uniform, right down to the little white cap on the backs of their bamboo heads. Not living, not even aware, as such, but quite capable of following orders. And their guns were real enough. The nurses scurried forward with inhuman speed, their bamboo feet scuffing across the floor, spreading out into a perfect semicircle to cover us. Suzie swept her shotgun back and forth, looking for a useful target, knowing she was outnumbered and outgunned, but refusing to be intimidated. I *was* intimidated, but I made a point of striking a defiantly casual pose, while waiting for the puppet master to show himself.

Whoever ran the nurses wouldn't miss an opportunity to gloat over the capture of two such famous faces as Suzie Shooter and John Taylor. If he'd been sensible, he'd have had the nurses shoot on sight, but the bigger the ego, the bigger the need to show off.

And sure enough, the crowd of bamboo nurses suddenly broke apart, silently opening a central aisle for their lord and master to make his entrance. Surprisingly, it was no-one I knew. Not one of the Major Players, not even one of the more ambitious up-and-comers. The man striding quite casually through his army of bamboo nurses was entirely unknown to me, and that doesn't happen often in the Nightside.

He was tall, well made, well dressed, in a rich cream suit; the kind usually favoured by remittance men banished by their families to hot and far-away places. At first I thought he was a young man, but the closer he got the more the little tell-tale details gave him away. The skin of his face was too tight, too taut, and his eyes were very old. Old and cold. His smile was a dead, mirthless thing, meant to frighten. This was a man who had seen the world, found it wanting, and taken his revenge. His movements had the surety and control that only comes from age and experience, and he walked like a wolf in a world of sheep. He had large, powerful hands, with long, slender fingers—surgeons' hands. And for all his grace, there was no mistaking the sheer brute power of his wide shoulders and barrel chest. He finally came to a halt, a respectful distance away, nodded to me and smiled at Suzie, ignoring the shotgun she was levelling on his chest.

"The famous John Taylor and the infamous Shotgun Suzie," he said, in a rich, deep voice with just a hint of an unfamiliar accent. "Well. I am honoured. I should have known that if anyone would find me out, it would be you." He laughed briefly, as though at some private joke. "Allow me to introduce myself. I am Frankenstein. Baron Viktor von Frankenstein."

He said it as though expecting a flash of lightning and a roll of thunder in the background. I didn't quite laugh in his face.

"That's a not uncommon name in the Nightside," I said. "The place is lousy with Frankensteins. I don't know how many nephews and nieces and grandsons I've run into down the years, along with any number of your family's monstrous creations. You'd think practice would make perfect, but I've yet to see any proof of that. They're nearly always complete fuck-ups. What is it with you and your family, and grave-yards, anyway? I'm sure it was all very cutting-edge, back at the dawn of medical science, messing about with body parts and batteries and cosmic radiation, but the rest of us have moved on. Science has moved on. You people should have gone into transplants and cloning, like everyone else. So you're another Frankenstein. What relation, exactly?"

"The original," said the Baron. "The first . . . to bring life out of death. To take dead meat and make it sit up and talk."

"Damn," said Suzie. "Colour me impressed."

"Doesn't that make you over two hundred years old?" I said.

The Baron smiled. There was no humour in it, and less warmth. "You can't spend as long as I have studying life and death in intimate detail and not pick up a few tips on survival." He looked around him at the rows of patients suffering silently in their beds and smiled again. "My latest venture. I know—voodoo superstitions and medical science aren't natural partners, but I have learned to make use of anything and everything that can assist me in my researches. Like these bamboo figures. Pretty little things, aren't they? And a lot more obedient than the traditional hunchback."

"I should have known a Frankenstein was involved when I saw this," I said. "Your family's always been drawn to the dark side of surgery."

"Oh, this isn't my real research," said the Baron. "Only a little something I set up to fund my real work. The creation of life from the tragedy of death. The prolongation of life, so that death shall have no triumph. What I do, I do for all Mankind."

"Except for the poor bastards strapped to those beds," I said. A thought came to me. "You're not from around here, are you? You came from the same reality as these people. That's why I never encountered you before."

"Exactly," said the Baron. "I came through a Timeslip."

"Why?" said Suzie. "Another mob with blazing torches? Another creature that turned on you?"

"I'd done all I could there," said the Baron, entirely un-moved by the disdain in Suzie's voice. "I found the Timeslip, and I came here, to the Nightside. Such a marvellous locality, free from all the usual hypocrisies and restraints."

"How did you stabilise the Timeslip?" I asked, genuinely interested.

"I inherited it. Apparently Mammon Emporium had their first premises here. They took their Timeslips with them when they moved to a bigger location . . . but they left one behind. Of such simple accidents are great things born. I shall do great work here. I can feel it." He wasn't boasting, or trying to convince himself. He believed it utterly, convinced of his own genius and inevitable triumph. He looked at me dispassionately. "May I enquire . . . what brought you here, Mr. Taylor?"

"One of your clients was very upset when you turned him away," I said. "Never underestimate the fury of professionally pretty people."

"Ah yes . . . Percy D'Arcy. He offered me a fortune, but I couldn't take it. There was nothing I could do for him, because in the other dimension he was already dead. Percy . . . another loose end that will have to be attended to. Fortunately, I have two very reliable people in charge of my security. I brought them with me, from my home dimension."

He snapped his fingers, and as though they'd been waiting just out of sight for his signal, a man and a woman came through the doors and strode lightly between the ranks of bamboo nurses to stand on either side of the Baron. The man was tall and blond, and wore black leather motorcycle leathers with two bandoliers of bullets crossing over his chest. The pump-action shotgun in his hands covered me steadily. The woman . . . was tall, dark-haired, and wore a long white trench coat. She grinned at me mockingly.

"Allow me to present Stephen Shooter and Joan Taylor," said the Baron, savouring the moment. "Where we come from, their legend is as extensive as yours, though perhaps in a more unsavoury fashion. Their destiny led them down different, darker paths. I've always found them very useful." He looked me over, taking his time, then studied Suzie just as carefully. "I would have enjoyed working with you. Opening you up, studying your details, seeing what I could have made of you. Surgery is an art, and I could have worked such miracles in your flesh, with my scalpels . . . But now that you have found me out, others are bound to follow. This operation must be shut down, and I must move on." He sighed. "The story of my life, really."

He gestured abruptly, and the bamboo nurses surged forward inhumanly quickly. They snatched the shotgun out of Suzie's hand and punched and kicked her to the ground. I went to help her, and they clubbed me down with their gun butts. It all happened so quickly. They gathered around us, beating at us with their gun butts, over and over again. I tried to get to Suzie, to shield her, but I couldn't even do that. In the end, all I could do was curl into a ball and take it.

"Enough," the Baron said finally, and the nurses fell back immediately. I was a mass of pain, aching everywhere, blood soaking and dripping from my face, but it didn't feel like anything important was broken. I looked across at Suzie. She was lying very still. I did, too. Let them think they'd beaten the fight out of us. I concentrated on breathing steadily, nursing my rage and hate, trying to find some part of me that didn't hurt like hell.

"Stephen, Joan, take care of these two," said the Baron. "Be as creative as you like, as long as the effects are permanent. When you're finished, come down to me. I have more work for you."

He turned unhurriedly and walked away. The whole army of bamboo nurses spun on their bamboo heels and stomped out after him. Still in perfect lock-step, the bitches. I sat up slowly, trying not to groan out loud as every new movement sent pain shooting through me. I hate being ganged up on— it's so undignified. There's no way you can look good afterwards. Suzie sat up abruptly, and spat a mouthful of dark red blood on to the floor. Then she looked round for her shotgun, and glared at the male version of herself as he waggled the gun mockingly at her.

"Mine! Finders keepers, losers get buried in unmarked graves."

The female version of me smirked, both hands thrust deep in her trench coat's pockets. I really hoped I didn't look like that when I smiled. She leaned forward a little, so she could stare right into my bloodied face.

"Wow. That had to hurt. But that's what happens when you choose the wrong side."

I ignored her, climbing slowly and painfully to my feet. Suzie got up on her own. I knew better than to offer to help. We stood together, shoulder to shoulder, more than little unsteady, and considered our counterparts. Stephen Shooter had all the menace of Suzie, but none of her dark glamour. Where she was disturbingly straightforward and driven, he gave every indication of being crude and brutal. Gun for hire, no morals and less subtlety. My Suzie could think rings round him, even as she was blowing his head off his shoulders.

He still had a whole face, untouched by scar tissue. He hadn't endured what she'd been through.

Joan Taylor looked far more dangerous. Simply standing there, with no obvious weapons, she looked entirely calm and confident. I hadn't realised how disconcerting that could be. It was strange, looking into her face and seeing so many similarities. I could see myself in her. Her gaze was cool and mocking, her smile an open insult. *Take your best shot,* everything about her seemed to be saying. *We both know it's not going to be good enough.*

"So," I said, making sure the words came out clear and casual, despite my smashed mouth. "My evil twin. I suppose it had to happen, eventually."

"Hardly," Joan said easily. "You and I are the perfect example of the only child. Self-sufficient, self-taught, a legend in our own lifetime by our own efforts. Was your mother...?"

"Yes. Did you . . . ?"

"Yes." Her smiled widened. "And I made her beg before I killed her."

I smiled. "We're not even remotely alike. My partner is a professional. Yours is a psychopath."

"Perhaps," said Joan. "But he's my psychopath."

Stephen Shooter giggled suddenly. A brief, disturbing sound. "It's true, it's true. I do enjoy my work. That's why I'm so good at it. Practice makes perfect."

"You talk too much," said Suzie.

"How did the two of you end up here?" I said, before things could get out of hand. I needed to keep Joan talking, buy myself some time, because I was counting on there being one major difference between us and them.

"We made the old home-town a touch too hot for us," Joan said coyly. "We'd spent years together as soldiers for hire, professional trouble-shooters, whatever euphemism floats your boat, but we made the mistake of taking out a very well-connected functionary called Walker. It was all his fault. Stupid old man, thinking he could tell us who we could and couldn't kill. We'd have done him for the fun of it, but luckily he had an awful lot of enemies . . . Stephen blew him in half with his shotgun, and we laughed about it all the way home. But it turned out Walker also had friends, rich and powerful friends, and, just like that, no-one loved us any more. So when the Baron very kindly offered us a regular gig and a guaranteed new start . . ."

"We killed a whole bunch of people, settled some old scores, burned down half the town, and escaped here before anyone knew we were gone," said Stephen. He was grinning, a loose, crafty smile with far too many teeth in it.

"We've been here for ages," said Joan Taylor. "Doing all sorts of things you wouldn't approve of. You'll probably take the blame for a lot of them. Everyone knows about you, but no-one knows about us. Though I can't say I believe half the things they say about you."

"Goody Goody Two-shoes," said Stephen.

"Any chance we can make a deal?" I said.

Joan raised an eyebrow. "Would you?"

"No," I said. "Your very existence offends me."

I lunged forward and punched her right in the face. She fell backwards, sprawling awkwardly on the floor. She hadn't even had the time to take her hands out of her pockets. I looked round, and Suzie had already taken her shotgun away from Shooter and back-elbowed him in the throat. I grinned. Sometime back, Suzie and I had both received werewolf blood, diluted enough that we were in no danger of turning were, but still potent enough that we healed really quickly. My aches were already fading away. I looked down at Joan Taylor and smiled as she scrambled angrily back on to her feet.

We stood facing each other, hands clenched into fists at our sides as we concentrated, both of us calling on our gifts. I opened my inner eye, my third eye, and studied her coldly, searching for some gap in her defences, something I could use against her. I could feel her doing the same thing. Strange energies flickered on and off in the air between us, a tension of unseen forces building and building until they had to explode somewhere. My gift versus hers. It was like arm-wrestling with invisible, intangible arms.

I was vaguely aware of all hell breaking loose in the hospital ward, as Suzie and Stephen went head to head. Shotgun blasts were going off all over the place, accompanied by the roar of grenades. Beds overturned, and patients were thrown out, disconnected from their supporting tech. Dark smoke drifted across the ward as equipment caught fire.

I couldn't let this go on. We were too evenly matched with our duplicates, and too many innocents were getting hurt. So I found a slippery patch under Joan's left foot, let her stumble and lose her concentration for a moment, then I yelled to Suzie.

"Hey, Suzie! Switch partners and dance!"

She grasped the idea immediately and turned her shotgun on Joan Taylor. And while Stephen Shooter hesitated, I used my gift to find the one pin that wasn't secure in his grenades. It popped out, Stephen glanced down, and there was a swift series of explosions, as the one grenade set off all the others. Small parts of Stephen Shooter went flying all over the hospital ward in a soft, pattering, crimson rain. Behind me there was the single blast of a shotgun, and when I looked round Joan Taylor was lying flat on her back, without a head. She probably wasted time trying to find a way to stop Suzie, the fool. No-one stops Suzie Shooter.

"They were good," I said. "But they weren't us. They hadn't been hardened and refined by life in the Nightside."

"They weren't us," Suzie agreed. She came over to me and looked closely at my face. "You took a hell of a beating."

35

"So did you. Thank the good Lord for werewolf blood."

"But you still tried to get to me, to protect me. I saw you. I didn't even think to do that for you. You've always been better than me, John."

"Forgive me?" I said.

She smiled briefly. "Well, just this once." She looked at Joan's headless body. "I've never cared for cheap knock-offs."

"Our dark sides," I said.

"Well, darker," said Suzie.

I considered the point. "Do you suppose . . . there might be better versions of us, somewhere? In some other world? More saintly selves?"

"You're creeping me out now," said Suzie. "Let's go find the Baron and shut him down."

"First things first," I said. "I've had enough of this place. No more suffering innocents. Not on my watch."

I raised my gift again, and studied the whole ward through my inner eye, until I could See the connection the Baron had forged with his science and his voodoo, between the patients in their beds and their more fortunate duplicates in the Nightside. A whole series of shimmering silver chains, rising from every patient and plunging through the ceiling. And having found them, it was the easiest thing in the world for me to break the weakest of the chains, with the slightest mental touch. Pushed out of its awful balance, the whole system collapsed, the shimmering chains snapping out of existence in a moment. The patients in their beds cried out with a single great voice, as all the traces of age and surgery and hard living disappeared; and, just like that, they were young and perfect again. They didn't wake up, which was probably as well. Let Walker send some people down to help them, and hopefully get them home again.

Suzie and I had other business.

I considered what must be happening, in all the best clubs and bars and parlours in the Nightside above, as rich and powerful faces were suddenly struck down with years, and the many results of debauchery and surgical choices. I visualised them screaming in pain and shock and horror as they all finally assumed their real faces. What better revenge could there be?

"You're smiling that smile again," said Suzie. "That *I've just done something really nasty and utterly justified and no-one's ever going to be able to pin it on me* smile."

"How well you know me," I said. "Now, where were we? Ah yes—the Baron."

"Bad man," said Suzie Shooter. She worked the action on her shotgun. "I will make a wicker man out of his nurses and burn him alive."

"I love the way you think," I said.

We found another door that opened on to another stairwell, leading down into hell. We crept quietly down the bare concrete steps. The Baron had to have heard the fire-fight above him; but he had no way of knowing who'd won. Suzie led the way, shotgun at the ready, and I struggled to maintain my gift, searching the descent below us with my inner eye for hidden traps or alarms. But the stairwell remained still and quiet, and there wasn't even a glimpse of a bamboo nurse.

The smell hit me first. A thick stench of spilled blood and spoiled meat, of foul things done in a foul place. It grew stronger as we descended the last few steps and found ourselves facing a simple wooden door. The air was hot and sweaty, almost oily on my bare skin. It was the heat of opened bodies in a cold room, the pulsing warmth of inner things exposed to the light. *Frankenstein*... I pushed quietly past Suzie, and tried the handle. It wasn't locked. I went inside, and Suzie was right there with me, silent as an avenging ghost.

We were in a great stone chamber, carved out of the very bedrock itself. Rough pitted walls and ceiling, and an uneven floor partly covered with blood-stained matting. Naked light bulbs hung down on long, rusting chains, filling the chamber with harsh and unforgiving illumination. There were shadows, but not nearly enough to hide what had been done in this place. Trestle tables had been set up in long rows, and each of them bore a human body, or bits of bodies. Men and women had been opened up, and the parts dissected. White ribs gleamed in dark red meat. Piles of entrails steamed in the cool air. Heavy leather restraining straps held the bodies to the tables. They had been alive when the cutting began.

The Baron had gone back to his old surgical experiments. Frankenstein, the living god of the scalpel.

He was standing at the far end of the room, wearing a blood-spattered butcher's apron over his cream suit, half-bent over the body on the table before him. It had been a young woman, though it was hard to tell that now. The Baron looked up at me, startled, his scalpel raised, dripping blood. We'd interrupted him at his work.

"Get out," he said. "You can't be here. I'm doing important work here."

"This isn't a surgery," I said. "It's a slaughter-house."

He straightened up, and, with almost prissy precision, put his scalpel down beside the woman's body. "No," he said calmly. "A slaughter-house is a place of death. This is a salon dedicated to life. Look beyond the obvious, Mr. Taylor. I am working to frustrate death, to cheat him of his victims. I take dead flesh and make it live again, all through my own efforts. You have no idea of the wonders and glories I've seen inside people."

He came out from behind the table to face Suzie and me, wiping the blood from his bare hands with a bit of rag. "Try to understand and appreciate what I'm doing here. I have gone far beyond merely duplicating nature. Now I seek to improve on her work. I use only the most perfect organs, reshaped and improved by surgical skills perfected over centuries. I . . . simplify things, removing all unnecessary details. And from these perfect parts I have built something new—a living creature completely in balance with itself. I see no reason why it should not live forever, and know lifetimes. It took me so long to understand . . . the key was to work not with corpses, but with the living! To harvest them for what I needed—the most fresh and vital tissues!"

"How many?" I said, cutting him off roughly. There was something almost hypnotic in the brute certainty of his voice.

"I don't understand," he said. "How many what?"

"How many victims, you bastard! How many good men and women died at your hands, to make your perfect bloody creature?"

He actually looked a little sulky, angry that I hadn't got the point, even after he'd explained it all so carefully.

"I really don't know, Mr. Taylor. I don't keep count. Why should I? It's the parts that matter. It isn't as if they were anyone important. Anyone who mattered. People go missing all the time in the Nightside, and no-one ever cares."

"He does," said Suzie, unexpectedly. "Part of why I love him. He cares enough for both of us."

The Baron looked at her uncertainly, then turned his attention back to me. "Progress always has a price, Mr. Taylor. Nothing is ever gained without sacrifice. And I sacrificed them." He gestured at all the bodies on all the tables, and smiled briefly. "I do so love an audience. A failing, I admit, this need to explain and justify myself...But I think I've rattled on quite long enough. Am I to understand that Joan Taylor and Stephen Shooter will not be joining us?"

"No," said Suzie. "They rest in pieces."

The Baron shrugged. "It doesn't matter. I still have my nurses."

He snapped his fingers, and a whole army of bamboo nurses appeared out of the bare stone walls, snapping into existence, to fill the space between us and the Baron. They surged forward, bamboo hands reaching out to Suzie and to me, but this time I was prepared. I'd been waiting for them. I took the salamander egg from my coat pocket, crushed it in my hand, and threw it into their midst. The egg exploded into flames, and a dozen nurses immediately caught fire. Yellow flames leapt up, jumping from nurse to nurse as the bamboo figures lurched back and forth, spreading the flames with their flailing arms. In a few moments the cellar was full of juddering, burning figures, a hellish light dancing across the bare stone walls. Suzie and I were back by the door, ready to make our escape if necessary, but the Baron was trapped with his back against the far wall. He watched helplessly as the nurses crashed into his trestle tables, overturning them and setting them on fire, too. And in the end he had no choice but to shout the command Word that shut them all down. The figures crashed to the floor and lay there, still burning. The sound of crackling flames was very loud in the quiet.

Suzie and I moved forward into the cellar again, stepping carefully around blackened bamboo shapes. The Baron studied me thoughtfully. He didn't look nearly as worried as I'd thought he would. He had the air of someone who still had a card left to play.

"Wait," he said. "I'm sure we can reason together."

"I'm pretty sure we can't," said Suzie.

"You must meet my latest creation," said the Baron. "See the results of my work. Creature, stand! Show yourself!"

And from a dark, concealing shadow in one corner, something stirred and stood up. It had been sitting quietly on a chair all this time, so inhumanly inert it went unnoticed.

41

Suzie moved quickly to cover the figure with her shotgun as it moved forward into the light. It was beautiful. Tall and perfect, utterly naked, it stood head and shoulders above us all, perfectly proportioned, no scars or visible stitches anywhere, thanks to modern surgical techniques. It had strong androgynous features, and it moved with a sublime and perfect grace.

I hated it on sight. There was something . . . *wrong* about it. Perhaps simply because it didn't move like anything human, because its face held no trace of human thoughts or human emotions. I felt the same way looking at the creature as I did when surprised by a spider. An instinctive impulse to strike out, at something with which I could never have any empathy.

"Isn't it marvellous?" said the Baron von Frankenstein, moving forward to place one large and possessive hand on the creature's bare shoulder. "Hermaphroditic, of course. Self-repairing, self-fertilising, potentially immortal."

No breasts and no obvious genitals, but I took his word for it. "Whose brain did you use this time?" I said finally.

"My own," said the Baron. "Or at least, all my memories, downloaded into a brain wiped clean of its original patterns. Computers have made such a difference to my work. You see, Mr. Taylor? Even if you kill me here, my work goes on. I go on, in every way that matters."

He patted his creature fondly on the shoulder. It turned its perfect head and regarded him thoughtfully, turned and placed its perfect hands on the Baron's face, and ripped the Baron's head right off his shoulders. The body fell jerking and kicking to the floor, the neck stump pumping blood, while the creature held the Baron's slack face up before its own. The Baron's eyes were still moving, and his mouth worked, though no sound came out.

"Now that I exist, you are redundant," said the creature, to the Baron's dying eyes. Its voice was like music; horrible music—with nothing human in it. "I have all your knowledge, all your techniques, so what use are you? Yes, you made me. I know. Did you think I'd be grateful?"

"I can't believe he didn't see that one coming," said Suzie.

The creature looked into the Baron von Frankenstein's eyes, satisfied itself that its creator no longer saw anything, and tossed the head aside. Then it turned slowly, thoughtfully, to consider Suzie and me.

"Nice operation the Baron had here," said the creature. "Think I'll take it over."

I shook my head. "Not going to happen."

"You can't stop me," said the creature.

Suzie shot it in the chest at point-blank range. The blast blew half its chest away, and the impact sent the creature staggering backwards. But it didn't fall, and when it regained its balance the huge wound was already repairing itself. The creature's mouth moved in something that would have been a smile on anything human.

"My creator made me very well. The best work I ever did."

I raised my gift, searching for the link that held all the creature's separate parts and pieces together, but there wasn't one. The Baron hadn't used science or sorcery to put his creature together, only expert surgical skills honed over lifetimes of work. I dropped my gift and looked at Suzie.

"We're going to have to do this the hard way. You ready to get your hands dirty?"

"Always," said Suzie Shooter.

So we took a scalpel each, slammed the creature to the floor, and took it apart piece by piece. There was a lot of kicking and screaming, and in the end we had to burn all the pieces separately to stop them moving, but we did it.

TWO

At Home with John and Suzie

Until Walker's people arrived, Suzie and I stuck around, talking to the newly awakened patients, and comforting them as best we could. Well, I did most of the talking and comforting. Suzie isn't really a people person. Mostly she stood at the door with her shotgun at the ready, to assure the patients that no-one was going to be allowed to mess with them any more. A lot of them were confused, and even more were in various states of shock. The physical injuries might have been reversed, but you can't undergo that kind of extended suffering without its leaving a mark on your soul.

Some of them knew each other, and sat together on the beds, holding each other and sobbing in quiet relief. Some were scared of everyone, including Suzie and me. Some . . . just didn't wake up.

Walker's people would know what to do. They had a lot of experience at picking up the pieces after someone's grand scheme has suddenly gone to hell in a hand-cart. They'd get the people help and see them safely back to their home dimension. Then they'd shut down the Timeslip, and slap a heavy fine on the Mammon Emporium for losing track of the damn thing in the first place. If people can't look after their Timeslips properly, they shouldn't be allowed to have them. Walker's people . . . would do all the things I couldn't do.

When Suzie and I finally left the Guaranteed New You Parlour, Percy D'Arcy was outside waiting for us. His fine clothes looked almost shabby, and his eyes were puffy from crying. He came at me as though he meant to attack me, and stopped only when Suzie drew her shotgun and trained it on him with one easy move. He glared at me piteously, wringing his hands together.

"What have you done, Taylor? What have you done?"

"I found out what was going on, and I put a stop to it," I said. "I saved a whole bunch of innocent people from . . ."

"I don't care about them! What do they matter? What have you done to my friends?" He couldn't speak for a moment, his eyes clenched shut to try to stop the tears streaming down his face. "I saw the most beautiful people of my generation reduced to hags and lepers! Saw their pretty faces fall and crack and split apart. Their hair fell out, and their backs bent, and they cried and shrieked and screamed, running mad in the night. I saw them break out in boils and pus and rot! *What did you do to them?*"

"I'm sorry," I said. "But they earned it."

"They were my friends," said Percy D'Arcy. "I've known them since I was so high. I never meant for this to happen."

"Percy..." I said.

"You can whistle for your fee!" said Percy, with almost hysterical dignity. And then he spun around and walked away, still crying.

I let him go. I saw his point, sort of. Some cases, no-one gets to feel good afterwards. So Suzie and I went home.

The Nightside doesn't have suburbs, as such. But a few areas are a little more safe and secure than anywhere else, where people can live quietly and not be bothered. Not gated communities, because gates wouldn't even slow down the kind of predators the Nightside attracts, but instead small communities protected by a few magical defences, a handful of force shields, and a really good mutual defence pact. Besides, if you can't look after yourself, you shouldn't be living in the Nightside anyway. Suzie and I lived together in a nice little detached house (three up, three down, two sideways) in one of the more peaceful and up-market areas. Just by living there, we were driving the house prices down, but we tried not to worry about that too much. Originally, there was a small garden out front, but since Suzie and I were in no way gardening people, the first thing we did was dig it up and put in a mine-field. We're not big on visitors. Actually, Suzie did most of the work, while I added some man-traps and a few invisible floating curses, to show I was taking an interest.

Our immediate neighbours are a Time-travelling adventurer called Garth the Eternal, a big Nordic type who lived in a scaled-down Norman castle, complete with its own gargoyles who kept us awake at night during the mating season, and a cold-faced, black-haired alien hunter from the future named Sarah Kingdom, who lived in a conglomeration of vaguely organic shapes that apparently also functioned as her star-ship, if she could only find the right parts to repair it.

We've never even discussed having a housing association.

Suzie and I live on separate floors. She has the ground floor, I have the top floor, and we share the amenities. All very civilised. We spend as much time in each other's company as we can. It's not easy being either of us. My floor is defiantly old-fashioned, even Victorian. They understood a lot about comfort and luxury. That particular night, I was lying flat on my back in the middle of my four-poster bed. The goose-feather mattress was deep enough to sink into, with a firm support underneath. Some mornings Suzie had to pry me out of bed with a crow-bar. Supposedly Queen Elizabeth I had slept in the four-poster once, on one of her grand tours. Considering what the thing cost me, she should have done cart-wheels in it.

A carefully constructed fire crackled quietly in the huge stone grate, supplying just enough warmth to ward off the cold winds that blew outside. The wood in the fire remained eternally unconsumed, thanks to a simple moebius spell, so the fire never went out. One wall of my bedroom is taken up with bookshelves, mostly Zane Grey and Louis L'Amour Westerns, and a whole bunch of old John Creasey thrillers, of which I am inordinately fond. Another wall is mostly hidden behind a great big fuck-off wide-screen plasma television, facing the bed. And the final wall holds my DVDs and CDs, all in strict alphabetical order, which Suzie never ceases to make remarks about.

I have gas lighting in my bedroom. It gives a friendlier light, I think.

A richly detailed Persian rug covers most of the floor. It's supposed to have been a flying carpet at some point, but no-one can remember the activating Words any more, so it's just a rug. Except I always have to be very careful about what I say out loud while I'm standing on it. Scattered about the room are various and assorted odds and ends I've collected and acquired down the years, often as part or even full payment for a case. A few purported Objects of Power, some antiques with interesting histories, and a whole bunch of things that might or might not turn out to be valuable or useful someday.

There's a musical box that plays top-twenty hits from thirty years in the future. Still mostly crap...Some *Tyrannosaurus rex* dung, in a sealed glass jar, labelled *For when any old shit just won't do.* A brass head that could supposedly predict the future, though I've never heard it utter a word. And a single blood-red rose in a long glass vase. It doesn't need watering, and it hisses angrily if anyone gets too close, so mostly I leave it alone. It's only there to add a spot of colour.

49

As I lay on top of the blankets on my huge bed, listening to the wind battering outside and feeling all warm and cosy, it occurred to me how far I'd come since I returned to the Nightside. Wasn't that long ago I'd been trying to live a normal life in normal London and being spectacularly bad at it. I'd been living in my one-room office, in a building that should have been condemned, sleeping on a cot pushed up against one wall. Eating take-away food and hiding under my desk when the creditors came calling . . . I'd left the Nightside to feel safe. And because I was afraid I was turning into a monster. But there are worse things than that. Failure tastes of cold pizza and over-used tea bags, and the knowledge that you're not really helping anyone, even yourself.

I'll never leave the Nightside again. For all its many sins, it's my home, and I belong there. Along with all the other monsters. And Suzie Shooter, of course. My Suzie.

I got up off the bed, with a certain amount of effort, and went downstairs to see what she was doing. We loved each other as best we could, but I was always the one who had to reach out. Suzie . . . couldn't. But then, I knew that going in. So down the stairs I went, and treading the patterned carpeting was like moving from one world to another. Suzie wasn't what you'd call house-proud.

Her floor looked a lot like her old place—a mess. Dirty and disgusting with overtones of appalling. It was somewhat more hygienic, because I insisted, but the smell always hit me first. Her floor smelled heavy, female, borderline feverish. I peered through the bedroom door in passing. It was empty apart from a pile of blankets in the middle of the floor, churned up like a nest. At least they were clean blankets. Since she wasn't there, I moved on to the living-room, careful to knock on the door first. Suzie didn't react well to surprises.

Suzie was crashed out on her only piece of furniture, a long couch upholstered in deep red leather. *So it won't show the blood,* Suzie had said when I asked, so I stopped asking. She ignored me as I entered the room, her attention fixed on the local news showing on her more modest television set. The room never ceased to depress me. It was bleak, and so empty. Bare wooden floor-boards, bare plaster walls, apart from a huge life-size poster of Diana Rigg as Mrs. Emma Peel in the old *Avengers* TV show. Suzie had scrawled *My Idol* across the bottom, in what looked suspiciously like dried blood.

Her DVDs were stacked in piles against one wall. Her Bruce Lee and Jackie Chan movies, her much-watched copies of *Easy Rider* and Marianne Faithful in *Girl on a Motorcycle.* She also had a fond spot for James Cameron's *Aliens* and his two *Terminator* movies. Plus a whole bunch of Roger Corman's Hells Angels movies, which Suzie always claimed were comedies.

She was wearing her favourite Cleopatra Jones T-shirt over battered blue jeans, and scratching idly at the bare belly between the two, while eating deep-fried calamari nuggets from a bucket. I sat down beside her, and we watched the local news together. The impossibly beautiful presenter was in the middle of a story about a proposed strike by the Nightside sewer workers, who were holding out for bigger flame-throwers and maybe even bazookas. Apparently the giant ants were getting to be a real problem.

SIMON R. GREEN

Next, a new Timeslip had opened up in a previously unaffected area, and already members of the Really Dangerous Sports Club were racing to the location, so they could throw themselves in and be the first to find out where they'd end up. Nobody was trying to stop them. In the Nightside we're great believers in letting everyone go to Hell in their own way.

And finally, a fanatical Druid terrorist had turned up in the Nightside with his very own backpack nuke wrapped in mistletoe. Fortunately, he had a whole list of demands he wanted to read out first, and he hadn't got half-way through them before Walker turned up, used his commanding Voice on the Druid, and made him eat his bomb, bit by bit. People were already placing bets as to how far he'd get before the plutonium gave him terminal indigestion.

Without looking away from the screen, Suzie reached out and placed her left hand lightly on my thigh. I sat very still, but she took the hand away again almost immediately. She tries hard, but she can't bear to be touched, or to touch anyone else in a friendly way. She was abused as a child, by her own brother; and it left her psychologically scarred. I would have killed the brother, but Suzie beat me to it, years ago. We're working on the problem, taking our time. We're as close as we can be.

So I was surprised when she deliberately put down her calamari bucket, turned to me, and put both her hands on my shoulders. She moved her face in close to mine. I could feel her steady breath on my lips. Her cool, controlled expression didn't change at all, but I could feel the growing tension in her hands on my shoulders, the sheer effort she had to put

52

into such a small gesture. She snatched her hands away and turned her back on me, shaking her head.

"It's all right," I said. Because you have to say something.

"It's not all right! It'll never be all right!" She still wouldn't look at me. "How can I love you when I can't touch you?"

I took her shoulders in my hands, as gently as I could, and turned her back to face me. She tensed under my touch, despite herself. She met my gaze unflinchingly for a moment, then lunged forward, pressing me back against the couch. She put both her hands on my chest and kissed me with painful fierceness. She kissed me for as long as she could stand it, then pushed herself away from me. She jumped up from the couch and moved away from me, hugging herself tightly as though afraid she'd fly apart. I didn't know what to say, or do.

So it was probably just as well that the doorbell rang. I went to answer it, and there at my front door was Walker himself. The man who ran the Nightside, inasmuch as anyone does, or can. A dapper middle-aged gentleman in a smart City suit, complete with old-school tie, bowler hat, and furled umbrella. Anyone else you might have mistaken for someone in the City, some nameless functionary who kept the wheels of business or government turning. But you only had to look into his calm, thoughtful eyes to know how dangerous he was, or could be. Walker had the power of life and death in the Nightside, and it showed. He smiled easily at me.

"Well," I said. "This is . . . unexpected. I didn't think you did house calls. I wasn't even sure you knew where we lived."

"I know where everyone is," said Walker. "All part of the job."

"As a matter of interest," I said, "how did you get past all the mines, man-traps, and shaped charges we put down to discourage the paparazzi?"

"I'm Walker."

"Of course you are. Well, you'd better come in."

"Yes, " said Walker.

I took him into Suzie's living-room. He was clearly distressed by the state of the place, but was far too well brought up to say anything. So he smiled brightly, tipped his bowler hat to Suzie, and sat down on the couch without any discernable hesitation. I sat down beside him. Suzie leaned back against the nearest wall, arms tightly folded, glaring unwaveringly at Walker. If he was in any way disturbed, he did a good job of hiding it. Surprisingly, he didn't immediately launch into whatever business had brought him to my home for the very first time. Instead, he made small-talk, was polite and interested and even charming, until I felt like screaming. With Walker, you're always waiting for the other shoe to drop. Usually he speaks to me only when he absolutely has to—when he wants to hire me, or have me killed, or drop me right in it. This new friendly approach...just wasn't Walker. But I played along, nodding in all the right places, while Suzie scowled so fiercely it must have hurt her forehead.

Finally, Walker ran out of inconsequential things to say and looked at me thoughtfully. Something big was coming—I could feel it. So I did my best to avert it with other business, if only to assert my independence.

"So," I said. "Did you get all the Parlour's patients safely back to their home dimension?"

"I'm afraid not," said Walker. "Less than half, in the end. Many didn't survive being separated from their life-support technology. Many more died from the shock of what had been done to them. And quite a few were in no fit physical or mental state to be sent anywhere. They're being cared for, in the hope that their condition will improve, but the doctors . . . are not hopeful."

"Less than half?" I said. "I didn't go through all that just to save less than half!"

"You saved as many as you could," said Walker. "That's always been my job—to save as many people as possible."

"Even if you have to sacrifice some of your own people along the way?" I said.

"Exactly," said Walker.

"Why should you get to decide who lives and who dies?" said Suzie.

"I don't," said Walker. "That's up to the Authorities."

"But they're dead," I said. "We were both there when they were killed and eaten by Lilith's monstrous children. So who . . . exactly . . . pulls your strings these days?"

"The new Authorities," said Walker, smiling pleasantly. "That's why I'm here. I need you to come with me and meet the new Authorities."

I considered him thoughtfully. "Now you know very well I've never got on with authority figures."

"These people . . . are different," said Walker.

"Why now?" I said.

"Because the Walking Man has finally come to the Nightside," said Walker.

I sat up straight, and Suzie pushed herself away from the wall. Walker's voice was as cool and collected as always, but some statements have a power all their own. I would have sworn the room was suddenly colder.

"How do you know it's really him and not just some wannabe?" said Suzie.

"Because it's my business to know things like that," said Walker. "The Walking Man, the wrath of God in the world of men, the most powerful and scariest agent of the Good, ever, has come at last to the Nightside to punish the guilty. And everyone here is either running for the horizon, barricading themselves in while arming themselves to the teeth, or hiding under their beds and wetting themselves. And every single one of them is looking to the new Authorities to do something."

Suzie paced up and down the room, scowling heavily, her thumbs tucked in the top of her jeans. She might have been worried, or she might have been relishing the challenge. She wasn't scared. Suzie didn't get scared or intimidated. Those were things that happened to other people, usually because of Suzie. She sat down abruptly on the edge of the couch, next to me. Close though she was, she still didn't quite touch me. I caught Walker noticing that, and he nodded slowly.

"So close," he said. "In every way but one."

I gave him my best hard look, but to his credit he didn't flinch. "Is there anything you don't know about?" I said.

He smiled briefly. "You'd be surprised."

"It's none of your business," said Suzie. "And if you say anything to anyone, I'll kill you."

"You'd be surprised how many people already know, or guess," said Walker. "It's hard to keep secrets in the Nightside. I am merely . . . concerned."

"Why?" I said bluntly. "What are we, to you? What have I ever been to you, except a threat to your precious status quo, or an expendable agent for some mission too dangerous or too dirty for your own people? And now, suddenly, you're *concerned* about me? Why, for God's sake?"

"Because you're my son," said Walker. "In every way that matters."

He couldn't have surprised me more if he'd taken out a gun and shot me. Suzie and I looked blankly at each other, then back at Walker, but he gave every indication of being perfectly serious. He smiled briefly, holding his dignity close about him.

"We've never really talked, have we?" he said. "Only shared a few threats and insults, in passing . . . or discussed the details of some case we had to work on together. All very brisk and businesslike. You can't afford to get too close to someone you know you may have to kill one day. But things are different now, in so many ways."

"I thought you had two sons?" I said. I didn't know what else to say.

"Oh yes," said Walker. "Good boys, both of them. We don't talk. What could we talk about? I've gone to great pains to ensure that neither they nor their mother has any idea what it is I do for a living. They know nothing about the Nightside, or the terrible things I have to do here, just to keep the peace. I couldn't bear it if they knew. They might look at me as though I were some kind of monster. I used to be so good at keeping my two lives separate. Two lives, two Walkers, doing my best to give equal time to both. But the Nightside is a jealous mistress . . . and what used to be my real life, my sane and rational life, got sacrificed to the greater good.

"My boys, my fine boys . . . are strangers to me now. You're all I've got, John. The only son of my oldest friend. I'd forgotten how much that time meant to me, until I met your father again during the Lilith War. Those happy days of our youth . . . We thought we were going to change the world; and unfortunately we did. Now your father is gone, again, and you're all I've got left, John. Perhaps the nearest thing to a real son I'll ever have. The only son who could ever hope to understand me."

"How many times have you tried to kill me?" I said. "Directly, or indirectly?"

"That's family for you," said Walker. "In the Nightside."

I looked at him for a long time.

"Don't listen to him," said Suzie. "You can't believe him. It's Walker."

"The words *manipulative* and *emotional blackmail* do spring to mind," I said. "This is all so sudden, Walker."

"I know," he said calmly. "I put it all down to midlife crisis myself."

"And where does all this leave us?" I said.

"Exactly where we were before," said Walker. "We'll still probably end up having to kill each other, someday. For what will no doubt seem like perfectly good reasons at the time.

But it means... I'm allowed to be concerned. About you, and Suzie. And no, you don't get a say in the matter."

"We're doing fine," said Suzie. "We're making progress."

She let one arm rest casually across my shoulders. And I hope only I could tell what the effort cost her.

"Let us talk about the Walking Man," I said. Everything else could wait till later, after I'd had more time to think about it. "He's never come here before. So, why now?"

"In the past, the Nightside's unique nature kept out all direct agents of Heaven and Hell," said Walker. "But since Lilith was banished again, it appears a subtle change has come over the Nightside, and many things that were not possible before are cropping up now with regrettable regularity."

"So all kinds of agents for the Good could be turning up here?" I said.

"Or agents of Evil," said Suzie.

"Well, quite," murmured Walker. "As if things weren't complicated enough..."

"Still," I said, "what's bringing the Walking Man here *now*?"

"It would appear he disapproves of the new Authorities," said Walker. "The group whose interests I now represent."

"That's why you're here!" I said. "Because if they're in danger, so are you!"

Walker smiled and said nothing.

"Who are they?" said Suzie. "These new Authorities? The old bunch were nothing more than faceless businessmen who ran things because they owned most of the Nightside. So, are we talking about their families? The next generation? Meet the new boss, same as the old boss, don't get screwed again?"

"The inheritors?" said Walker, with something very like a sniff. "They wish. We saw them off. One quick glimpse of what actually goes on here, and they couldn't sell their holdings fast enough. No...Certain personages in the Nightside have come together to represent the main interests in this place. Essentially, the Nightside is now determined to run itself."

"Who, exactly?" I said. "Who are these brand-new *self-appointed* Authorities? Do I know them?"

"Some of them, certainly," said Walker. "They all know you. That's why I'm here."

"How can you serve people from the Nightside?" I said, honestly curious. "You've never made any secret about your feelings for us. You always said the best thing to do would be to nuke the place and wipe out the whole damned freak show once and for all."

"I've mellowed," said Walker. "Just possibly, these new Authorities can bring about real change, from within. I would like to see that, before I die. Now, come with me and meet the new Authorities. Hear what they have to say; learn what they mean to do. Before the Walking Man tracks them down and kills them all."

"But what do they want with me and Suzie?" I said.

Walker raised an eyebrow. "I would have thought that was obvious. They want you to use your gift to find the Walking Man, then find a way to stop him. Shall we go?"

THREE

Not Really Fitting In at All at the Adventurers Club

I let Suzie finish setting up the house's defences while Walker and I stood outside in what used to be the garden, not looking at each other. Suzie always likes arming the hidden charges and taking the safeties off the concealed weaponry and contemplating the mayhem and general carnage that will undoubtedly ensue if anyone is dumb enough to try to get into the house while we're out. One very professional burglar actually made it all the way to our front door once, and the door ate him. The letter-box was spitting out bone fragments for weeks afterwards.

I was still thinking about what Walker had said. *You're my son, in every way that matters.* You can't just drop an emotional bomb-shell like that into the conversation and expect everyone to act all business-like afterwards, as though nothing had happened. Unless you're Walker, I suppose. That calm, collected, cold-hearted functionary, who only runs the Nightside because he doesn't trust anyone else to do the job properly. Who always has an agenda, and a secret goal hidden inside every end game. Was he telling the truth this time? With Walker you could never tell, until it was too late. And what did I feel about him, after all these years? He's always been there, in the background of my life, sometimes helping, sometimes watching, sometimes sending his dogs after me. He's tried to have me killed on several occasions, but I never took that personally. For Walker, it was always just business.

I respected him. Even admired him on occasion, from a safe distance. But you couldn't like Walker. He wouldn't let you. He never let anyone get close enough to see the real him.

Suzie slammed the front door shut and muttered the last few activating Words, then I led us down the safe path, through the mine-field. Walker strode casually along beside me, swinging his furled umbrella like a walking-stick. Typical of the man. You could set fire to his old-school tie, and it still wouldn't affect his stiff upper lip. Walker was old school all the way, and proud of it. Family means a lot, to people like him. It's all they've got outside duty.

Once we were safely out on the street, Walker drew his gold watch from his waistcoat pocket and looked at me thoughtfully.

"I'm about to share one of my greatest secrets with you, John, Suzie. So do pay attention. I don't tell them to just anyone. So, basically, Timeslips don't just happen. Well, actually yes they do, suddenly and violently and all over the place. Bloody things are always popping up exactly where they're least needed and making trouble for everyone . . . But, there is a reason, a pattern, behind their appearances, and some people have learned to control them. Like Mammon Emporium . . ."

"Like the one we found in Frankenstein's cellar," said Suzie, determined not to be left out of things.

"Well, quite," said Walker. "They learned how to stabilise Timeslips, for their own profit. The old Authorities learned how to control them, for their own purposes. And the old Authorities didn't just give me my Voice—they also gave me this." He indicated the gold pocket-watch in his hand. "A Portable Timeslip. A doorway to everywhere, in and out of the Nightside. So that I can be wherever I need to be, whenever I need to be there. And sometimes just a little bit in advance."

"That explains a lot," said Suzie.

"I'll be damned," I said, staring at the watch. I'd seen it in Walker's hands a hundred times before and never thought twice about it. Typical of the man, to hide his greatest secret in plain sight.

"I'm only revealing this to you now because we have to get where we're going without being observed," said Walker. "I hope I can depend on both of you to be discreet about this?"

"Oh sure," I said cheerfully. "Right up to the point where I need to blackmail a favour out of you. So, where are we going?"

"Uptown," said Walker. "Clubland, to be exact. The

Adventurers Club. That distinguished home away from home for all the great heroes, gallants, and adventurers who pass through the Nightside. And most of them have, at one time or another."

"Why not the Londinium Club?" I said. "It's older, more established, and more exclusive than any other club in the Nightside, and it's always been the home base of all the real Powers That Be."

"Precisely," said Walker. "Far too connected with the old order. The new Authorities intend to make a clean break with all the old ways of doing things and are determined to send a clear message, right from the start. So, the Adventurers Club it is."

He fiddled with the rolled gold fob on the side of his watch, and the lid flew open, revealing an impenetrable darkness within. A deep, deep dark that seemed to draw my gaze in, till it felt like I was standing on the edge of an abyss and might fall in at any moment. And then the darkness leapt up and out, enveloping us all, and when it fell back again, we were somewhere else.

Uptown is the very best part of the Nightside, where all the very best people go. The most exclusive and exciting night spots, the most expensive bars and restaurants, and all the richest, most famous and powerful and totally up themselves people you could ever hope not to meet. And all the most exclusive, members-only, circle the wagons to keep out the riffraff clubs in Uptown gather together in Clubland. Where distinguished and discreet establishments cater to every need, enthusiasm, and obsession known to man. Some are nearly as old as the Nightside itself, while others deal in fads and fancies that come and go like mayflies. But they all have one thing in common. Membership is by invitation only. Plebs need not apply.

Walker led Suzie and me through the packed streets, and everyone gave way before us. Some because they recognised Walker, some because they recognised me, and quite a few because Suzie always looks dangerous even when she's just wondering what's for dinner. Walker nodded easily to famous and powerful faces, and they nodded respectfully back. He was one of them. Suzie and I quite definitely weren't. They did give us plenty of room. Which on the whole I think I preferred.

I gave my attention to the various clubs we passed along the way—the famous and the infamous, the outrageously exotic and the determinedly obscene. Names you could drop to impress your friends, or infuriate your enemies. Members-only clubs are the ultimate extension of the Old Boys Network, and it is in these very private back rooms that all the real decisions get made. In between the very best drinks and drugs and debauchery, of course. You go to clubs like them to do things behind closed doors that you'd never even think of discussing in polite society, to do the things of which your friends and family would never approve.

Like the Caligula Club, dedicated to exploring the furthest reaches of pleasure and pain, the most extreme forms of sensation. Or Club Dead, exclusively for the mortally challenged. A club for zombies, vampires, mummies, and quite a few of the Frankenstein clan's creations. (Club motto: *We belong dead.*) The Blue Parrott exists to cater to the Nightside's bird-watchers. Oh yes, we have them, too. You'd be surprised at some of the strange species that turn up here, and bird-watchers from all over the world come to the Nightside to observe ancient, rare, and impossible species that can't be found anywhere else. Everything from the dodo to the pteranodon, the giant roc to the fabled Oozalum bird. But no pigeons... There are no pigeons in the Nightside; or at least, not for long. Something eats them.

Then there's Pagan's Place, for barbarian warriors who want to better themselves, and right next to that, the Adventurers Club. Older than all the others put together, the original Club was supposedly founded back in the sixth century, and has been a watering hole for heroes between quests ever since. You wouldn't have thought any real hero would be seen dead in a place like the Nightside, but something about its reputation draws them here, possibly like moths to a flame, and the Adventurers Club is where they gather. Getting in is not easy. In fact, simply getting past the Doorman can be an adventure in itself. I think you have to slay an ogre and rescue a princess just to be allowed to use the rest rooms.

Still, every adventurer with a name or a reputation worth the knowing is supposed to have passed through its doors at one time or another. Why? Perhaps because the Nightside is the single greatest challenge any hero can face, the Mount Everest of challenges, and you can't call yourself a real hero until you've tested yourself against it. I only know about the

Club because my sometime friend Julien Advent has been a Member in good standing on two separate occasions. First, when he was the greatest hero and adventurer of the Victorian Age, then again after a Timeslip brought him here in the nineteen sixties. Julien's a good man and a revered personage; I planned to drop his name at every opportunity and hope some of his respectability rubbed off on me.

I said as much to Suzie, but she just shrugged. She's never cared about being respectable.

"Julien's not the oldest Member in the Club, though, is he?" she said.

"Not by a long way. I think that honour goes to Tommy Squarefoot. Of course, he's a Neanderthal."

Walker led us right up to the Adventurers Club Doorman, who stood tall and broad and very large before the closed Club doors. He was supposed to be a were sabre-tooth tiger, and given the sheer size of him, I was perfectly prepared to believe it. He stood aside for Walker, because everyone does, but gave first Suzie and then me his best cold, assessing look as we passed. Suzie glared right back at him, and he actually blushed a little and looked away.

"He likes you," I said solemnly to Suzie.

"Shut up," said Suzie.

"He likes you. He's your special Doorman friend."

"I have a gun."

"Never knew you when you didn't."

"Children, children," murmured Walker as he led us into the gorgeously appointed lobby. "Try not to show me up..."

I decided immediately to piss in the first potted plant I

saw, on general principles, but I got distracted. The interior of the Adventurers Club was as impressive as I'd always thought it would be. The Club proper was all gleaming wood-panelled walls, waxed floors, portraits and chandeliers, and proudly antique furnishings. Familiar faces passed by on every side, or gathered together to chat happily in the luxurious meeting rooms, or consult the leather-bound volumes of Club history in the huge private Library, or just brag to each other in the Club bar about their latest exploits.

Chandra Singh, the monster hunter, and Janissary Jane, the demon killer, were discussing new tracking techniques in the Library. They completely ignored me as I peered in through the open door. Jane was wearing her usual battered combat fatigues, which I knew from personal experience would smell of smoke, blood, and brimstone up close. Because they always did. She'd fought in every major demon war in the last twenty years, in as many different time-lines and dimensions, and while she'd been on as many losing as winning sides, she was a true professional, feared and respected by all who knew her. Especially when she had a few drinks in her.

Chandra Singh was tall, dark-skinned, and distinguished, with a sophisticated style and a truly impressive black beard. He was wearing his usual height-of-the-Raj finery, all splendid silks and satins, topped with a jet-black turban boasting the biggest single diamond I'd ever seen. Chandra hunted monsters in and around the Indian subcontinent, with a passion and enthusiasm unmatched anywhere in the world. His wall of trophies was legendary. He says he does it to protect the innocent and keep them safe, but I think he just likes killing monsters.

Well hell, who doesn't?

Walker dropped Suzie and me off in the bar while he went upstairs to tell the new Authorities we'd arrived. I didn't argue. I felt like I could use several large drinks, with an even larger drink for a chaser. The bar itself was almost overpoweringly luxurious, and I was impressed despite myself. No expense had been spared to make the Adventurers Club bar the envy of all lesser mortals, and it openly boasted every comfort known to man. The bar itself was a work of art, in gleaming mahogany and brightly polished glass and crystal, with a whole world of extraordinary potables lined up, just waiting to be ordered by some hero who'd worked up a serious thirst slaughtering everything in sight. Suzie, who had never been impressed by anything in her entire life, marched straight up to the bar, ordered a bottle of Bombay Gin, and put it on Walker's tab. I drifted in beside her, studied the bottles on display, and ordered an heroic measure of the most expensive brandy I could see. Also on Walker's tab. Having thus happily attended to the inner man, I put my back to the mahogany bar and took a good look at my fellow imbibers.

A dozen good men and women stood scattered about the oversized bar, in various garb from various times and places, all intent on each other and thoroughly ignoring Suzie and me. So I just as deliberately ignored them, giving my full attention to the various displays and trophies and portraits that adorned the bar. The walls were positively crowded with

portraits of old Club Members who'd distinguished themselves down the years. There were Admiral Syn, Salvation
Kane, Julien Advent, Owen Deathstalker, in a whole series of
clashing styles and periods. And the bar was positively lousy
with impressive trophies.

The shadow of a Leopard Man, imprisoned in a great block
of transparent lucite. A hollowed-out alien's skull, put to use
as an ash-tray. Something I didn't recognise from the Black
Lagoon, stuffed and mounted, and a severed demon head,
unconsumed by ever-burning flames. Several of the Club
Members lit their cigars off it. And up on the far wall, proudly
presented, the withered and mummified arm of the original
Grendel monster. Donated by Beowulf himself, apparently. (I
told you the Club dated back to the sixth century.)

Most of the famous faces were quite happy to pretend Suzie
and I weren't there, but two braver adventurers made a point
of coming over to say hello. Augusta Moon was a professional
trouble-shooter, and a noted dispatcher of problem super-
natural menaces. She was also an impressively large middle-
aged woman who looked like she should have been running
a girls' finishing school somewhere in the Home Counties.
Augusta was large and loud and famous for not giving a
damn. She dressed like an old-fashioned maiden aunt, in a
battered tweed suit, with a monocle screwed firmly into her
left eye. She also carried a stout walking-stick topped with
silver, and wasn't above poking people with it to make her
point. Augusta greeted me with a firm handshake, accompanied by her usual bark of a laugh, loud enough to shake the

furnishings. She had the good sense just to nod to Suzie, who nodded back. Augusta shrugged cheerfully.

"What the hell are you doing here, John? Thought you had more good taste than to show up in a dump like this. Place has gone severely downhill, since they started letting in people like us. Eh? Eh? Bunch of stiffs for the most part, old thing, haven't a clue how to have a good time. Had that Charlston Blue Blade in here the other day, really big noise by all accounts, but he damn near fainted away when I pinned him in a corner and inquired about the possibility of a little nookie!"

She laughed again, a loud, uncomplicated, and only faintly threatening sound. "Did you hear about my latest exploit? Jolly good sport, and a nice day out into the bargain. I was down in Cornwall on a walking holiday, just seeing the sights and putting the wind up the locals, when word came of a possible manifestation of the old god Pan. Well! Wasn't going to let that one by, was I? You mention Pan these days, to your modern high-tech hero, and all they can come up with is the goaty fella with the pipes and the hairy legs and the maiden fixation. No, no, Pan is where we get the word *panic* from. The spirit of wild and remote places that strike terror into the human heart for no good reason. Well, thought I, just the thing to shake up the old constitution, so I get myself down there and have a good old poke around.

"Didn't take me long to track down the source. An old village church, not far from Land's End. Norman architecture mostly, though not in the best of condition. Only thing holding it together was the ivy. Anyway, turned out that back in the day the locals had captured this terrible beastie and imprisoned it in a dimensional trap under the church, to be used as a defence against marauding Norsemen. Except, of course, the bally Vikings never did get that far south, so the beastie was left there and eventually forgotten. You can see the rest coming, can't you? The trap was finally breaking down, and beastie was flexing his muscles and preparing a break-out. The locals were picking up on the dread thing's thoughts of escape and revenge, and reacting accordingly, even if they didn't know why.

"So I broke into the church, kicked the trap apart, and let the beastie out, then slapped the nasty thing down with vim and vigour. Mercy killing really, poor old chap. No place left for olde-worlde monsters, in this day and age."

"How did you kill it?" I asked, professionally curious.

Her head went right back as she laughed her appalling laugh again. She brandished her walking-stick before me. "Clubbed it to death with this, old thing! Blessed oak and a silver handle, nothing better for beating the brick-dust out of a tall dark nasty!"

Some heroes are more frightening than others. I turned, with a certain amount of relief, to the only other adventurer who was prepared to be seen talking with the likes of me. Sebastian Stargrave, also known as the Fractured Protagonist, who claimed to have been three other Members of the Adventurers Club at different times in his confused time-line. Sebastian was tall and fragile, with an air of defeated nobility. A pale face under stringy jet-black hair, with eyes like coals coughed up out of Hell. He never smiled, and an air of quiet melancholy hung about him like an old tattered cape. He wore shimmering, futuristic golden armour, cut close to the skin, that murmured and whispered to itself, and rose up in a tall, stiff collar behind his head. Sebastian had been back and forth in Time so often, explored so many different timetracks and been so many different people, that he'd quite forgotten who he originally was. I've seen five different versions of him discussing the problem at the Hawk's Wind Bar & Grille, trying to work out where they might have come from originally. He may, or may not, have done many amazing and impressive things, in his time. He was quite certainly crazy as a bagful of badgers, and dangerous with it. I smiled and shook his frail hand, and said pleasant things because everyone does. Sebastian's been down on his luck for so long he brings out the protective instinct in most of us. Especially Augusta, who was always ready to clap him on the back and offer bluff, well-meant advice. Which is probably why he avoided her as much as he did.

Sebastian started one of his long, wandering quest stories, but none of us had the patience for that, so Augusta butted in and fixed me with a blunt glare through her gold-rimmed monocle.

"So, you and Suzie gal are here to meet the new Authorities, eh? Auditioning, are you?"

"Possibly," I said. "What do you make of them, Augusta?"

She snorted loudly, polished off the last of her single malt in one good gulp, and shrugged good-naturedly. "Someone's got to be in charge, I suppose, so why not some of our own, for a change? Doubt they'll last, though. Far too full of good intentions, and we all know where they lead. And you've got to be a little crazy to think you can run a madhouse like this. Eh? What?"

All of a sudden, a new figure appeared out of nowhere, right in front of us, and everyone in the bar fell silent to look at him. He was short and stout, dressed in black from head to toe, with ten alien power rings on his fingers, and I knew him immediately. Bulldog Hammond—burglar, thief, and quite possibly the most useless criminal in the Nightside. He lucked into those powerful alien rings and immediately became convinced he could use them to make himself a criminal mastermind. Unfortunately, the rings didn't come with an instruction manual, and he was still trying to figure out how to use them properly.

His eyes bulged in his silly face as he looked around and realised he wasn't where he'd meant to be. He fiddled desperately with his teleport ring but couldn't make it work again. He bestowed a strained smile on the barful of heroes and adventurers glaring at him, while giving every indication of a man who desperately needed a toilet.

"Ah. Yes. Hello, all! Sorry about this, got the coordinates wrong again. You know how it is I meant to burgle Pagan's Place next door and this explanation isn't going at all well is it?"

I had to smile. "You really did pick the wrong club to break into, Bulldog."

"Oh shit it's John Taylor. Hi! Yes! Is Suzie with you by

any chance oh hell she's right behind me isn't she? I really don't feel very well."

Augusta Moon glared furiously at him. "I know you, Hammond! Nasty little sneak thief! You stole the Golden Frogs of Samarkand from my little sister Agatha, didn't you?"

"Who me? What makes you think that was me? They weren't real gold anyway and I really think I'll be getting along now."

"Agatha cried on my shoulder for a week over those bloody frogs!" said Augusta. "Can't stand her most of the time, but family is family. Come here, you worm, so I can bestow beatings."

She raised her walking-stick, and Bulldog Hammond whimpered pitifully and grabbed at one of his rings. A force shield sprang up around him, enclosing him inside a cube of shimmering energies. Augusta gave it a good prod with the point of her stick, grunted once, then lifted her stick and whacked the hell out of the energy cube. The shield held, while Bulldog cowered inside and made high-pitched noises of distress. Augusta belaboured the force shield with all her considerable strength, and strange energies discharged on the air as the magic of her stick met the science of the shield. Everyone else watched, entranced. Many were laying bets. Suzie stepped lazily forward, her shotgun in her hands.

"No, Suzie," I said quickly. "The key word here is ricochets. There's all kind of delicate and expensive-looking shit in here, and I just know they'd make me pay for any breakages."

"Getting soft, John," said Suzie. But she did lower the shotgun.

Bulldog was still trying one ring after another, as the force shield shook and trembled under Augusta's unceasing assault. And then a series of brightly coloured rays shot out from one ring, piercing the force shield and flying across the room. Everyone threw themselves out of the way, but the rays did no obvious damage to anyone they touched. Instead, they worked their alien magic on all the trophies scattered around the bar. The muscles on Grendel's severed arm swelled and bulged, and the huge fist hammered against the wall. A suit of armour drew its sword, a tall potted plant lashed about with its sting, a small statue of a demon started playing with itself. Some artefacts exploded, some melted, some disappeared; and some launched open attacks on the Club Members.

A great painting of a strange alien jungle suddenly came alive and formed a window into that world. Terrible shrieks and cries came clearly to us, along with a gusting wind that stank of carrion. And through this newly opened gateway to another world, a whole cloud of ugly flying things burst into the bar; dark, hairy shapes with flapping batwings, glaring eyes, and huge, snapping teeth. They shot back and forth in the confined space, biting fiercely at everything in reach. There was chaos in the bar as everyone defended themselves as best they could.

Suzie Shooter opened fire with casual skill, her shotgun blasting the nasty flappy things out of mid air one after the other, never missing once; but still more and more came flooding through the open doorway. The Club Members fought the flying horrors with all kinds of weapons, and even their bare hands, but the growing numbers came close to overwhelming them. Augusta struck about her with her walking-stick, while loudly singing a psalm, and blood and bat brains flew on the air as she connected again and again. Bulldog cringed inside his force shield crying, "Sorry! Sorry!" I took a pair of chaos dice from my coat pocket and rolled them back and forth in my hand, and just like that the flying horrors couldn't seem to find me. I glared around. I don't carry weapons, as such. I don't usually need them. But I had to do something to stop this, before people started getting hurt. Even the greatest of heroes and adventurers can be brought down by sheer force of numbers.

Janissary Jane and Chandra Singh came rushing in. Jane had an energy gun in each hand, and shot the flying horrors out of the air with deadly speed and skill. Chandra had a long, curved sword, and danced amongst the swarming creatures, cutting them out of mid air with swift graceful strokes that were a work of art. Blood flew on the air as he worked his way into the very centre of the mayhem, grinning broadly all the while.

A batwinged nightmare bigger than all the rest came sweeping in out of nowhere and snapped its jaws shut on Suzie's shoulder. She didn't even flinch, but kept on firing. The teeth worked fiercely, gnawing into the black leather. I grabbed the thing with both hands and tore it away from her shoulder. The leather was torn, but I didn't see any blood. The thing struggled in my hands, its wings flapping fiercely, struggling to turn itself round so it could get at my fingers. I crushed it, my fingers sinking deep into its hairy body. It exploded in blood and bits, and died still trying to bite me.

I threw the bloody mess aside, and only then realised I'd dropped my chaos dice to help Suzie. I wasn't protected any more. Except by my gift. I sheltered behind Suzie as I concentrated on opening my inner eye. It was the work of a moment to find the energies holding the gateway open. Bulldog had accidentally cancelled them out. Then it was the easiest thing in the world to find the right combination to slam the gateway shut. The opening was immediately only a picture again, and no more creatures came flying through.

The Club Members made short shrift of the remaining flapping things, and the suit of armour and the potted plant, and all the other problems...then everything was quiet in the bar again, apart from the muffled curses of heroes and adventurers checking their wounds and trying to get their breath back. The floor was a mess of dead flappy things, with blood and hair and organs pulped into the rich carpet. One by one, we all turned to look at Bulldog Hammond.

He gulped hard and turned off his force shield. He then raised both hands high above his head and turned to me.

"Mr. Taylor, sir! I really would like to surrender now please. Oh yes and very definitely. Haul me off to jail I'll go quietly please don't let them kill me."

"People could have died here," I said.

"I know and I'm really very very sorry! It's all their fault for having so many nice and desirable things and for tempting such a weak-spirited soul as me and why is that large woman glaring at me like that?"

"I've got bat blood on my best suit!" snapped Augusta, brandishing her walking-stick. Blood and brains dripped off the end. "I know dry-cleaning isn't going to get it out! Come here and take your medicine, you appalling little man."

"I don't think I will if that's all right with everyone," said Bulldog.

"The rings, Bulldog," I said firmly. "Hand them over. You can't be trusted with them."

"But without them I won't be a master criminal any more!"

"You insist on hanging on to them, and you'll end up as one more bloody mess on the carpet."

"I see your point," said Bulldog. And he quickly stripped the rings from his fingers and dropped them on to my waiting open palm. I hefted them thoughtfully, then slipped them into my coat pocket.

"Very good," I said. "Now go and sit quietly in that corner, and wait here till Walker comes to collect you."

"You really think we're going to let that little snot get away with this?" said Augusta.

Several other Club Members made noises of agreement. I looked around me, taking my time. "He's just a small man who made a big mistake. It's over. Let it go."

"Why should we?" said Sebastian Stargrave in his quiet, deadly way.

"Because he's under my protection," I said. "Anyone here have a problem with that?"

No-one said anything. And then, one by one, they turned away and set about clearing up the mess. Because while they were all quite definitely heroes and adventurers...I was John Taylor; and you never knew. Bulldog went off to sit in the corner, Suzie put her shotgun away, and I retrieved my chaos dice from the blood-soaked carpet. Augusta Moon and Sebastian Stargrave ostentatiously turned their backs on me and drifted off together. Janissary Jane stood before the jungle painting, studying it thoughtfully. And Chandra Singh came forward, cleaning his long blade with a length of silk.

He nodded easily to me, extremely white teeth flashing in his great black beard. "Good to meet you at last, Mr. Taylor. I know you by reputation, of course, and I am pleased to discover it is not exaggerated." He turned his smile on Suzie and actually beamed broadly at her. "Miss Suzie, a pleasure to make your acquaintance again."

And to my surprise, Suzie actually smiled briefly at him. "Chandra. Killed any good monsters recently?"

He laughed, a rich and carefree sound. "I have been to many places in the world, and seen many monstrous things. Some I had no choice but to kill; some I captured to protect innocent lives; and some I photographed and let go. Not every creature is a monster, if you catch my meaning."

"You two know each other?" I said, trying to keep it casual.

"I watched his back, on a few hunts," said Suzie. "I was his native guide in the Nightside."

"Miss Suzie is a most excellent shot," said Chandra. "We worked well together. And I am hoping that you and I will also be able to work together, Mr. Taylor. You have been summoned here to hunt the Walking Man, am I not correct?"

"Could be," I said. "How would that concern you? I thought you only hunted monsters."

Chandra Singh nodded soberly. "Such has been my calling for many years, yes. I am a Sikh, Mr. Taylor, from the Punjab. I am what my people call a khalsa, or holy warrior. I stand against the forces of darkness, in all their forms. Does that perhaps remind you of anyone?"

"The Walking Man," I said. "Both of you serve your god in violent ways."

"Exactly, Mr. Taylor. I feel a great need to meet this Walking Man, and talk with him, and discover if he is indeed what they say he is."

"And if he is?" I said.

Chandra smiled his great smile again. "Then perhaps I shall sit at his feet and learn wisdom. But I think that unlikely. If he has done even some of the things they say he has, he would seem to be as much a servant of the dark as the light. And I will oppose him to my last breath. So, I ask your permission to accompany you and Miss Suzie as you track him down."

"What do you think, Suzie?" I said.

"He kills monsters," said Suzie. "Better to have him where we can see him, than maybe sneaking up on us. And I am kind of curious to see what will happen when two holy warriors go head to head."

"All right," I said to Chandra. "You're in. We split the fee three ways, and you're responsible for your own expenses. Agreed?"

"Most certainly, Mr. Taylor. I shall be very interested to see how you work, close up."

"If the Walking Man truly is a servant of the Christian God, where does that leave you?" I said, honestly curious.

"God is God," said Chandra. "Creator of us all. I do not think the Supreme Being cares what name we give him, as long as we talk to him. And listen."

Walker finally came down to fetch me and Suzie, looked around at the general blood and mess, and gave me a stern look.

"Can't take you two anywhere."

"Entirely not my fault," I said. "See Bulldog Hammond over there, sitting very quietly in the corner?"

"Ah," said Walker. "I suppose none of this is Suzie's fault either?"

"Of course not," I said. "Or there'd be dead bodies piled up all over the place."

"Good point," said Walker. "Come with me. The Authorities are waiting."

"What took you so long?" I said. "I was under the impression they were expecting us."

"We had things to discuss first," said Walker. "Like whether the situation really was bad enough to justify hiring you and Shotgun Suzie."

"Good point," said Suzie.

Walker nodded respectfully to Chandra Singh. "Always good to see you again, Chandra. Keeping busy?"

"Of course, Mr. Walker. There is never any shortage of monsters in the Nightside."

They bowed to each other briefly, then Walker led the way upstairs.

"I didn't know you knew Chandra," I said to Walker.

"Of course," he said. "I went to Eton with his father. Splendid chap. First-class geneticist these days, by all accounts."

The Nightside is full of unexpected connections. Heroes and villains, gods and monsters, we all know each other. Sometimes as friends, sometimes as enemies, sometimes as lovers. Sometimes all three. It's that kind of place.

I let Walker lead the way up the back stairs, just in case. Only a fool turns his back on Walker. Suzie brought up the rear. And in a small private room at the top of the Club, surrounded by the very best security measures the Adventurers Club had to offer, I finally came face-to-face with my new would-be lords and masters. They sat around a long, polished table, trying to look like people in charge. My breath caught in my throat as I saw their faces, and I thought my heart would stop. I knew them. I had seen them all together before, and not in a good way.

Julien Advent, the legendary Victorian Adventurer, now editor of the *Night Times*. Jessica Sorrow, the Unbeliever. Annie Abattoir, spy, assassin, and high-class courtesan. Count Video, lord of the binary magics. King of Skin, in all his sleazy glory. And Larry Oblivion, the dead detective. I had seen these people gathered together in one place before, in a future time-line where they had been the last survivors of Humanity, and my Enemies. They sent terrible agents back through Time to try to kill me, before I could bring about the awful devastated future in which they lived. I had gone to great pains to avert that particular time-line, to save their souls and mine, but here they were, gathered together again for the first time.

It had to mean something.

I strolled into the room and gave them all my best unimpressed look, on general principles. Never let them see you're hurting. And never let them think they've got the upper hand, or they'll walk all over you. Suzie didn't look impressed either, but then, she never does. Count Video spotted the shotgun holstered on Suzie's back and stirred uncomfortably.

"Hold everything. I thought we agreed—no weapons at meetings!"

"You want to try to take it away from her, be my guest," said Annie, amused.

Of course then everyone at the table had to make their views known, and I took the opportunity to gather my shattered thoughts. It didn't matter whether this particular grouping had any future significance; I had to deal with them here and now. So ... Julien Advent I knew of old. We'd worked together, on various cases. Julien was a good, honest, and highly moral man, which meant he tended not to approve of me. Or at least, some of my methods. He's far too good a man for the Nightside. I think he only stays because he's never been known to back down from a fight. As always, he was dressed in the height of Victorian finery, all stark black-and-white, with the only touch of colour the apricot cravat at his throat, held in place by an ornate silver pin supposedly presented to him by Queen Victoria herself. He looked to be a handsome man of about thirty, and had appeared so for several decades.

Jessica Sorrow's appearance was altogether more disturbing. Called the Unbeliever because for many years she didn't believe anything was real except herself, and she believed that so fiercely that if any particular thing or person caught her attention...she disbelieved in them until they stopped existing. A very scary and dangerous personage, until I helped defuse her. She still had a powerful presence, a kind of anti-charisma that fascinated and appalled at the same time. Barely five feet tall, she sat curled up in her chair like a feral child, horribly emaciated and corpse pale. Her eyes were very big in her face, her colourless mouth little more than a slit. She wore a battered brown leather jacket and leggings, the jacket hanging open to reveal her bare, sunken chest, to which she tightly hugged the teddy bear I'd found for her. Her old childhood friend, perhaps her only friend, it helped her ground herself in reality. Given the fierce, unsettlingly blank look in her dark eyes, I wouldn't have put money on her stability, but just the fact that she was there, interacting with other people, was a good sign. She cocked her head suddenly to one side, and looked at me, and knew me. For a moment, her expression was almost human. She smiled briefly. Her eyes didn't blink nearly often enough.

Annie Abattoir was altogether easier on the eye. A ripe, voluptuous woman in her midforties, Annie was an accomplished seductress and heart-breaker, and many other things beside, most of which could not be discussed in polite company. Six-foot-two, broad-shouldered and imposing, with a sharp sensual face, she wore a ruby red evening gown, cut daringly low at front and back, that went well with her great mane of copper red hair. She was beautiful and sexy and effortlessly charming, and she knew it. She wore long white evening gloves; presumably to disguise how much blood she had on her hands.

Count Video was a Major Player, when he could get his act together, and an old adversary of mine. And a real pain in the arse. Tall and stiff, he wore a stylish suit with little grace and less poise. I could still see the staples and stitches on his neck and face from where he'd had his skin ripped off during the Angel War, then reattached afterwards. The skin also puckered around the odd silicon node, or patch of implanted sorcerous circuitry, which powered his impressive binary magics. Plasma lights sputtered on and off around him, as some drifting thought or impulse rewrote reality on some basic level. He was good-looking enough, in a sulky sort of way, and would probably be dangerous if he ever got around to growing a pair.

King of Skin was more than a man but less than a god. Or possibly the other way round. It was hard to tell. Wrapped in his usual sleazy glamour, people only saw of him what he wanted them to see. He could charm or enchant you with a word or a look, or show you what you feared most. He could make nightmares real and send them chasing through the street after you, or grant you something very like your heart's desire, though it might look very different in the morning. Except mostly . . . he couldn't be bothered. A nasty man with nasty tastes and worse habits, King of Skin was also a Major Player, when he chose to be. For today's meeting, he had chosen to appear as the young Elvis, in Ann-Margret drag.

And, finally, there was Larry Oblivion. The dead detective, the post-mortem private eye. He looked in pretty good shape, for a zombie. Word was he'd been betrayed and murdered by the only woman he ever loved. She brought him back as a zombie, and he killed her for it. Just another love story, in the Nightside. Tall and well built, he wore the very best suit Armani had to offer. He had a colourless, stubborn face under lank, straw-coloured hair, and his icy blue eyes burned with something much worse than life. Up close, I knew he would smell faintly of formaldehyde. He had a good reputation as a private eye. Almost as good as mine.

His brother was missing, presumed dead. Because of me.

And these were the new Authorities—my old Enemies. Did that mean something? Had I escaped one awful destiny, only to see the start of another? Or had I really escaped anything at all? Julien Advent excused himself from the increasingly bad-tempered discussions and came over to join me. Walker made a point of moving politely away, while Suzie made a point of standing firmly at my side, glaring at everyone impartially.

"Good to see you again, John," Julien said easily. "I know we're going to achieve great things together."

Suzie sniffed loudly. We both ignored her.

"You always were the optimist," I said. "I thought you didn't approve of me?"

"Mostly I don't," said Julien, with his usual frankness.

"But on the whole you do more good than harm, in your own disconcerting and quite appalling way."

"That's right," I said. "Smooth-talk me."

Julien regarded me seriously. "We need you, John. No-one else can do what needs doing."

He broke off as Jessica Sorrow drifted over to join us, still hugging her teddy bear to her. Even the great Julien Advent got nervous around the Unbeliever. I sensed as much as saw Suzie reaching for her shotgun and shook my head urgently. Jessica stopped right in front of me and fixed me with her dark, bottomless gaze. She was so skinny there was hardly anything of her; in fact, her leather jacket probably weighed more than she did. She smiled briefly, almost shyly, and when she finally spoke, her voice was like a whisper from another room.

"You helped me, John. Or at least, the bear did. I'm so much more together, these days."

"I'm glad to hear that," I said.

She looked me over slowly, consideringly. "Something bad happened. Something so bad I had to make myself forget everything, just to be rid of it. I don't even know if my name really is Jessica. I'm better now. More . . . focussed. Being here, being a part of this, helps."

"We're all very pleased to have you here with us, Jessica," said Julien. And being him, he probably meant it. I had to wonder how the others felt, having the Unbeliever in their midst. Must be like sitting down with an unexploded bomb and wondering if you could hear ticking. I left Julien and Jessica talking and moved over to the long table. They'd run out of things to argue about, for the moment, and were scowling coldly at each other. Until I arrived, then they all switched immediately to glaring at me. I gave them my best cheerful smile.

"Hi, guys. Where's the buffet?"

"We should never have invited you here," said Larry Oblivion, his voice remarkably normal for a dead man. He scowled past me at Jessica Sorrow. "We should never have invited her, either. I don't trust her."

"Hell, darling, I don't trust anybody here," said Annie Abattoir. If a cat could purr with a mouthful of cream while screwing another cat, it would sound like Annie. "But if I can put aside my prejudices, and my quite-justified paranoia where some of you are concerned, to try and make this work, so can you. Oh hush, dead man. We've heard it all before. Don't make me come over there and sit on you."

"We all bring something to the table," Julien Advent said firmly, as he and Jessica seated themselves again. "I bring respectability, and the power of the press. Jessica is here to frighten our enemies. Annie has practised her appalling profession for every side there is, and a few she made up specially, and so has important contacts everywhere. Count Video and King of Skin are both Major Players, and command respect. And Larry has built quite a reputation for public service, since his death."

"Nothing like dying to provide a real wake-up call to the conscience," said Larry. "Heaven and Hell seem so much closer..."

"If you wanted a professional private investigator, why didn't you ask me?" I said, a bit put out.

"You've never been much of a team player, John," Julien said kindly. "And to be honest, given your...family history, no-one in the Nightside is ever going to feel comfortable with you in charge."

"He has a point," said Suzie, leaning back lazily against the wall with her arms folded. "I'll still shoot them all, though, if you like."

"Maybe later," I said. I can never tell when she's joking about things like that. Maybe she can't either. I indicated Walker, still standing politely off to one side. "What about him? Why isn't he a part of the new Authorities? He's got more experience in running the Nightside than all of you put together."

"They asked me," Walker said calmly. "I declined. My feelings about the Nightside are no secret, and I have to admit; my recent attempts at imposing some kind of order on the various Beings of the Street of the Gods...didn't work out too well. I was called in to organise, regulate, and modernise all the various churches, religions, and Beings, but despite my best efforts, things...deteriorated quite rapidly. It's not my fault the make-overs didn't take. Worshippers can be so literal, and very stubborn. And then the Punk God of the Straight Razor got involved, and it all went to Hell in a hurry."

"I remember that," I said. "For a while you couldn't move in some parts of the Nightside for Beings running out of the Street of the Gods, crying their eyes out."

"Well, quite," said Walker. "Either way, I feel I can best serve the interests of the Nightside as a functionary, not a decision-maker." He smiled briefly. "Unless the new Authorities should prove unworthy or incompetent, in which case I will move in to shut them down."

"You would, too, wouldn't you?" I said. "Suddenly and violently and with malice for all."

"It's what I do best," said Walker. "I have always found the possibility of sudden death tends to concentrate the mind wonderfully."

The new Authorities gave every indication of being united for the first time, as they glared at Walker.

"Let's get down to business," I said. "You brought me here because of the Walking Man. Why don't you people want him here? Would it really be so bad if he were to wipe out some of our more prominent scumbags and generally take out the trash?"

"This Walking Man tends to favour the scorched earth policy," murmured Walker. "And bad as this place undoubtedly is... there are some things here worth preserving."

I smiled. "You are mellowing, Walker."

"Told you," said Walker. "Terrible, isn't it?"

"What exactly do we know for sure, about the Walking Man?" I said, looking round the table.

Julien Advent took the lead, as always. "Throughout history, there has always been the legend of the Walking Man. That once in every generation, a man can make a deal with God to become more than a man. He can swear his life to God, and if that man will swear to serve the Light and the Good with all his heart and all his will, forsaking all other paths, such as love or family or personal needs... then that man will become stronger, faster, and more terrible than any other man. He will be invulnerable to all harm, as long as his faith remains true and he walks in Heaven's path. God's will in the world, God's warrior, the wrath of God in the world of men, sent forth to punish the guilty and stamp out evil wherever he finds it. Called the Walking Man because he will walk in straight lines to get where he has to go, and do what he has to do, and no-one will be able to stop him or turn him aside."

"Some Walking Men have killed kings," said Walker. "Some have overturned countries and changed the fate of the world. Others have followed more personal paths, clearing the world of evil one death at a time. Some stick to the shadows, some lead armies; and now one has come to the Nightside."

"If some of them have been so important, why don't I know their names?" I said.

"You probably do, if you think about it," said Julien.

"Ah," I said. "Like that, is it?"

"Mostly," said Julien. "There have never been that many, down the centuries. Perhaps because no normal man would take such a deal, giving up love and friends and everything that makes life worth living."

"They're killers," said Larry. "Cold-blooded, cold-hearted killers. Judge and jury and executioner. No mercy, no compassion, no pity."

"And only he gets to decide what's evil and what isn't," said Count Video. "He doesn't care what the law has to say. He doesn't have to. He answers to a higher power."

"No shades of grey for the Walking Man," said Annie. "Only stark black and white, all the way. You can see why so many people in the Nightside might be feeling a tad nervous, now that he's here."

"So as far as he's concerned, just by being here we're all guilty," I said. "I can see why you thought you needed me." I considered the matter for a while. "What do we know about the current Walking Man?"

"Nothing," said Larry Oblivion. "Not even his real name. He's invulnerable to all forms of remote viewing. We've tried science and sorcery, seers and oracles, and computers, gone cap in hand begging answers from important personages on all sides, and no-one knows anything. No-one wants to know anything. They're all afraid of being ... noticed. All we know for sure is that he's on his way here. Hell, he could be here right now, walking our streets, and we wouldn't know it till the bodies started piling up."

"He punishes the guilty," Jessica Sorrow said quietly. "And so many here are guilty of something."

"But ... if no-one can see him, what makes you so sure he's coming?" I said.

"Because he told us," said Annie.

"Sent me a very nice handwritten letter," said Julien. "In my capacity as editor of the *Night Times*. Advising us of his purpose and intentions, and that he would be here within twenty-four hours. Which time is almost up. He wanted me to publish his letter, so everyone would know he was on his way and could put their affairs in order before he got here. Very considerate of him, I thought."

"Yes," I said. "You would. Are you going to publish his letter?"

"Of course!" said Julien. "It's news! But...not just yet. We don't need a panic. Or people taking advantage of the situation to settle old scores. We're hoping you can...do something, before matters get out of hand."

I looked around the table. "What, exactly, do you want me to do?"

"I would have thought it was obvious," said Julien. "We want you to find the Walking Man and stop him from bringing death and destruction to the Nightside in general, and us in particular. He was quite clear in his letter that he intends to kill the new Authorities to send a message to the rest of the Nightside."

"How am I supposed to stop the wrath of God?" I said. Not unreasonably, I felt.

Larry Oblivion smiled. "That's your gift. We're confident you'll...find a way."

I suppose I asked for that. "What's the fee?" I said.

"One million pounds," said Julien. "And...we'll owe you."

I nodded. "Sounds about right." I looked from face to face. "You're all powerful people. And you know even more powerful people. Some of them so powerful they aren't people at all. So why put your faith in me?"

"Walker recommended you," said Julien. "And you do have a reputation for winning out against impossible odds."

"You of all people should know better than to believe everything you read in the papers," I said. I sighed, heavily. "All right. But let us be very clear about this. What *exactly* do you mean, when you say you want me to stop him? Do you mean reason with him, overpower him, or kill him?"

"You are authorised to use any and all means necessary," Julien said carefully.

"Hell, you can try bribing him if you think it'll do any good," said Annie. "Do whatever it takes, we'll clean up the mess afterwards. If you've tried being reasonable, and he doesn't want to know, feel free to stick a gun up his nostrils and blow his bloody head off."

"Love to," said Suzie, and we all looked at her.

"I'm still worried about the whole unstoppable, invulnerable, wrath of God bit," I said.

"This from a man who's fought angels from Above and Below," said Larry. "At least, according to him."

"I know my limits," I said, matching him stare for stare. "I can find the Walking Man. I can talk to him. I can use all kinds of tricks to confuse and divert him...but after that, your guess is as good as mine. We're in unknown territory here."

"Scared?" said Count Video.

"Bloody right I'm scared!" I said. "When the angels came here to fight their war over the Unholy Grail, their powers were strictly limited by the nature of the Nightside, and they still killed thousands of people and wrecked the place! And now Walker tells me the Nightside's nature has changed, and we don't even have that protection any more. If I had any sense, I'd go home and hide under the bed until this is all over. As it is...Look, when we talk about the wrath of God, we should be bearing in mind what happened to Sodom and Gomorrah, two cities destroyed by God for the sinfulness of their inhabitants. And I'll bet good money they weren't up to half the stuff that happens here on a regular basis, half price at weekends."

"He's still just a man," said King of Skin. His voice was deep and rich and irredeemably sleazy. "Every man has his weaknesses."

"I'll be sure to mention that to him," I said. "From a safe distance. Come on, I'm good, people, but even I can't go up against the direct will of God. Just saying that out loud is enough to make me nervous of a plague of boils on my nether regions."

"You do have a Biblical background," Julien said carefully. "Your mother was Lilith, first wife to Adam."

"Yeah, right—the one who rebelled against God's authority, got kicked out of Eden, went down to Hell and slept with demons, and gave birth to monsters," I said. "Really don't plan on mentioning that connection to the Walking Man, thanks all the same."

"It's only a parable anyway," said Suzie, unexpectedly. "A simple way to comprehend a much more complex reality."

We all looked at her for a moment. Suzie can always surprise you.

"Jessica Sorrow," I said. "The Unbeliever…It seems to me that you're the only one here with a strength of belief, or rather unbelief, to match the Walking Man. Maybe if we put the two of you together, you'd…equal out."

"That was then," said Jessica, fixing me with her deep, dark, unblinking eyes. "I'm much better now."

There was a certain amount of uncomfortable shifting about in the room, as everyone disagreed vehemently without actually saying anything.

"We're saving Jessica as our last resort," said Julien. "Our most dangerous weapon."

"Damn," said Suzie. "I thought that was me."

Julien flashed her a sympathetic smile, then gave me his best grave and concerned look. "It has to be you, John. You're the only one we can trust to do this."

"You keep saying that," I said. "I'm still not convinced."

"I still don't get this," Suzie said stubbornly. "I mean, God's wrath, fast and strong, yes, get all that. But what does he actually *do*?"

"Anything he wants," said Walker. "He's as strong as he needs to be, and as fast. He can kill with any weapon, or with his bare hands. No door can keep him out, no argument can turn him aside, and nothing in science or magic can protect you from him."

"Yeah," said Suzie. "But is he bullet-proof?"

"As long as he walks in Heaven's path, nothing in this world can touch him," said Julien.

"Even blessed or cursed bullets, with crosses carved in the end?" said Suzie.

"He wouldn't even blink," said Walker.

Suzie smiled suddenly. "Then I guess I'll have to try harder."

SIMON R. GREEN

"I've just had a cunning and downright disturbing thought," I said. "If the nature of the Nightside has changed, could we perhaps contact the Opposition, and have them send one of their agents to take on the Walking Man?"

"Let's you and him fight," said Count Video. "I like it."

"Are you crazy?" said Julien. "Two Walking Men, going head to head in the Nightside? Remember how much damage the angels did? We're still rebuilding!"

"Well, what about the Street of the Gods?" I said, doggedly. "Isn't there any Being there who feels strong enough to—"

"Not one," said Walker. "The whole Street is discussing moving itself out of phase with the Nightside, until this is all over, and it's safe for them to return."

"There's always Razor Eddie," said Suzie.

There was another silent uncomfortable moment, as everyone considered the implications of that.

"The Punk God of the Straight Razor has always been a very just man, in his own appalling way," I said finally. "He might decide to go along with the Walking Man. Eddie's always practised a zero-tolerance policy where the really bad guys are concerned. In a strictly hands-on, blood and brains all over the walls, sort of way."

"I still say we should defend ourselves!" King of Skin said abruptly. "Each of us is a Power, in our own right. We need to show the Nightside that we are a force to be reckoned with! We don't need to hide behind the likes of John Taylor. We should go abroad now, in all our awful glory, and grind this Walking Man beneath our feet!"

"No!" Julien Advent said firmly. "This is no time to be proud! We can't stop him. Not alone, or all together. He is the wrath of God in the world of men. There is no greater Power upon the Earth today! Our only hope is that John can out-think or out-manoeuvre him."

"We're doomed..." said Count Video.

"Hold everything," I said. "Are we missing the obvious here? Why not send Walker? He can use his Voice on the Walking Man and command him to leave the Nightside and never come back."

"Wouldn't work," said Walker. "My Voice derives its authority from that original Voice, that said *Let there be light*. I doubt it would have any effect on one who is a lot closer to the source of that Voice than I will ever be."

We waited, but that was all he had to say. Trust Walker to give you an answer that left you with more questions than you started with. Another thought occurred to me, and I looked hard at Walker.

"It's just like old times, this, isn't it? You recommended me for this job because I'm expendable. If I can stop the Walking Man, fine. If I can't, you'll have learned something from the encounter you can use to brief the next poor fool you send after him. You haven't changed a bit, Walker."

"I'd go myself if I could," said Walker. "But I can't stop him. At least you've got a fighting chance. And if he should kill you, John, I will find a way to make him pay."

"How very reassuring," I said. "You didn't have to bother with the emotional manipulation, you know. I would have done this anyway."

"John, I didn't—"

"Not now, Walker," I said. "Not now."

I fired up my gift, concentrating on my inner eye, opening it wide so that my Sight soared high above the Nightside. Bright lights shone amongst dark buildings, and hot neon blazed like bale-fires in the night that never ends. The streets turned slowly under me as I searched, until I spotted one single spark that shone so much more brightly than all the others. I plunged down, closing in on my target, until finally I found him, the Walking Man, strolling down a main street with laughter on his lips and cold, cold death in his eyes. And then he stopped, and turned, and looked right at me.

"Well hello there! Come and find me, John Taylor. Before I find you."

FOUR

Justice, for All

I have been hated and feared, loved and adored, but being looked on with sheer naked jealousy was a whole new experience to me. I decided to enjoy it while it lasted. It seemed like half the Membership of the Adventurers Club had crowded into the bar to watch Suzie and me descend the stairs from our meeting with the new Authorities. Some were trying to look without being seen to be looking, some just happened to be glancing in our direction, but most were glaring right at us with stares that could have punched holes through an elephant. I could see jealousy, curiosity, intrigue, and barely suppressed fury in the famous faces turned in our direction, and I loved every moment of it. All these heroes and adventurers, with their magnificent histories and legends, but it was Suzie and me who got to meet with the new Authorities first.

It should have been me, all the faces said, and I gloried in it.

I bestowed upon them all my most cheerful and enigmatic smile and walked through the bar without saying a single word. Let them wonder, let them marvel . . . I was the man on the spot, and they weren't. It's the little victories that keep me going. Suzie, as usual, gave no indication of giving a damn what anyone thought of her, good or bad. In fact, it was entirely possible she hadn't noticed any of the jealousy around her. Such small things were beneath her.

Walker followed us through the Club, and out on to the street again, also without saying a word to anyone. But then, Walker never says anything without a purpose. I like to think he escorted us out as a mark of respect, and not because he was afraid we might take offence and start something.

Outside in the street, leaning quite casually against the Club's oversized Doorman, Chandra Singh was waiting for us. He favoured us all with his great flashing smile and came forward, his every movement as smooth and lithe as a jungle cat scenting a kill.

"I trust your meeting with our new Authorities went well, Mr. Taylor, and that you are now fully empowered to track down the infamous Walking Man."

Walker sighed. "You really cannot keep a secret in this place . . ."

"You still want to help out on this?" I said to Chandra. "Knowing how dangerous the Walking Man can be?"

"Of course!" Chandra said happily. "I love a good hunt."

I considered him thoughtfully. Chandra Singh had an excellent reputation as a tracker, fighter, and holy terror in trouble spots all over the world, and I could certainly use his expertise. But I had to wonder if his motives were quite as clear-cut as he made out. Whether he only wanted in on this . . . for a chance to go head to head with the Walking Man to test his faith, one holy warrior against another.

What the hell, I could always use a good stalking horse. And someone big to hide behind. Suzie and I could always throw him to the wolves if necessary.

"All right," I said. "You're in. Try not to get in our way."

Chandra laughed. "No, Mr. Taylor, you must try to keep out of mine."

"Men," said Suzie. "Why don't you just get them out and measure them?"

Walker started talking over her before she'd even finished. He'd always had problems with Suzie's directness.

"You found the Walking Man with your gift, John. Can you tell us what he looked like? Most people only ever get to see the Walking Man if they're about to die at his hands, which makes it very difficult to get a clear description."

Suzie and Chandra looked at me curiously, too, so I thought about it. "He's tall and lean," I said finally. "And he swaggered down the street like he owned it. He wore a long duster coat, earth brown, battered and worn as though through long exposure to the elements. I couldn't tell you how old he is; he had a blunt, square face, heavily lined, as though life had cut harsh experiences deeply into him. He smiled all the time, a bright, mocking smile, as though all the world was crazy and only he knew why. His eyes . . . looked right through me. As though I was just another obstacle in his path, something to be knocked down and walked over if I got in his way. I've lived most of my life in the Nightside, gone head to head with gods and monsters and worse, and I am here to tell you . . . I have never seen anything as scary as that man. So sharp, so intense, so focussed. . . . He looked like every human weakness had been scoured out of him—by life, or death, or maybe even God himself."

"I never knew you to be so eloquent, John," murmured Walker.

"Yeah, well," I said. "Stark terror will do that to you."

"You want to let this one go?" said Walker. "Step aside, and let someone else talk over?"

"No," I said.

"Hell no," said Suzie.

Chandra just gave us his broad grin again, his eyes twinkling and happy. I was beginning to get a bit worried about Chandra.

Walker took out his pocket-watch, fiddled with the fob, and immediately the three of us were on our way. The transition was as unpleasant as before—darkness, total and complete, but with the enduring sense that there was something else in there with us. Something imprisoned in the dark, waiting for its chance. It could have been just my imagination, but that's not the way to bet in the Nightside. The three of us reappeared half-way down the street where I'd Seen the Walking Man in my vision. He wasn't there any more. No-one in the busy street paid any attention at all to our sudden arrival. In fact, I got the impression from the faces of people around me that sudden arrivals were so common as to be utterly unfashionable.

"An impressive way to travel," said Chandra Singh, quickly checking his person to make sure everything had arrived safely.

"You have no idea," I said. "Really."

We were standing on one of the main shopping streets, in the wildly expensive area usually referred to as the Old Main Drag. The kind of exclusive establishments where nothing has a price tag, because if you have to ask, you can't afford it. The neon signs were delicate and restrained, the window displays were works of art, and you had to make an advance appointment just to get sneered at by the sales staff. The Timeslip had deposited us right in front of one of the most famous stores. The elegant sign said simply PRECIOUS MEMORIES, the single window was covered with steel shutters, and there wasn't a clue anywhere as to exactly what the shop sold. Again, either you already knew, or you were in the wrong place. Precious Memories only supplied its very expensive products to those in the know. An exclusive place, offering exclusive services, for very exclusive people. I'd heard of the shop and what it offered because I make it my business to know about such things.

"Memory crystals," I said to Suzie and Chandra. "These people can impress real, *you are there*, POV memories on to a single crystal, which can then replay the experience in its entirety. Complete sensory recordings of any experience, to be enjoyed as many times as you wish."

"What kind of memories?" said Chandra. "What kind of experiences?"

"No-one knows," I said. "Except the few fortunate customers. The suppliers go to great pains to keep it all very hush-hush. There are any number of guesses, of course. Important events from the point of view of the protagonist. Any and all kinds of sex, by any and all kinds of people. Gourmet meals, enjoyed by the experienced taste buds of a real epicure. The rarest of wines, on an educated palate. Whatever interests you... Precious Memories is supposed to be able to supply you absolutely any experience you can name, from climbing Mount Everest to diving in the Mariana Trench. For the right price, of course. But, no-one knows for sure.

"The customers never talk. Part of the deal. The crystals are very expensive, and there's only a limited supply. There's a waiting list to get on the waiting list. Precious Memories is in a position to pick and choose, and it does. So even though there is intense curiosity everywhere as to what the experience is like, no-one ever talks."

"Oh come on," said Suzie. "This is the Nightside. Someone always talks."

"A few customers dropped a hint or two, and were immediately cut off," I said. "They killed themselves."

"Ah," said Chandra. "The practice is addictive, perhaps?"

"Could be," I said. "The crystals are supposed to be a safe way of observing or experiencing very extreme and unsafe things. Though, of course, that's not for everyone. When you come to the Nightside, the risk is part of the game."

"The door's open," said Suzie.

"Yes," I said. "I Saw the Walking Man push it open, quite easily, as though all its locks and security measures were nothing to him."

We looked at the door, standing slightly ajar.

"It seems . . . very quiet in there," said Chandra. "I think we have a duty to investigate the situation."

"Right," said Suzie. "Try and stay out of the way when I start shooting."

I pushed the door in, with one hand. No reaction, no alarms, no sound at all from inside. Not good. I led the way in, Suzie and Chandra pressing close behind me. The lobby of Precious Memories was perfectly normal—comfortable chairs, a nice carpet, tasteful prints on the walls, and an impressive state-of-the-art reception desk. All perfectly normal. Except for the bodies lying everywhere, and the blood splashed thickly across the walls, soaking into the rich carpet. Dozens of men and women, in expensive clothing, lying broken and bloodied with staring eyes, reaching out for help that never came. All of them shot to death, and not too long ago.

I moved cautiously forward, stepping over and around the bodies. Everything was still, and silent. Suzie had her shotgun in her hands. Chandra had his long, curved sword. Dead men and women covered the floor of the lobby, cut down where they stood. Huge chest wounds, gaping holes in backs, heads blown apart. The stench of spilled blood was so strong I could taste it in my mouth, and it squelched up out of the carpet as I trod on it. More blood ran down the walls, along with the occasional grey splash of brains. Some of the dead looked to be clients, some staff. Young and old, they'd all been murdered with brutal efficiency. Heart shots, head shots, and in the back if they'd tried to run. Even the receptionist was dead, sitting slumped in her chair behind her desk. She was just a teenager, but the Walking Man had shot her through the left eye.

Chandra Singh moved quickly through the lobby, kneeling here and there to check for a possible pulse, searching increasingly desperately for anyone who might have survived. Suzie swivelled back and forth, searching for a target, for someone she could shoot. The dead didn't bother her. She'd seen worse. I stood in the middle of the lobby, looking around for some sign of where the Walking Man might have gone, but the bodies kept drawing my attention back to them. Forty-eight in total, mostly men. Gathered together in the lobby for some kind of meeting. Some had been gut-shot, their insides splashed across the carpet. Some looked like they'd tried to surrender. It hadn't saved them. *The wrath of God in the world of men* . . . What could have been going on here to make him so angry? There was another door, at the far end of the lobby, with a single bloody hand-print on it.

"This is an abomination," said Chandra Singh, quite simply. "There cannot be any justification for such . . . slaughter, such human butchery."

"This is bad," I said. "Even for the Nightside."

"He walked in and killed everyone he saw," said Suzie. "What could they have been guilty of, to make him so angry? Or were they just in his way?"

"I hunt monsters," said Chandra. "I have dedicated my life to protecting people from the things that prey on them. I never thought I would see the day when I would end up on the trail of a human monster. How could a man of God do something like this?"

I moved over to the reception desk. Set directly before the dead receptionist was a single memory crystal. Someone had drawn an arrow in blood on the desk top, pointing to the crystal. We all gathered together before the desk and studied the crystal carefully, without touching it.

"Did he leave this here, for us?" said Chandra. "His . . . explanation, or justification, for this atrocity?"

"Could be a clue as to where he's gone," said Suzie. "Hope so. I really want to kill this one."

"I'll try it," I said. "If it looks like it's a trap, or the memory's . . . getting to me, slap the bloody thing out of my hand."

"Got it," said Suzie.

She put her shotgun away, and moved in close beside me as I nerved myself to pick up the crystal. It looked like such a small, innocent thing, but I didn't want to touch it. I didn't trust it. And . . . I wasn't at all sure I wanted to see what was in it. The things the Walking Man had done here. But in the end I picked it up anyway. Because that was the job.

To my surprise, a giant screen appeared, floating in mid air in the middle of the lobby. And from Suzie and Chandra's immediate reactions, it was clear they could see it, too.

"This isn't what I was expecting," I said.

"He must have modified the crystal," said Chandra, frowning. "I didn't know you could do that."

"You can't," I said. "At least, not without access to really high tech."

"He probably just touched it," said Suzie. "And it had no choice but to do what he and his god wanted."

We thought about that. What could be so terrible, that we couldn't experience it first hand, but only on the screen?

"How do we activate the thing?" said Suzie.

"I don't know," I said. "Maybe you just say *Start!*"

And the huge screen came to life and showed us awful things.

It wasn't a memory. Or a sensory experience. It wasn't even POV. It showed us a view of the lobby, with men and women standing around, talking quietly. They all seemed quite happy, and relaxed. Ordinary men and women, going about their ordinary business. They had no idea what was coming. No idea who was coming for them. They all looked round in surprise as the door suddenly opened, all the locks and security measures disengaging by themselves. And then the Walking Man strode in, with a smile on his lips and murder in his eyes, his long duster coat flapping about him like some Wild West preacher come to dispense brimstone and hellfire.

The men and women were still looking at him, puzzled and a little taken aback, like hosts presented with an unexpected guest. I wanted to call out and warn them, but there was no way my voice could reach them. The Walking Man's coat opened by itself, falling back to reveal a simple white shirt over worn blue jeans and two large pistols holstered head to head across his flat stomach. The guns seemed almost to leap into his hands as he reached for them; old-fashioned

Wild West pistols, with long barrels and wood grips. Peace-makers, the guns Wyatt Earp and his brothers used to tame helltowns like Tombstone. The Walking Man was still smil-ing when he began killing people.

He strode forward into the lobby, shooting the men and women before him with casual, practised skill. No warnings, no chance to surrender, no mercy. He shot them in the head or in the chest, and he never needed more than one bullet. The screaming started then, as surprise turned to shock, and to horror. People fell back as bodies crashed to the floor, and blood and brains flew on the air. The Walking Man never missed, and he never shot to wound, and though he fired and fired without pausing his guns never ran out of bullets. By now the lobby was full of shouting and screaming and plead-ing, and the sound of continuous gunfire. Some tried to run, and the Walking Man shot them in the back, or in the back of the head.

The huge guns bucked and roared in the Walking Man's hands, but his aim was always perfect, and he never grew tired. His smile actually widened a little as he worked his way through the lobby, as though the killings invigorated him. Bullets slammed into bodies like sledgehammers, throwing men and women backwards, or slamming them to the ground. Arms flailed wildly amongst spurting blood, and heads exploded in flurries of blood and brains. The Walk-ing Man stepped over kicking bodies, to get at those who remained.

Some pleaded, some protested, some even sank to their knees and begged for their life, tears streaming down their faces. The Walking Man killed them all anyway. A few tried to fight back. They drew guns and knives, and even beat at him with their bare hands. But bullets bounced off him, knives couldn't cut him, and he didn't seem to feel their blows. He was the wrath of God in the world of men, and no-one could stop him doing anything he wanted.

Some men pulled hysterical women before them, to use as human shields. The Walking Man killed the women, then the men behind them. Until finally he stood in the centre of the lobby and looked around him. No-one had escaped. The floor was heaped with the dead, the last of their life's blood soaking into the rich carpeting. The only sound came from the teenage receptionist, crying loudly, hopelessly, in her chair behind her desk. The Walking Man shot her through the left eye. Her head snapped back, and her brains stained the wall behind her.

He walked unhurriedly across the lobby, sometimes kicking bodies out of his way, until he came to the door at the far end. He paused there a moment, then picked up a dead man's arm to press the bloody hand against the door, leaving a clear bloody handprint. A sign of where he'd gone. The view on the screen followed him through the door and down the steps he found there, to the next level. At the bottom of the steps, another heavy door, with state-of-the-art electronic locks and security devices. The Walking Man looked at them, and, one by one, the locks snapped open and the security devices disengaged. The door swung slowly open as he approached it.

The Walking Man entered a long, narrow room full of computers and assorted technology. Someone had money for the very best. The Walking Man passed them by, indifferent. He did pause to consider hundreds of memory crystals growing in a thick, shimmering liquid bath, inside a wide glass-and-steel lattice. The equivalent of a DVD-pressing plant, perhaps. The technicians working in the room looked round sharply as he entered, then rose quickly from their chairs and backed away as they saw the guns in his hands. One of them hit an alarm, and a raucous electronic howl filled the room. Armed men came running into the room from the other end. They had semi-automatic weapons, and body armour. They opened fire the moment they saw the Walking Man—short, controlled bursts, just the way they'd been trained.

He killed them all anyway. Guards and technicians, armed and unarmed. His bullets punched clean through the body armour as easily as through the technician's white lab coats. Weapons couldn't touch him, couldn't stop him. He walked unhurriedly forward and killed everyone before him. Once again there was shouting and screaming, and pleas for mercy, and blood and brains on the air and on the floor, but the Walking Man never stopped smiling. A cold, grim, satisfied smile. When they were all dead, he systematically smashed the crystal lattice, and half-formed crystals splashed on to the floor, and the Walking Man crushed them under his boots.

Another door, at the far end. More stairs, down to the next level. The defences there were really hard core. They would have stopped anyone else. As the Walking Man reached the bottom of the stairs, heavy-duty gun barrels protruded from both walls and opened fire on him. The din in the confined space was appalling, as the guns pumped out thousands of rounds per minute, but he strode unflinchingly through the smoke and the noise, and none of the bullets could touch him. His coat wasn't holed or tattered, or even scorched by proximity to the red-hot gun barrels. The guns finally fell silent, and the Walking Man went on.

Further down the hallway, energy guns slid smoothly out of the walls, future or alien technology from some Timeslip or another. They blasted the Walking Man with all kinds of energies and radiations, strange lights flaring in the dimly lit hallway, and none of it affected him in the least. He grabbed one gun barrel as he passed, ripping it effortlessly from its mounting. He examined it briefly, then threw it aside, never slowing his pace for a moment.

Force shields sprang into being before him, shimmering walls to block his way. He strode through them, and they burst like soap bubbles. Poison gasses belched into the hallway from hidden vents, and he breathed them in like summer air and kept going. A trap-door opened abruptly beneath his feet, revealing a bottomless pit, but he kept walking, as though the floor was still there to support him.

Finally, he came face-to-face with a massive steel door. Ten feet tall, eight feet wide. Just to look at it was to know it was thick and heavy and solid. Tons of steel, held in place by massive bolts. The Walking Man stopped, and considered the door thoughtfully. Far behind him, the alarms were still shrieking dimly. The Walking Man put away his guns and placed both his hands flat against the steel door. He frowned slightly, and his fingers sank slowly, unstoppably, into the solid steel as though it were so much mud. He buried his hands in the metal, took a good hold, and tore the door apart, splitting it from top to bottom. The steel screeched like a living thing as it broke, forced to left and right like a pair of curtains. The Walking Man pulled his hands free with hardly an effort and walked on.

Cyborg guards came running to meet him, huge ugly men with crudely implanted technology. They were big and muscular with unfamiliar tech thrust inside their bodies, some of it still protruding through puckered skin. Home-made cyborgs, not from any future time-line. They came at him with augmented hands—steel claws and energy guns protruding from their wrists and palms. But the guns couldn't touch him, and the claws couldn't cut him. The Walking Man tore their implants right out of them, ripping the tech out with his bare hands, then smashed it over their misshapen heads. He beat them to death, with simple brute efficiency, one after the other, until there weren't any more. He stood over their broken bodies for a moment, his hands dripping blood and motor oil, then he went on, into the rough stone cellar at the base of the building.

A long run of basic kennels held some twenty or more dogs. Large, powerful creatures in good condition. They all barked loudly at the Walking Man, protesting his presence. They could smell the blood and death on him. They moved restlessly back and forth in their kennels, uneasy as he approached them. Some actually backed away, disturbed by his intensity, while others threw themselves at the steel mesh of their kennel doors, barking and snarling and slavering, desperate to get at him. The doors were all firmly padlocked.

The Walking Man was in no danger from them. He killed them all anyway. He walked slowly from one end of the kennels to the other, shooting each dog in the head. Some defied him to the last, some backed away with their tails between their legs. The last few crouched down, abasing themselves before him, pissing themselves and wagging their tails hopefully. He killed every last one of them.

Finally, he turned to face us, looking out of the screen as though he could see the three of us watching him. And perhaps he could. It took me a moment to realise he wasn't smiling any more. He put his guns away, and said, "This is why."

The scene moved past him, past the dead dogs in their kennels, to give us a clear view of the whole cellar. It was full of cages, rows and rows of them, maybe four feet square at most, simple steel mesh in steel frames. And in each of these cages was a child. Naked, bruised, and beaten, shivering, with a hopeless face and empty eyes. A bowl of water, and straw on the floor to soak up the wastes, and that was all. Not even a bucket to shit or piss in. Children, kept like animals. Worse than animals. Small children, none older than nine or ten. The youngest looked to be a little girl about four years old. None of them were crying, or asking for help, because they'd learned the hard way that didn't work. They looked at the Walking Man with blunt animal curiosity. They didn't expect to be rescued. All hope had been systematically beaten out of them. The cages weren't big enough for them to stand up. They sat or crouched listlessly, in their own filth. Waiting for whatever this man wanted to do to them.

"These children were snatched off streets all over London,"

said the Walking Man. "Brought here to the Nightside, to be raped, tortured, mutilated, and, eventually, murdered. All so that the experience could be impressed on a memory crystal, then sold to those who delight in such things. A real *you are there* experience, for sale to the very highest bidders. This was the product Precious Memories dealt in, for its very select clientele. Utter degradation, from a safe distance. They didn't do anything, after all. They just watched. Over and over again, until the thrill wore off. Long after the child was dead and gone. That's why everyone here had to die. They all knew what was going on. They all profited. They were all guilty. After the children died their slow, horrible deaths, their bodies were fed to the dogs, for disposal. And that's why they had to die, too."

He moved into view again, unlocking the cages one by one. None of the children tried to leave. They cowered back, afraid of the Walking Man, as they'd learned to be afraid of all men. Even with the doors open, they wouldn't, couldn't, leave. When the Walking Man had finished, he turned back to look at us.

"Help them," he said. "Get them out of here. Get them to safety, and comfort, and heal those who can be healed. Get them home. I can't stay here. I still have work to do. I have to track down everyone who was on Precious Memories' customer list, and kill them all."

The viewscreen disappeared, and the three of us were left together in the lobby full of dead people. I snatched my hand away from the memory crystal. I was shaking so hard I couldn't speak. Suzie moved in close beside me, comforting me as best she could with her presence. I looked around at the dead men and women. I couldn't believe I'd ever felt sorry for them. After what they'd done ... the Walking Man showed them more mercy than I would have. He'd given them quick, clean deaths. I felt cold, so cold, right down to my soul. Bad things happen in the Nightside. That's what it's for. But this ... systematic, business-like brutality, to feed the worst appetites of humanity ... a concentration camp for children ... He was right. The Walking Man was right, to kill every last one of them.

I must have said some of that aloud, because Chandra Singh nodded quickly. When he spoke, his voice was thick with outrage.

"Perhaps ... I have been hunting the wrong kind of monster, all these years."

"We have to go down there," said Suzie. "Into the cellar. We have to help the children."

"Of course we do," I said.

We went down into the cellar. Sometimes we stepped over the bodies, sometimes we kicked them out of our way. At the bottom level, the smell hit us first. It drifted through the broken steel door like a breeze gusting out of Hell. A bad smell, of death and horror, of human filth and children's suffering. Of piss and shit, sweat and blood. Of terrible things, done in a terrible place. A harsh, reeking, animal smell.

The children were still there, in their cages, trapped in the world that had been made to hold them. Suzie and Chandra approached the cages slowly and cautiously, speaking softly to the children, trying to coax them out. I got on the phone to Walker. I told him what had happened there, then I told him to send help. All the help the children would need. There must have been something in my voice, because Walker didn't argue or waste my time with unnecessary questions. He promised me help was on the way, and I hung up on him.

Chandra was having some success reaching the children, with his great smile and his warm, friendly voice. And perhaps because he was dressed so differently from what they were used to seeing. Suzie did better. They weren't as afraid of a woman. I tried to help, but I was too close to what they'd been taught to be afraid of. It seemed to take forever for Walker's people to arrive. Down there, in that hell. When the doctors and nurses and shrinks finally turned up, we'd still only managed to coax seven of the children out of their cages. Five boys, two girls. They looked at us with wide, traumatised eyes, still too disturbed to talk, just beginning to hope that maybe their long nightmare was finally coming to a close.

One of the girls, a small bruised child of maybe five or six, impulsively hugged Suzie, who was kneeling before her. I moved forward to take the child away, but Suzie stopped me with a look. She slowly closed her arms around the girl and hugged her back. The child nestled against Suzie's breast, safe at last. Suzie looked up at me.

"It's all right, John," she said. "I can do this. I can hold her. It's like holding me."

I guess one abuse survivor can always recognise another.

The doctors and the nurses and the shrinks did what they could. I got the feeling they'd seen this kind of thing before. They seemed to know what to say. One by one, the children began to emerge from their cages. Some could even say their names. Walker finally showed up and looked the scene over. His expression never changed, but his eyes were colder than I'd ever seen them.

"We don't have social services, as such, in the Nightside," he said finally. "Not much call for them. But I've got people coming in from all over, including a few telepaths and empaths. They'll get the children stabilised, then I'll arrange for them to be taken back into London proper. Back to their homes, eventually. Hopefully. The children will get everything they need, John. You have my word on that."

"Search the computers here," I said. "There has to be a complete list of Precious Memories' customers, distributors, everyone involved in this filthy business who weren't here when the Walking Man came calling. Find them all, Walker, and punish them. No exceptions, no excuses, no mercy. No matter how well connected some of them may be. Because if the Walking Man doesn't kill them, I will."

"He's been sighted again," said Walker. "At the Boys Club. Do you know it?"

"Of course I know it," I said. "It's back in Clubland. Send us there."

"I'm not going," said Suzie. I looked at her, and she met my gaze steadily, still holding the small child in her arms. "I need to be here, John. To see they all get the help they need. I can help. I understand."

"Of course you do," I said. "Stay. Do what you can. I'll take care of things."

"I will go with you," said Chandra Singh. "I need to talk to this Walking Man. What kind of a man is he? What kind of man can go into places like this and kill everyone he finds? What must that do to a man, to his state of mind? To his soul?"

"He wants us to know," I said. "That's why he showed us everything. He's teaching us to see the world as he does. Black and white, right and wrong, and no shades of grey. A world where the guilty will be punished."

"He still has to be stopped," said Walker. "All cats are grey in the Nightside. And not all of them deserve to be judged so harshly."

"Are there other places like this, in the Nightside?" I asked him. "Did you know about this place?"

"No," said Walker. "But I can't say it surprises me. The Nightside exists to serve sinners. All kinds of sin. There are places worse than this, and if you keep following the Walking Man...I've no doubt he'll show you just how dark the night can get."

FIVE

Bad Boys and Wayward Girls

Walker's Portable Timeslip delivered Chandra Singh and me right into the middle of Clubland, and we took a moment to lean on each other while our heads and stomachs settled. Passing through that unnatural darkness was getting worse. The latest one had felt like being trapped in a plummeting lift, while it was on fire, and something really bad was gnawing its way through the lift floor to get at me. Only more so.

"That...was most unpleasant," Chandra said finally.

"Yeah," I said. "And Walker's been doing that every day for years. Explains a lot about the man."

I led the way through the relatively sophisticated streets of Clubland (where you could still get mugged but at least the fellow would have the decency to wear a dinner jacket) and headed for the Boys Club. Chandra was inexperienced in the ways of the Nightside, so it fell to me to explain to him just what kind of a place the Boys Club was. Basically, it was a particularly nasty and wholly corrupt establishment where all the Nightside's most pre-eminent gangsters, crime lords, Mr. Bigs, and general scumbags went to be with their own kind. To spend their money ostentatiously, practise very basic one-upmanship, usually involving guns, and boast of their latest successes and ill-gotten gains. Taste, restraint, and charm are notable by their absence, at the Boys Club.

"The law knows of this place, and does nothing?" said Chandra.

"This is the Nightside," I said patiently. "There is no law here, and less justice, unless you make some for yourself. Walker and his people only ever step in when things are really getting out of hand, and then only to restore the status quo. This is a place where people come to do the things they're not supposed to, and pursue the pleasures they're not supposed to want. Forbidden knowledge, forsaken gods, and all the fouler kinds of sex. And where there's business, you can be sure there's always someone taking a cut. By force if need be."

"And these...people belong to the Boys Club," said Chandra.

"The nastiest, vilest, and most unpleasant representatives of their kind," I said.

Chandra Singh considered this. "Why not just kick in the

123

door and toss in half a dozen incendiaries?" He smiled briefly. "Being a monster hunter teaches you to be practical, above all else."

"You could kill everyone in there," I said. "And most of us have thought about it, at one time or another, but they'd all be replaced within the hour. There's never any shortage of people on the way up, eager for a chance to prove they can be even nastier and more unpleasant than the scumbags they're replacing."

Chandra looked at me seriously. "Why do you stay in this terrible place, John Taylor? I have heard stories about you . . . but you do not seem such a bad man. What keeps you in the Nightside?"

"Because I belong here," I said. "With all the other monsters."

I increased my pace. Part of me was worried that we'd get there too late and find another massacre. And part of me wondered if that might be such a bad thing . . . But not everyone in the Boys Club deserved to die. Just most of them.

The Club finally loomed up before us, flashy, gaudy, and weighed down with a really over-the-top Technicolor neon sign. Nothing to indicate what the Club was for, of course; either you already knew, or you had no business being there. Membership was strictly by invitation only, an acknowledgment by your peers that you'd made it, that you were finally big enough and important enough to be one of the Boys.

And there, waiting outside the front door for us, was the Walking Man. He was leaning casually against a lamp-post in his long duster, with his hands in his pockets, smiling easily, one foot planted on the neck of the Club's unconscious Doorman. Chandra and I came to a halt, maintaining a respectful distance. The Doorman was big enough to be part troll, but there he was lying facedown in the gutter, without an obvious wound on him. The Walking Man nodded to us, then we all stood there for a while, taking the measure of each other.

The Walking Man looked just as I remembered him to, but in person there was so much...more to him. He had an air, a presence, an almost overwhelming intensity to him, as though he was the only real man in a world of fakes and posers. His eyes were bright and merry, his smile was full of mischief and bravado, and everything about him exuded an almost spiritual insolence. *I am here to do absolutely appalling things in the name of the Good,* his stance positively shouted. *And what are you going to do about it?* He had the look of a man who would do anything he felt like doing, and do it with a laugh on his lips and a song in his heart. This was no sombre driven warrior of God come to do his duty, no cold and dour executioner. This man enjoyed what he did.

Dead men and women, and dogs. And children in cages.

"John Taylor," the Walking Man said finally, in a happy, cheerful voice. "Thought you'd be taller."

"I get that a lot," I said.

"Who's your friend?"

"I am Chandra Singh, monster hunter!" Chandra said proudly.

"Good for you," said the Walking Man.

Chandra bristled just a bit, as he realised his name and

cherished reputation meant nothing to the Walking Man. He drew himself up to his full height, the better to show off his magnificent Raj silks and the diamond flashing in his turban.

"I, too, am a holy warrior," he said hotly. "I also do God's work, striking down those who would threaten the innocent!"

"How nice," said the Walking Man. "Try not to get in the way."

Chandra suddenly realised he was being teased and gave a great bark of laughter.

I was concentrating on the Walking Man's face. There was something of the impish, the almost devilish, about his mocking gaze and easy smile. He wasn't at all what I'd expected. He was far more complicated, and therefore far more dangerous.

"I can't just let you walk in there and kill everyone," I said bluntly. "This isn't like Precious Memories, where everyone was guilty. There are bad people in the Boys Club, but not everyone is bad enough to be worth killing."

"That's my decision to make, not yours," said the Walking Man. "This is what I do. You're just along for the ride."

"I know the Nightside better than you ever will," I said.

"You're too close," the Walking Man said kindly. "You can't see it clearly any more. You need me, to do what you've never been able to do."

"I'll stop you if I have to," I said.

He flashed me a bright smile and shot me a merry look,

one professional to another. "You're welcome to try. Now, let the fun begin!"

We just walked in. The Doorman was currently making low, sad moaning sounds in the gutter, clearly in no shape to ask to see our Membership cards. The door swung open by itself. (At least the Walking Man hadn't killed the Doorman outright. I told myself there was hope in that.) There were, however, a number of large and very competent-looking security guards waiting for us in the lobby, their muscular forms all but spilling out of their expensive suits. The Walking Man sauntered in like he owned the place, nodding briskly to the security guards. They nodded back, responding instinctively to his arrogant authority, before catching themselves and moving quickly forward to block our way. The Walking Man stopped, and looked them over, his smile openly mocking.

I looked around the lobby. They'd redecorated the place since I was last there, but it was still big and flashy and overstated, like most of the Club Members. Chandra and I moved in on either side of the Walking Man, and several of the security men got a bit twitchy when they recognised me. It was because of my last visit that they'd had to redecorate the lobby. But still, they were just thugs with guns, for all their nice suits, and I'd spent my whole life running rings round goons like them.

The most senior thug took a step forward, fixing me with his best intimidating stare. "You know you're not allowed in here, Mr. Taylor. You upset the nice gentlemen and their ladies. You are banned. And that goes for your friends as well, whoever they are."

"I am Chandra Singh, holy warrior and mighty monster hunter!" said Chandra, getting a little peeved at his lack of fame in the Nightside. "I have got to get myself a better agent..."

"And I am the Walking Man," said the Walking Man cheerfully. "Come to judge your souls."

The security men went very pale. Several started perspiring, several more began shaking, and one actually whimpered. All their attention was on the Walking Man. Chandra and I might as well have not been there. It would seem what had happened at Precious Memories had already reached the Boys Club. Nothing travels faster than bad news, especially in the Nightside. The thug in charge swallowed audibly.

"I think we'd all like to run away now, sir, if that's all right with you."

"Go," said the Walking Man, gesturing grandly. "I can always find you later if I need you."

The body-guards departed, but they didn't just leave— they ran as if Death herself was on their trail, actually fighting each other to get through the door first. I'd never had that effect on people, on the best night I ever had. I felt distinctly jealous.

"Doesn't the lobby seem so much bigger, without them in it?" said the Walking Man. "Shall we go in?"

"Why not?" I said. "I think you've done all the damage you can here."

He laughed.

I opened the doors into the main Club area, and the Walking Man swaggered through with his hands still stuffed deep in his coat pockets. He couldn't have looked more at ease if he'd been walking into his own front room. Chandra and I took up our positions on each side of him again. Though whether to support or restrain him, I hadn't actually decided.

Entering the Club's huge recreation area was like walking into the world's sleaziest circus, all bright lights and glaring primary colours, with all kinds of beasts on display. People sat at tables, or milled around in the open central area, or propped up the massive bar. Music blasted out of concealed speakers, almost drowned out by the sheer din of so many people shouting and laughing at once, doing their best to convince themselves and everyone around them that they were having a great time. There was a lot of looking around, to see what everyone else was doing, in case it looked like more fun, and a constant checking of who was with whom.

There were gambling tables—cards, craps, roulette—as well as display boards giving the odds for every kind of bet, on anyone and anything. And there were other games, not so nice. Like the great pit in one corner, for bare-knuckle fights, knife fights, or drunks who thought they could take on creatures of varying size and nastiness. The betting action was really hot around the pit, whose sides were dark with layers of dried blood. Expensively dressed women clutched at men's arms, and oohed and aahed and squealed delightedly at the sight of blood. Men struck poses in expensive suits, and women stalked back and forth in the very latest fashions, all of it for show. To say *Look at me. I've arrived. I belong here.* Except they wouldn't have needed to try so hard if they'd really believed it.

Sitting at their tables, the Boys watched the circus go by with the blank, expressionless faces of those who'd seen it all before. The Boys: Big Man, Mr. Big, the Big Guy . . . the men who ran everything, owned everything, and cared for nothing but themselves. You could all but smell the testosterone in the air. They were all big, fat, ugly men, crammed sloppily into exquisitely cut suits. Men who didn't care about their appearance any more because they didn't have to. Women were drawn to them by money, power, status, and even the harsh glamour of what they were. There have always been such women, sometimes coming completely cold-bloodedly, sometimes drawn like moths to a flame.

The women came and went, but the Boys remained. Accompanied by women in wine-stained blouses and smeared makeup, laughing at everything they thought might be funny, clinging to their meal ticket's arm, snuggling up against them, kidding themselves they were important be-cause their men were important.

And, of course, every Boy had his own little court, his circle of sycophants and admirers, business partners and advi-sors, and whole armies of stone-faced body-guards. Men to carry out commands, or run errands, to listen while their lord and master spoke, and never ever do or say anything other than what was expected of them. And if no-one in that circle was ever entirely comfortable or at ease, because they knew they could be replaced at any minute, or dragged off and shot on a moment's whim. Well, that was the price they paid for being so close to the Boys. For believing, hoping, that power might trickle down, just like money.

The Boys Club—the only place to be if you were a part of every sick and dirty business in the Nightside.

The din was deafening, people laughing and shrieking and shouting above each other, all trying to convince themselves of what a great time they were having. Drinking and gambling and indulging themselves...but always keeping one eye on the Boys, who might or might not deign to notice them, do business with them, raise them up out of their empty little lives and into the Inner Circle...All the fun of the fair in the Boys Club, for nasty desperate little men and women.

Spangled girls swung on trapezes overhead, or danced long-leggedly on the raised stage. Waiters bustled back and forth, bearing the very best food and drink in the world to people the waiters knew didn't appreciate it. There was even a heated indoor swimming pool, steam rising gently around young men and women showing off their perfect bodies in the briefest of costumes, for the enjoyment of the Boys. They, too, hoped to be noticed and made use of, in one way or another.

The scene was unrelentingly tacky and tasteless, but no expense had been spared, with every imaginable luxury laid on. The best of everything, or what these people thought of as the best. These large men, with their large appetites, indulging themselves to their limits, just because they could. And all around them, men on the way up and men on the way down, always ready to do anything that might be required of them. No matter how degrading. You left your pride behind when you went calling on the Boys.

Surprisingly, many of the body-guards were women. Beautiful women in beautiful clothes, with cold faces and colder eyes, all of them armed to the teeth. Presumably the latest fad or fashion. The Boys liked to keep up with such things. I even spotted a few combat sorceresses, with their Clan affiliations tattooed above their right eyes. Which meant they were professionally trained, and guaranteed incredibly dangerous.

The Walking Man strode right into the midst of everything, and people on every side fell back to give him room. They might not know who he was yet, but one predator can always recognise another. The Walking Man headed straight for the Boys themselves, and all the body-guards tensed, their hands suddenly full of many guns. The combat sorceresses eased gracefully into attack position. Chandra Singh and I strolled casually along beside the Walking Man, not deigning to notice any of it.

And then I stopped abruptly, as I recognised one of the body-guards. Tall and lithe, dark-skinned and elegant, Penny Dreadful dressed like a flapper from the 1920s, in a tight scarlet dress, long, swinging beads, and neat little hat. She nodded easily to me, and I nodded back. Penny and I had been friends and enemies, and about everything in between, at one time or another. Just two hard-working professionals, getting by in the Nightside. Penny Dreadful was an old-school enchantress. She could make you do anything. She could make you do awful things, to yourself, or to your friends or loved ones. She never killed anyone. Mostly, after she'd finished with them, they killed themselves.

Penny was the most amoral woman I have ever met, and I've met a few. She would work for anyone, good or bad, as long as she was paid in advance. Penny genuinely did not care. She was only ever in it for the money. The complete professional. She worked with me on a case once. After I paid her to do it. We got along okay.

"Hello, Penny," I said. "Keeping busy?"

"You know how it is, John darling. A girl has to eat."

She had a little girl's voice, with a charming French accent. Word had it she'd danced at the Crazy Horse, in her younger days. She twirled her beads at me artlessly.

"Still," I said. "The Boys Club? As a body-guard? A bit below you, isn't it, Penny? You used to work for a much better class of scumbag."

She shrugged. "The money's good. Needs must, when your creditors bay at your heels. Please don't start anything, John. I'd hate to have to stop you. Really I would."

"If you've quite finished chatting up the staff," said the Walking Man. "I have death and destruction to be about."

"John Taylor," said a slow, growling voice, and we all looked round. We'd ended up in front of Big Jake Rackham's table. He sat sprawling in a vast overstuffed chair as though it were a throne, surrounded by the pinched, unfriendly faces of his court. He was large, rather than fat, with brute, powerful features and eyes that didn't give a damn about anything. Big Jake Rackham ran the sex trade in the Nightside, taking his cut from every business that operated. No-one indulged in the sins of the flesh in the Nightside without putting money in Rackham's pocket. He was middle-aged but looked older, the awful experiences of his life etched deep into his face. His hair was receding, so he wore it in a long, greasy ponytail down his back. It had been a long time since he'd beaten enemies and rivals to death with his bare hands, but no-one doubted he was still capable of it.

I knew him. He knew me. He leaned forward abruptly, fixing me with eyes as cold and dark as any shark's.

"How did you get in here, Taylor? You're banned. You killed Kid Cthulhu, and handed Max Maxwell over to Walker. You have interfered in my business and cost me money. You must be mad to force your way in here. You must know I'll have you killed for such an affront."

I looked at him, holding his gaze, and he couldn't look away. He stiffened as he realised he wasn't in control any more. I looked at him, and his whole body began to tremble. He cried out, as bloody tears trickled down his cheeks from his bulging eyes, and still he couldn't move a muscle. When he started to whimper, his body-guards trained their guns on me, but didn't dare open fire without a direct order from Rackham. In the end, Penny Dreadful stepped forward and put herself between Rackham and me, blocking my gaze. I smiled at her, and nodded slightly. Behind her, Big Jake Rackham had collapsed in his chair, struggling for breath.

"What did you just do, John?" murmured Chandra.

"I stared him down," I said, not bothering to lower my voice. "Scumbags should know their place."

I looked around, and several people winced, or tried to hide behind each other. A few actually made warding signs against the evil eye. The whole of the Club had gone quiet, like animals around a watering hole sensing the arrival of a lion. Someone had shut off the music, all the games had been stopped, and everyone's attention was fixed on me. I don't think I've ever seen so many unhappy faces, or had so many guns trained on me at one time. It made me feel rather better, after being ignored by the lobby's security men. I smiled condescendingly on one and all, ostentatiously taking all the ill will and threats in my stride. Never let them see you sweat. It helped that I really had done many of the awful things they thought I'd done. Nobody wanted to be the first to start anything, because none of them were entirely sure of what I might do...

More of the body-guards were moving forward, putting their bodies between us and their masters. The Boys paid extremely well to be protected. I looked thoughtfully about me, and many of the heavily armed men and women actually flinched, but none of them fell back. That's the trouble with real professionals; it takes more than a bad reputation to hold them off. Chandra moved round to protect our rear, his long, curved sword ready in his hand.

"What am I to do, John Taylor?" he murmured in my ear. "I can't fight women! It would be...unseemly!"

"Then you're going to be at a serious disadvantage in the coming unpleasantness," I said. "Because these women will quite definitely kill you, given half a chance."

"Really?" said Chandra, tugging at his long black beard and beginning to smile. "How very...exotic."

The Walking Man stepped forward and struck a dramatic pose, and it was as though a great spotlight had fallen upon him. Everyone forgot all about me and Chandra, and turned their complete attention to the Walking Man. I don't think they could have looked away if they'd wanted to. Suddenly he was the most important, significant, and dangerous man in the room.

"Hello boys, hello girls, anyone else see me afterwards," he said, smiling happily about him. His hands weren't anywhere near his guns, but his stance dared anyone to start anything. "Sorry to put such a crimp in your celebrations, but I'm afraid the party's over. No more good times for bad little boys and girls."

He paused, looked at the table beside him, took a firm hold on the edge of the tablecloth and whipped it off the table with a dramatic snap. Everything on the table flew through the air and crashed to the floor. The Walking Man smiled brilliantly, and dropped the table-cloth.

"I meant to do that. Now, where was I?"

He strolled between the tables, and the body-guards fell back despite themselves, giving him plenty of room to go wherever he wanted. His every movement made it clear he'd known they would. The sheer confidence in the man was unsettling, even disturbing. He stopped at every table to talk with every Boy, and he always had something to say about them.

"I am the Walking Man," he said grandly. "Latest in a long line of utter bastards, completely dedicated to slapping down villains and scumbags and brown-trousering the ungodly. I am the wrath of God in the world of men, walking in straight lines to punish the guilty, wherever they may be found. And there are so many guilty faces here tonight! Let's start with you, Big Jake Rackham."

He stopped right in front of the big man and shook his head sadly, like a teacher disappointed by a determinedly under-achieving student.

"Big Jake. Self-made man and proud of it. Everyone knows you run the sex trade in the Nightside. Everyone knows you take a cut from every sordid little transaction: every blow from every pimp; every disease from every hooker; every mugged and rolled client. Every woman driven to an early grave... But, does everyone know what you do to your gorgeous wife, Jezebel, because you can't do anything else with her?"

He moved on to Marty DeVore, also known as Devour, though never to his face, of course. Marty with a thin, weaselly figure with an endless appetite for acquiring new businesses. Whether the original owners wanted to sell or not. The Walking Man clapped him familiarly on the shoulder, and DeVore shrank away from the touch.

"Dear old Marty DeVore," said the Walking Man happily. "Such an unrelenting sinner. Your sheer enthusiasm for awfulness never ceases to impress me. You made your original money in slavery, of course, selling anyone and anything to anyone and anything. Everyone knows that. But do they know what you like to do for a bit of relaxation, Marty? How you bribe mortuary staff to let you lie down with dead bodies, with the prettiest corpses, and have your wicked way with them? Especially if they're the wives and daughters of your friends and enemies?"

He moved on to the Hellsreich brothers, the twins, Paul and Davey. Big blond blue-eyed Aryan types, young and healthy and rotten to the core. Heading right to the top, through endless alliances and very secret behind-locked-doors deals. Everyone wanted to hang on to their coat-tails.

"Paul and Davey," said the Walking Man, moving suddenly between them so he could put an arm across both their shoulders. "Does my heart good to see such young men striving for success. You deal in insurance, or more properly protection, taking money to pay yourselves not to do nasty things to your customers. And you're so good at making deals that profit everyone! Everyone knows that. But, do they know you murdered your loving parents to get the money that got you started? Who could ever trust you again, knowing a thing like that?"

And finally he came to Josie Prince. One of the few women to be accepted by the Boys as their equal. Slim, elegant, stiff-backed in her formal evening gown, she looked like everyone's stern, grey-haired granny. She'd strangled her eldest son with her bare hands to take over his business because he wasn't making enough money for her. Josie Prince was a debt-collector, the kind who sent the leg-breakers round if you were a day late paying back what you owed.

The Walking Man swept her a low, sarcastic bow. Her stern, disapproving features didn't give an inch. He straightened up with a snap, sat in her lap, and threw an arm across her bony shoulders.

"Sweet Josie Prince, as I live and breathe! Old in years and dyed in sin, right down to the bone. I know what I need to know, when I need to know it, so I can do my job, but just knowing what you do makes me sick to my stomach. You deal in enforcement and intimidation, in torture and brutality and murder. Everyone knows that. But does everyone here know you founded and funded Precious Memories? Do they know why your youngest son killed himself?"

Everyone in the Boys Club looked at Josie Prince, as the Walking Man rose easily to his feet and strode away. Even some of her own body-guards looked at her with loathing. Josie Prince's face didn't change at all.

Suddenly, Big Jake Rackham was on his feet, shouting denials and abuse and threats. The other Boys quickly rose and joined in, saying that the Walking Man was a liar, spreading rumour and gossip for his own purposes. Others were on their feet, too, protesting and threatening, perhaps for fear the Walking Man would come after them next. And the Walking Man just stood there, in the middle of the Boys Club, smiling happily at the bedlam he'd caused. Dozens of guns and worse weapons were trained on him from all sides. And he didn't give a damn. He looked smoothly self-satisfied, a man happy in his work. Then he glanced at me, and I realised it had all been for my benefit. He could have just walked in and started shooting; but he wanted me to know why. He started speaking again, and immediately everyone fell silent again. They couldn't help it. There was something about the Walking Man that demanded your attention.

"You're all guilty," he said. "You all profit from the sin and suffering of others. You all know where your money comes from, and how much blood it has on it, and you've never done anything about it. Your sin is you didn't care."

His hands suddenly came up full of guns, and before anyone knew what was happening the bodies were already falling. He shot Big Jake Rackham and Marty DeVore while they were still standing by their chairs. Josie Prince tried to run, and he shot her in the back of her head, blowing her face right off. He turned his guns on the Hellsreich brothers, but they were already hiding behind their overturned table. Body-guards on all sides opened up with all kinds of weapons, and I hit the ground, rolling away in search of my own cover. The Walking Man might be bullet-proof, but I sure as hell wasn't. Chandra Singh roared a cheerful challenge in his own tongue and waded into the nearest body-guards with his long, curved sword. Blood flew on the air as he cut them down with swift, skilful strokes, moving so fast no-one could get a bead on him.

Bullets pounded into the Walking Man from all sides, only to ricochet away harmlessly. He didn't even feel the impact. He aimed and fired, aimed and fired, picking off his targets quite casually, smiling his terrible unforgiving smile. He was punishing the guilty, and loving every minute of it. Most of the Boys were already dead, the rest running for the exits, though I knew they would never reach them. Body-guards' bullets slammed into the overturned table I was hiding behind, and I decided I needed to find new cover. I scrambled away on all fours, head well down to avoid the bullets flying overhead, and found a female body-guard moving towards me with an energy gun in her hand. I backed away quickly. I've never been much of a one for physical combat, mostly because I'm no good at it. I've always preferred out-smarting people, or intimidating them, or being somewhere else when the shit actually hits the fan.

Another female body-guard came running at me, firing a semi-automatic weapon. The bullets didn't even come close. I can move really quickly when I have to. The two body-guards came together to get a clear shot at me. I rose, whipped the tablecloth off the overturned table, and threw it over both of them. They struggled with the cloth, and it was the easiest thing in the world for me to move in and bang their heads together. I may not be much of a fighter, but I'm a sneaky bastard.

I risked a quick look around. Chandra Singh was holding his own against a whole crowd of opponents, stamping and dancing amongst them, swinging his long sword with glee and gusto. He grinned broadly as enchanted blades shattered against his sword, and magics and curses exploded as he cut them out of the air. As long as he worked in close, no-one could use their guns for fear of shooting their own people, but I had to wonder how long that would last. Still, for a man who said he didn't want to fight women, he certainly seemed to be getting the hang of it. Bodies fell to the left and to the right as he cut his way through the enemies crowding around him.

They all fell back suddenly to let a combat sorceress

approach him, a short and stocky Asian woman in a black dress, with the Tiger's Claw ideogram tattooed above her right eye. That meant serious magic, and nasty with it. She pulled a spitting and sparking magic out of nowhere and threw it at Chandra. It roared through the air, burning up half a dozen body-guards in its path on its way to Chandra Singh. He laughed aloud and sliced the magic in two in mid air with one slash of his blade. The magic exploded, its sorcerous fires spraying everywhere. People ran screaming, with their flesh on fire. The combat sorceress began a staccato incantation in a language I didn't recognise. Chandra advanced on her, step by step, pressing against some invisible resistance. The sorceress's voice rose with urgency as he drew nearer, then she stopped short, and looked down at the blade buried in her stomach. Chandra Singh pulled the sword back, and her guts fell out on to the floor. The sorceress tried to say something, and Chandra cut her head off with one sweep of his blade. He turned away, not bothering to watch her hit the floor.

The Walking Man hadn't moved from his last position. He didn't need to. He just fired his guns, his old-fashioned long-barrelled Peacemakers that never ran out of ammunition, and blood flew on the air as men and women crashed to the floor and did not rise again.

What was left of the Boys Club Membership was in full rout. Fighting each other to get to the exits, trampling the fallen underfoot, screaming and shouting and trying to use each other as human shields. The exit doors were all sealed shut, though no-one had given any such order. Most of the body-guards were dead already. The Walking Man didn't care whether they stood and fought or turned and ran. He killed them all, starting with the worst and working his way down, choosing his targets through some hidden knowledge of his own. The remaining body-guards grouped together and hit the Walking Man with everything they had. But bullets couldn't touch him, enchanted blades shattered against his shabby coat, and magics and curses discharged harmlessly about him. He ignored the body-guards, unless they got in his way, then he shot them dead.

He was smiling widely, and it was not the kind of smile you expected to see on a man of God.

But as big as the Club was, and large though the Membership was, eventually he ran out of targets. The last body was thrown against a wall by the impact of the bullet and slid lifelessly to the floor, and the shooting stopped. The Walking Man lowered his guns and looked about him. The dead were piled up everywhere, men and women lying sprawled without dignity across the blood-soaked floor. The biggest heaps lay before the sealed exits, where the panicked Membership had tried to crawl over the bodies of the fallen to get to doors that would not open. A handful of the living still remained, hiding, crouched behind overturned tables and other cover, keeping silent, hoping not to be noticed. They should have known better. The Walking Man looked about him and casually picked them off, one by one, his bullets ploughing right through the cover to kill the prey concealed behind them.

The Hellsreich brothers rose abruptly from where they'd been hiding, clasped hands, and shrieked in unison a brutally simple spell of Unbinding. They'd finished it before the Walking Man could even turn his guns upon them. A great blue pentacle appeared on the floor of the Club, half-hidden under the dead bodies. The lines blazed brightly, a harsh actinic blue that seared the eye, steaming with released ectoplasm. The floor under the pentacle exploded, throwing dead bodies aside like leaves, ragged splinters flying through the air like shrapnel. And up through the great dark hole there rose a demon from the Pit, free to do its awful will in the world of men. The Boys Club's last act of malice, a terrible revenge on anyone who dared to bring them down.

It was a traditional, old-school demon, twice the size of a man, with blood-red skin, goat's horns and hooves, and very sharp teeth. It had the shape of a man, and the proportions of a man, but there was nothing human in its stance or in its glowing slit-pupilled eyes. Steam rose up from its scarlet skin, the air all around it heated past endurance by its very presence. It stank of shit and blood and brimstone, because it chose to. The Walking Man looked at me and Chandra Singh.

"You deal with it," he said. "I'm busy."

And he went back to looking for hidden prey, shooting them where he found them.

I was giving serious thought to finding some cover of my own when Chandra Singh started forward, swinging his long blade casually before him. The demon considered the monster hunter with interest, its long spade-tipped tail swinging lazily. Chandra shouted a challenge in his own tongue and brought his sword round in a long, sweeping arc that would have sliced most things in two, only to see his blade rebound harmlessly from the demon's scalding skin. The vibrations almost tore the sword from Chandra's hands, but he hung on stubbornly and struck at the demon again and again, grunting with the effort of his blows. The demon stood there and laughed at him soundlessly.

I searched frantically through my coat pockets for anything that might help, but I had nothing on me that could stop a demon from the Inferno. This was no ordinary demon, this was the real deal, a Lord of Hell. Where had the Boys Club found the power to summon something like this? Unless the founder of the Club really was who some people swore he was . . . You could hurt a demon like this with holy water, or give it pause with a crucifix, provided you had the faith to back it up, but nothing short of a full-scale exorcism could banish it from this plane. I racked my brain . . . and then shouted at Chandra, as he paused in his attack, bent over and breathing harshly.

"Chandra! The pentacle! It's a gateway between this place and the Pit! That's how they summoned it here! Break the pentacle, and the gateway will close!"

Chandra raised his sword and brought it slamming down on the nearest pulsing blue line. His enchanted blade sheared clean through the blue line, breaking the connection and short-circuiting the summoning. The gateway began to close, and the demon sank back into the darkness below, pulled inexorably back to where it belonged. It turned its horned head unhurriedly to look at the Walking Man.

"We know you in Hell," it said, in a voice like screaming

children. "We will meet again, Walking Man. All murderers end up in Hell. Even the ones who say God told them to do it."

The Walking Man shot the demon dispassionately between the eyes. Its horned head snapped back under the impact, then it shook its head, gargled for a moment, and spat out the bullet. It was still laughing as it disappeared back beneath the floor, a terrible, soul-destroying sound. It cut off abruptly as the last of the pentacle lines faded away, and the floor was a floor again, though with a bloody big hole in it now. The Walking Man looked at it for a while, his face unmoved. But he wasn't smiling any more.

I went over to Chandra, and he leaned heavily on me, his sword hanging down as though it had become too heavy to lift.

"Nice call, John," he said faintly.

"Nice cut," I said.

The Boys Club was still and silent. There was blood and dead bodies everywhere, even in the swimming pool, where the perfect bodies of young men and women floated facedown in bloody waters. The Hellsreich brothers stood together, holding their hands high in the air in surrender. The Walking Man regarded them thoughtfully.

"You've killed hundreds of men and women," I said. "Isn't that enough?"

"No," said the Walking Man. "It's never enough."

"We're just businessmen!" protested Paul Hellsreich. "We provide a service, we protect our customers from the vicissitudes of fate!"

"We're insurance men!" said Davey Hellreich. "We never killed anyone!"

"We'll go legitimate!" said Paul. "We'll pay taxes! We promise!"

"You don't have to kill us!" said Davey. "We're not worth it!"

"It's always worth it," said the Walking Man.

"You should turn them over to Walker," I said quickly, as he started to raise his guns again. "They have surrendered."

"To Walker?" said Paul. "And end up in Shadow Deep? I think I'd rather be shot."

"No problem," said the Walking Man.

"To hell with that," said a new voice. "I've never let a client down yet."

We all looked round in surprise as the owner of the charming French accent came forward. God alone knew where she'd managed to hide, but Penny Dreadful had survived the massacre without a drop of blood on her. She moved carefully through the carnage, stepping daintily over dead bodies, and came to a halt facing the Walking Man.

"Penny," I said carefully. "Get out of the way. You don't have anything that can stop the Walking Man."

"I took their money," she said. "Swore to guard them against all dangers, to put my body between theirs and all harm. That's the job."

"She took their money," said the Walking Man. "Even knowing where it came from. That makes her as guilty as them."

"No it bloody doesn't!" I said. "She's a professional, that's all! Just like me. And Chandra."

"You side with the sinners, you die with the sinners," said the Walking Man. "It really is that simple."

"No it isn't," I said. "Not here. Not in the Nightside. We do things differently here."

"I know," said the Walking Man. "That's the problem. Sin is sin. You've lived here so long you've forgotten that."

"She is brave, and honourable, and trustworthy, in her way," I said. And I moved slowly and deliberately forward, to stand between Penny and the Walking Man. "She's done good things."

"I'm sure God will take that into consideration," said the Walking Man. And he shot right past my ear. I spun round, but it was already too late. Penny was falling to her knees, a dark and bloody third eye in the middle of her forehead. I caught her before she hit the floor, but she wasn't breathing any more. I knelt before the Walking Man, holding my dead friend in my arms. I heard two more shots, but didn't look round to watch the Hellsreich brothers fall. I didn't want to let Penny go, even though I knew there was nothing I could do. Her body leaned heavily against me, like a sleeping child. She didn't deserve to die like this. Even if she had been the infamous Penny Dreadful, and done all the things she'd done, she didn't deserve to die like this.

I finally put her aside, got back on my feet, and glared at the Walking Man, who stared impassively back. I started towards him, and Chandra was quickly there to grab my arm and stop me.

"No, my friend! Not now. We're not ready."

"Let go of my arm," I said, and he let go immediately.

I was breathing hard, my whole body tense with the need to do...something. I knew he'd kill me if I took another step forward, but right then, I wasn't sure I cared, as long as I took him down with me.

"What about God's mercy?" I said finally, in a harsh voice I barely recognised. "What about his compassion?"

"Not my department," said the Walking Man. He decided I wasn't going to do anything after all and put away his guns.

"What gives you the right to condemn anyone to Hell?"

"I don't send anyone to Hell. I send them to judgement."

"Who are you, to take such responsibility upon yourself?" said Chandra Singh.

The Walking Man smiled; and for the first time it was a simple, human smile. "About time you asked. Very well, just for you; the secret origin of the Walking Man. My name is, or more properly was, Adrien Saint. No-one special. Just a man with a job and a wife and two small children. Mr. Average, I suppose. No great ambitions. All I wanted was to get on with my life and look after my family.

"A teenage joy-rider in a stolen car hit my wife and my two children head-on, when he lost control taking a corner too fast. Cut my wife in half, and dragged my children under his car for almost half a mile before he finally had to stop. He ran away, with his friends. The police couldn't identify any of them.

"I survived. You couldn't call it living, but I survived. Lost my job, my house, my money...and then one of the few friends I hadn't driven away found me a place in a monastery, in the countryside. A place for solitudes and contemplatives, and those hiding from a world that had become unbearable. It was a good place. I found a kind of peace there, if not comfort. And then one day, while helping to catalog the library, I found a very old book that told me all about the deal a man can make with God, to be his man, to be his Walking Man, and punish the guilty.

"I made the deal. Didn't hesitate for a moment. I went back into the world transformed, with God's will and God's wrath burning within me. I found the teenage joy-rider, with God's help. Sitting on a sofa, watching television, as though nothing had happened. I beat him to death with my bare hands, and his screams comforted me. I went round to his friends, and killed them all. There's a fine line between justice and revenge, but as long as it ended up with dead joy-riders, I didn't care.

"And then...I went travelling in the world, seeing it as it really was, walking up and down in it, dispensing justice. Until finally I was ready to come to the Nightside, and bring the wrath of God to the most sinful place on Earth."

"No wonder you're always smiling," I said. "This has never been about justice for you. It's always been about revenge. Every time you fire your guns, you're killing joy-riders, over and over again."

The Walking Man smiled briefly. "You think I don't know that? I'm obsessed, not crazy."

"You sure about that?" I said.

He actually laughed. "Well, I hear voices in my head telling me to kill people in God's name, so I suppose there has to be a chance that I'm a complete loony tune; but I don't think so. Not as long as I remain untouchable by all the evil in the world."

"What brought you to the Nightside, at this particular time?" said Chandra.

"I know what I need to know, when I need to know it. When God was sure I was ready, he showed me the secret ways into the Nightside."

"You talk often with your god?" said Chandra. He sounded genuinely curious. "What is that like?"

"Comforting," said the Walking Man.

"I often speak with my god," said Chandra. "He speaks to me through dreams, and prophecies and omens. And he has never once insisted I commit murder in his name."

"You kill monsters," said the Walking Man.

"Only when I have to. And then, only to protect the innocent."

"Yes!" said the Walking Man. "Exactly! I punish the guilty to avenge and protect the innocent. I kill the killers before they can kill again! The law might not be able to touch these evil men, but I can. And I do. Think of me...as a champion of last resort. The last person you can go to for justice, when the ways of the world have failed you. What I do is never murder, because I have a valid legal warrant for all that I have done, and will do, from the highest court of all. The Courts of the Holy."

"Penny wasn't evil," I said.

"Get over her," said the Walking Man, not unkindly. "I will do worse before I'm done because I must. The Nightside is an abomination in the world of men, and it must be humbled and brought down. There are too many temptations here, too many evils operating openly. It gives people...the wrong idea. That they can sin and get away with it."

"You don't believe in free will?" I said. "Or free choice? God gave them to us. Everyone who comes here knows the score, knows what they're getting into. You could say the Nightside keeps all the real sin and temptation in one place, away from the rest of the world."

"Shows how little you know about the rest of the world," said the Walking Man. "You argue well, John, but none of this matters. I will do what I will do, and no-one can stop me. I am here to clean up the Nightside, scour the filth right out of it, from top to bottom. Including your presumptuous new Authorities. As soon as I've finished the tasks I've set myself, I will kill these new Authorities, to put the fear of God into the Nightside. And you, John Taylor...are either with me, or against me."

"That's why you let me see what you do, and why," I said. "You want me to understand. To approve."

"I want you to stay out of my way," said the Walking Man.

"Many people whose opinion I respect tell me that the Nightside serves a purpose," I said slowly. "There are good people here. I won't let you hurt them. This is my home."

"Not for long," said the Walking Man. He pulled his old mocking insolence about him, flashed me a smile, then turned his back on me and walked away.

"Bastard son of a bitch," I said, after a moment.

"Well, yes," said Chandra. "By the way, you have blood all down the front of your trench coat."

I looked. Penny's blood, from where I'd held her.

"Not for the first time," I said.

We stood alone in the middle of the Boys Club, surrounded by the dead. The air seemed very still, very calm, as though a thunderstorm had just passed.

"I couldn't stop him," I said finally, unable to keep the helplessness out of my voice. "Even though I knew what to expect, even though I thought I was prepared for what he was, and what he did . . . I still couldn't stop him."

"Who are we, to stand against the will of God?" said Chandra Singh, reasonably. "And the men and women of this establishment were very definitely people who needed killing."

"Not all of them," I said. "The world is undoubtedly a better place with most of these people gone, but some of them were just . . . ordinary men and women, doing their jobs, drawing a pay-cheque to pay the bills and look after their families. Getting by, as best they could. Yes, they knew where the money came from . . . but whatever evil they did by working here was a small thing. Not worth dying like this."

"Like your Penny Dreadful?" he said.

"She was never mine," I said, automatically. "Penny was always her own woman. I never approved of her, but I liked her. She took no shit from anyone. And she really did do some good things in her time, even if she had to be paid to do them." I looked around me, and a slow, steady anger burned within me. "They didn't all need killing, Chandra. Some of them could have been saved."

153

"Of course! That's why you stay, isn't it?" said Chandra, with the enthusiasm of a sudden insight. "To try and save those you care about. Like your Suzie Shooter."

"Don't go there," I said, and when I looked at him, he fell silent.

No telling where that conversation might have gone because that was when King of Skin suddenly materialised out of mid air before us. Chandra and I both fell back a little, startled, as King of Skin skipped and swaggered among the dead bodies, sniggering and cackling and looking very pleased with himself. He stopped suddenly, and looked back over his shoulder at Chandra and me.

"I've been here all along," he said, in his hot breathy voice. "Hidden by my power and my nature, watching and listening. Know thy enemy! He does like to talk, this Walking Man, and says so much more than he realises. He has a weakness, and it's a very old one. Pride! He cannot ever admit to being wrong . . . Destroy his faith in the righteousness of what he does, even for a moment, and he will crumble . . . Oh yes!" He was suddenly right in front of me again, wrapped in his sleazy glamour, laughing right in my face. "Because of what I was, and what I am, I see the world very clearly. I see the Nightside for what it is, and not for what people on both sides like to think it is, or should be . . . That's why Julien Advent insisted I be a part of his precious new Authorities. Because I will always see what needs to be done, and the best way to do it, no matter how upsetting."

And just like that, he was gone again. Or at least, I presumed so. With King of Skin, you could never be sure.

I thought about Adrien Saint, the current Walking Man, so sure in his vocation. Could he really bring down the whole Nightside? Not by shooting the bad guys one by one... That would take him years, maybe centuries. So he must be planning something else. Something more... apocalyptic. Could he perhaps be the one to bring about the bleak dead future I'd encountered in the Timeslip? Where all the world was dead, and even the stars were going out? Could he be the real cause of that, and not me? Was that why the members of the new Authorities were the same people who had been my Enemies in that terrible future?

I had to stop the Walking Man. For many reasons. But how do you stop the will and wrath of God?

I was going to have to do some research.

SIX

The Only Thing Worse Than Asking Questions of God

We set fire to the Boys Club before we left. It seemed like the least we could do.

Afterwards, Chandra Singh and I stood outside in the street and watched the place burn. It went up very nicely. A crowd gathered around us to enjoy the spectacle. We like free entertainment in the Nightside. A street trader soon turned up to provide the crowd with snacky things on sticks, and in no time at all we were all variously toasting and roasting things in the flames of the burning Club. There's nothing like a good pork, beef, and quite probably something else sausage you've personally blackened in a fire. Chandra politely declined to get involved and looked around uncertainly.

"Shouldn't the fire brigade be here by now?"

"No such thing in the Nightside," I said cheerfully. "The surrounding clubs have their own fire-insurance spells, so the blaze won't spread. And in a high-rent area like this, reconstructive magics come as standard. This time tomorrow, there'll be a whole new club standing here. Minus the Boys and their lackeys, of course."

"What about the Walking Man?" said Chandra, apparently determined to be upset about something. "Shouldn't we be hot on his trail before he causes another massacre?"

"If he'd been planning something imminent, he'd have told us," I said, around a mouthful of sausage. "The man does love an audience. No, we've got time to do a little research. I need to talk with some Christian authorities, someone who can give us more detailed information...on the Walking Man in general, and the present incumbent in particular. Trouble is, there aren't that many truly Christian people in the Nightside, apart from some rather extreme groups on the Street of the Gods, and a handful of missionaries."

"Wouldn't we be better off in a library?" said Chandra, tactfully. "You have some of the most famous libraries in the world here."

"I think you mean infamous," I said. "Not to mention downright dangerous. Some of our libraries have books that read people. And edit them. No, I think we need a more personal touch for something like this. Which rules out the big organisations, like the Salvation Army Sisterhood. They'd only feed us the party line. We need to talk to the missionaries, the holy rollers, and the dedicated individuals. Like Prestor Johnny, Saint Gorgeous, Kid Christ, or the Really Righteous Brothers."

"They sound . . . rather eccentric," said Chandra. Still being tactful.

"Well, yes," I said. "You've got to be a little weird, not to mention certifiably strange, to want to spread the good word in a place like this. But we've always attracted more than our fair share of determined and highly individual religious zealots. Like Tamsin MacReady, the current rogue vicar. Yes, I think she's our best bet. Ooh look—are those marshmallows?"

"The rogue vicar?" said Chandra, refusing to be sidetracked.

I finished the last of my sausage, discarded my stick, and wiped my greasy fingers on the coat of the person standing next to me. I strode away from the burning Boys Club, and Chandra walked along with me. A mothman had turned up, circling overhead, attracted by the light, and already people were using it for target practice.

"Direct agents from Above and Below have always been banned from the Nightside," I said patiently. "Lilith designed it that way. Even the bigger organisations have trouble operating here, not least because the Street of the Gods offers mighty and ineffable Beings you can actually have a conversation and even do business with. But there's a long tradition of rebel priests and rogue vicars who come here against standing orders, to test their faith and their mettle against the Nightside. Half-mad missionaries and holy terrorists, no practice too extreme, variously successful and always a pain in the arse. Tamsin MacReady is the latest in a long line of hard-nosed optimists. She probably knows all there is to know about the Walking Man. If only I can persuade her to talk to me."

"Would I be correct in assuming that there is some bad feeling between you?" said Chandra.

"Sort of," I said. "The previous rogue vicar was a man called Pew. My mortal enemy, for many years. He's dead now, because of me."

"I can see that would cause problems," said Chandra.

Because I was in a hurry to get some information on the Walking Man before the bodies started dropping again, I broke one of my oldest rules and hailed a passing taxi-cab. Normally I know better. You can't trust the taxis in the Nightside. Partly because you can never be sure who the drivers are really working for, or reporting back to . . . but mostly because taxis are just too bloody dangerous. Some of them run on powdered virgin's blood, some of them interrupt their journeys to fight duels with cabs from rival firms, and some of them eat their passengers. Not everything that looks like a cab is necessarily a cab. But this was an emergency, so . . .

An old-fashioned black London taxi-cab pulled sharply out of the endless roar of Nightside traffic and screeched to a halt before me. I recognised the firm, Infernal Taxis. Their proud motto—*We promise you a Hell of a ride!* I held the door open for Chandra so he could get in first, just in case. I let him get settled comfortably and only then got in after him. You can't be too careful.

A sign inside the cab said *Please refrain from smoking or the driver will rip your lungs out.* Fair enough. I'd barely settled back into the scuffed leather seat beside Chandra before the driver slammed through the gears and forced his way back into the flow of traffic through brute force and intimidation. He body-slammed a few slower-moving vehicles out of his way, and heavy-duty automatic weapons deployed from the gleaming black bonnet to threaten any other vehicles that didn't move fast enough, or looked like they were getting too close. Which was also fair enough. Offensive driving is the norm in the Nightside if you want to reach the end of your journey alive, or even in one piece. I relaxed a little, feeling that I was in safe hands.

The driver was human enough, from the waist up. From the waist down, his torso plugged directly into the driving seat. Cables, wires, and tangles of translucent plastic tubing full of pulsing liquids connected him to the cab on both a physical and a mental level. Basically, he was a cyborg, and the cab was an extension of his truncated body. He drove it with his thoughts, but he kept his hands on the steering wheel to reassure his passengers. He kept a bonsai pine tree on his dash-board to serve as an air-freshener.

Chandra took one look at the driver's situation, and immediately lost his temper.

"Who did this to you, sir?" he demanded loudly. "Give us

the man's name, and I promise you we shall hunt him down and inflict dire punishments upon him!"

"Will you relax?" I said. "He paid for it himself. You can make serious money driving a cab in the Nightside, if you live long enough. Being a cabby here is a vocation, like mountain-climbing or spree killing. You leave him alone, Chandra, he's quite happy."

"Too right, squire," said the cabbie, without looking round. His skin was as pale and puffy as a mushroom, but his voice was disturbingly hale and hearty. "I had that Walker in the back of my cab the other day, you know. A real toff. Lousy tipper, mind. Where to, squire?"

"I need to speak to the rogue vicar," I said. "Take us to the Vicarage."

The driver sucked in a sharp breath between his yellow teeth. "Ooh no, I don't think so, squire. I don't go that far into the badlands. Far too dangerous."

I leaned forward so he could get a good look at me in his mirror. "I'm John Taylor. How dangerous do you think it's going to get in here if you don't do what I tell you to?"

"Oh bloody hell," said the driver.

He sniffed loudly, put his mental foot down, then sulked in silence for the rest of the way. Which suited me well enough. He'd only have wanted to talk politics, and how there were far too many elves in the Nightside these days. Chandra was apparently lost in his own thoughts, so I just stared out the window at the traffic. It was the usual mixture of vehicles—from the past, present, and future—thundering through the Nightside on their way to somewhere more interesting. Ambulances that ran on distilled suffering. Articulateds with unfamiliar logos emblazoned on their sides, transporting goods too dangerous or too disturbing even for the Nightside. Demon messengers on souped-up motorcycles, with hellfire flying out their exhausts. And a whole bunch of things pretending to be vehicles, for reasons of their own.

At least there are never any roadblocks to slow things down, mostly because the road is tougher than the traffic, and bites back if it gets annoyed. In fact, certain sections have been known to eat slower-moving vehicles, to encourage everyone else to get a move on. The whole road system in the Nightside is basically one big Darwinian struggle for survival, with only the strongest making it to the end of their journeys. Hell, sometimes you can actually watch vehicles *evolving*, right before your eyes. Some have become so advanced they're now purely conceptual—just the idea of vehicles in motion...

And no, there aren't any traffic lights. Anywhere. We tried putting some in a few years back, and they all retired with nervous breakdowns.

"Hello," said the driver suddenly. "Don't remember seeing that before..."

I immediately leaned forward to take a good look over his shoulder. Anything new and unexpected in the Nightside is automatically considered dangerous until proven otherwise by exhaustive testing. Up ahead a new bridge straddled the road, all gleaming steel and bright lights. The rest of the traffic seemed to be going out of their way to avoid it. I frowned.

"Is there another way we can take, driver?"

"Not one that doesn't add an hour or more to our journey," said the driver. "That new bridge crosses the only main road into the badlands. What do you say, squire? How much of a hurry are you in?"

"We're going in," I said. "Take it slow and steady. And if anything even looks at you in a way you don't like, feel free to shoot the crap out of it."

"Got that right, squire."

"Are we in trouble, John?" said Chandra.

"Maybe," I said. "That bridge wasn't there yesterday. It could have dropped out of a Timeslip, or it could be a projection from another dimension. Or it could just be a new bridge. I have absolutely no idea as to who's in charge of traffic improvements. Mostly, they just . . . happen."

The bridge and the tunnel it made remained reassuringly solid and ordinary as we approached the entrance. The lights inside were bright and steady. The taxi slowed right down as we passed under the bridge and entered the tunnel . . . then the beast revealed its true colours. The smell hit me first, even through the cab's closed windows—rotting meat spoiling in digestive juices. The lights lost their electric fierceness and sank into the blue-white glare of bioluminescence. The walls of the tunnel rippled slowly, the blue steel look replaced by a soft organic pink. And the road ahead and under us was suddenly the rough red meat of an endlessly long tongue. Sharp bones protruded from all sides of the tunnel, like the cutting parts of a meat-grinder. The tunnel was alive . . . and we were driving right down its throat.

The driver slammed on his brakes, but the tongue convulsed, rising and falling beneath us, carrying us on. The driver opened up with all his guns, but the heavy-jacketed bullets did little damage to the walls, which absorbed them. Thick pearly digestive juices were already dropping from the ceiling, hissing and fizzing on the cab's metal surfaces. The driver swore loudly, and threw the cab into reverse. Its wheels dug deep into the red meat of the road, and churned madly, but still we were carried deeper into the tunnel. I yelled for the driver to open the windows, and they juddered down slowly.

Chandra immediately leaned right out of his window, so far out I had to hold on to his legs for fear he'd fall. He stabbed the red road with his sword, the tip digging deep into the red meat, leaving a long, bloody furrow behind us. The tongue convulsed, throwing the taxi this way and that, but we were still being pulled in. I hauled Chandra back into the cab and concentrated on raising my gift. I forced my inner eye all the way open, the better to See the situation we were in. It only took me a moment to find what I was looking for, and hit the tunnel in its weakest spot. The red road whipped out from under us, the whole tunnel shaking violently. The taxi's wheels dug into the road again, and just like that we were backing out of the tunnel at speed. The starry skies reappeared above us as the taxi accelerated back into the Nightside traffic, which made every angry noise conceivable as it fought to avoid us. Chandra looked at me.

"All right, what did you do?"

I grinned, just a little smugly. "I used my gift to find its gag reflex..."

The taxi finally lurched to a halt, and we watched the living bridge melt away into mists. Getting around in the Nightside can be murder sometimes.

The taxi took us deep into the badlands, the roughest, most desperate and desolate part of the Nightside. So rough that even the more adventurous tourists find excuses to avoid it, and only the hardiest sinners venture in, looking for the pleasures and satisfactions they can't find anywhere else. The techno fetishists, looking to have sex with computers. Volunteers for drug-testing labs, only too willing to take on the latest pharmaceutical heavens and hells, just to be first in line for the latest trip. Innocence for sale on every street corner, only slightly shop-soiled. Sin eaters, soul eaters, sleep eaters. The darkest delights and the deepest damnations, for all those foolish enough to think they've already hit bottom. There's always further to fall, in the Nightside.

The buildings slouch together for support, with brickwork blackened by decades of traffic, or maybe just the general environment. Broken windows, holes patched with faded newspapers, doors hanging permanently half-open because the locks were broken long ago. Street-lights that sometimes worked, and the burned-out skeleton shapes of dead neon. Heaps of garbage everywhere, that sometimes moved, revealing the homeless. Many of them had missing limbs. You can sell anything in the badlands.

And, finally, long after we'd had to shut the cab's windows to keep out the smell, when it seemed we'd reached the sleaziest scummiest depths of the badlands, the taxi eased to a halt outside the Vicarage, the only civilised-looking building in the middle of a row of destitute properties. The streets looked wet and sticky, and something told me that had nothing to do with the recent rain. I've walked through alien jungles that looked less dangerous and forbidding. Exactly where a Christian missionary would be most needed...

Chandra and I stepped out of the taxi, which had parked under the only working street-light. I'd barely shut the cab door before the cabbie revved up and roared away, so desperate to get out of the badlands that he hadn't even paused to ask for his fare. Not that I'd had any intention of paying, of course.

Various figures stirred in the darkest parts of the shadows, deliberating whether Chandra and I were easy targets. Chandra drew his sword with a dramatic gesture, and the long curved blade burned supernaturally bright in the gloom. The figures shrank back, dim silhouettes disappearing into the concealing night. One predator can always recognise another. Chandra smiled briefly and sheathed his sword. I knocked on the Vicarage door. It was an old-fashioned brass knocker, in the shape of a lion's head, and the sound it made echoed on and on behind the closed door, as though travelling unguessable distances. There were no lights on anywhere, and I began to wonder if this was really such a good idea after all. But after a worryingly long pause, the door swung abruptly open, and bright, golden light spilled out into the street, like the illumination of Heaven itself. And standing in the doorway was a healthy, happy, young lady in a baggy brown jumper over worn-in riding britches and boots. She had short, tufty red hair and vivid green eyes, and she grinned broadly at Chandra and me as though we were two old chums who'd come to tea.

"Hello!" she said, in a bright cheerful voice. "I'm Sharon Pilkington-Smythe. Come in, come in! All are welcome here. Even you, John Taylor! No sin too great to be forgiven, that's our motto!"

"You know me?" I said, the moment I could get a word in edgeways.

"Of course, sweetie! Everyone knows you. You're right at the top of *People we intend to save by whatever means necessary before we die.* Now in you come, don't be bashful, all are welcome in the Vicarage! Don't know your friend."

Chandra drew himself up to his full impressive height and stuck out his beard. "I am Chandra Singh, holy warrior, mighty monster hunter, and legend of the Indian subcontinent!"

He was clearly gearing up to say a lot more, but Sharon butted in before he could get going.

"Gosh!" she said, with that particular mixture of innocence and ignorance that can be especially galling. "A real live monster hunter! We really could use you round here. If only to keep the local rat population under control. You can't keep using land-mines; it upsets the neighbours. Come in, Chandra, you're just as welcome as John Taylor, and probably more so. I should go easy on the whole monster-killing bit when you meet the vicar, though—not really her thing."

"She doesn't approve of killing monsters?" said Chandra.

"Well, I don't give a damn myself," Sharon said airily. "Carve them all up and make soup out of them, see if I care. But the vicar takes her beliefs very seriously. To her, a monster is only another lost soul that needs saving. The sweet and soppy thing. Come on, come on in both of you, and I'll take you to meet Tamsy!"

Sharon Pilkington-Smythe stepped smartly back, encouraging us both to enter with emphatic arm gestures, and Chandra and I allowed ourselves to be ushered in, if only to stop her talking. She slammed the door shut behind us with casual violence, and there was the sound of many heavy-duty locks, chains, and bolts closing by themselves. I can't honestly say it made me feel any safer. Sharon led the way down an excessively neat and tidy hallway that wouldn't have looked out of place in a traditional country vicarage, the kind that only seems to exist on the lids of biscuit tins these days. Gleaming linoleum covered the floor, while pretty flowered prints adorned the walls. The light was a pleasant golden glow, warm and comforting. The whole scene couldn't have seemed more cosy if it tried. I didn't trust it an inch. Half a dozen puppies scrambled suddenly out of a side doorway, furry little bundles with oversized paws, falling over each other to get to us. And, of course, nothing would do but Chandra had to stop and make a fuss of them. They were still too young for me to guess their breed, and some of them clearly hadn't had their eyes open long. Chandra knelt and petted them all happily. He held one up before his face, and the puppy wagged its stumpy tail ecstatically. Chandra looked at me.

"Would you like one, John?"

"Thanks," I said. "But I've already eaten."

Chandra gave me a disapproving look and put his puppy down. Sharon herded them all back through the side door with brisk efficiency, then closed the door firmly. She looked at me reproachfully, and I stared right back at her. Actually, I'm quite fond of dogs, but I had a reputation to maintain.

Sharon led us down the hallway and ushered us into a nice comfortable parlour, which contained everything you'd expect to find in a cosy vicarage parlour, but rarely do outside of a Jane Austen novel. Bright and open, with flowered wallpaper, tasteful prints on the walls, and the usual mixture of rough-and-ready furniture. The big surprise was the huge bay-window, which opened out on to a view of wide-open fields and low stone walls. Bright sunlight flooded in through the open window, beyond which I could hear a church-bell ringing in the distance. I didn't ask Sharon what was going on there because she so obviously wanted me to. So I nodded, and smiled, and said nothing. I can be really mean-spirited sometimes. The door opposite opened, and in came the current rogue vicar, Tamsin MacReady. She'd just been baking her own bread. I could tell, because she brought the smell in with her. How homey can you get?

The rogue vicar was a tiny little thing, barely five feet tall and slender with it. She looked like a strong breeze would blow her away, but there was something about her, a strength, a gravitas, that suggested hidden depths. Which was only to be expected. Delicate blossoms don't last long in the badlands. Tamsin had sharply defined features, softened by kind eyes and a winning smile, with frizzy blonde hair held in place by a cheap plastic headband. She wore a simple grey suit, with a white vicar's collar. She extended a hand for me to shake, and it was hardly bigger than a child's. I shook it carefully, and so did Chandra, then we all sat down in the surprisingly comfortable chairs.

"Well," the vicar said sweetly. "How nice. Two such important men, come all the way here to visit me. John Taylor and Chandra Singh. Monster, and monster hunter. What can I do for two such vaunted figures?"

"Just looking for a little advice," I said. "So you're the new rogue vicar, Tamsin?"

"I have that honour," she said. "I am Pew's replacement. Sharon, sweetie, there's blood all down the front of Mr. Taylor's coat. Be a dear and see to it, would you?"

And, of course, everything had to stop while I stood up and took off my coat, and handed it over to Sharon to be cleaned. She accepted the coat with a brisk, flashing smile, held it carefully between finger and thumb, and darted out of the room. I sat down again. I could have warned her about the coat's built-in defences, but I had a feeling Sharon could look after herself. Just as the coat could. And, in fact, Sharon was back almost immediately, without the coat, clearly not wanting to be left out of anything. She settled herself on the arm of the vicar's chair, one arm draped across Tamsin's shoulders.

Tamsin MacReady made a big deal out of serving us all tea and biscuits, from a silver tray that I would have sworn wasn't there on the table a moment ago. The tea service was delicate bone china, and I handled the cup carefully with my little finger extended, to show I wasn't a complete barbarian.

Chandra insisted on pouring the tea, putting the milk in first and frowning at me when I added more than one teaspoon of sugar. I waited patiently until everyone was settled again, then addressed the vicar while Chandra chomped happily on a mouthful of biscuits.

"Why are you here, vicar?" I said bluntly. I was finding pretending to be civilised very wearing, especially when the clock was ticking its way down to another massacre.

"People need me," said Tamsin, quite equably. "I choose to live here, amongst the lowest and worst of human kind, because they need me the most. People tend to forget that our Lord came down to earth to live among sinners because they needed him most. And since most of them can't or won't come to me, I must go out amongst them."

"Isn't that dangerous?" said Chandra.

"Oh no," said Tamsin. "Not while I've got Sharon."

Sharon wriggled happily on the arm of the chair, and the vicar patted her arm companionably.

"She's my partner. All gals together, ever since school. Inseparable, really, though I often fear Sharon hasn't got a truly Christian bone in her entire delightful body. Have you, dear?"

"I'll believe whatever you believe, Tamsy," Sharon said doughtily. "And Heaven help anyone who tries to hurt you while I'm around, that's what I say."

"Sharon is my body-guard," Tamsin said fondly. "She is so much more than she seems."

She'd have to be, I thought, but had the good sense not to say so out loud.

"I bear the word of the Lord to those who need it most," said the vicar. "I listen, offer advice and comfort where I can, and if I can lead just one sinner back into the light, then my time here will have been well spent. Though of course I hope to save rather more than that. Still, I am a missionary, not a crusader. The way of the sword is not mine."

"It is mine," said Sharon. "Though I don't usually limit myself to a sword."

"Not much like your predecessor, then," I said. "Pew always saw himself as a holy terrorist, fighting the good fight by any and all means necessary."

"Dear Pew," said Tamsin. "He is sorely missed."

"He was my teacher, for a time," I said. "Before he decided I was an abomination."

"I know," said Tamsin. "I've read his diaries from that period. He had great hopes for you, for a time."

I raised an eyebrow despite myself. "I didn't know Pew left any diaries."

"Oh yes. Fascinating reading. He wrote quite a lot about you. Before he gave away his eyes, in return for knowledge. About you. Do have another biscuit, John, that's what they're there for."

"I don't have time for distractions," I said bluntly. "What can you tell me about the Walking Man?"

Tamsin and Sharon shared a look. "We heard he was here, at last," said Tamsin. "It's said . . . he talks directly with God, who talks directly with him." She looked directly at Chandra. "I understand you are a khalsa, Mr. Singh. A holy warrior.

What brings you here, to the Nightside? At this time in particular? Did you know the Walking Man was going to be here?"

"Like you, I go where I am needed," said Chandra. "My life is a holy quest, for purpose and meaning, in the service of my god."

"Have you ever tried looking for your god on the Street of the Gods?" said Tamsin.

"No," said Chandra. "Have you?"

They both laughed, politely. A new subtle tension had entered the Vicarage parlour. It was getting in the way, so I intervened.

"The Beings on the Street of the Gods aren't gods at all, strictly speaking," I said. "Some of them are other-dimensional travellers, some are psychonauts from higher dimensions, some are aliens or icons or manifestations of abstract concepts. You get all sorts in the Nightside. Many of the older Beings are descendants of my mother Lilith, from when she went down to Hell and lay down with demons, and gave birth to monstrous Powers and Dominations. It's probably a lot more complicated than that, but there's a limit to how much weird shit the human mind can cope with."

"So...some of these Beings are related to you?" said Chandra.

"Only very indirectly," I said. "We're not close. Like so many other relationships in the Nightside, it's complicated."

"There is only one Supreme Being," said Tamsin.

"Yes," said Chandra. "There is."

"And the one true God has one true nature."

"Yes," said Chandra. "I would agree with that."

"But your god and mine are very different," said Tamsin. "I preach love and understanding and living peaceably with one another; and you follow the way of violence. We can't both be right. Is that why you came here to the Nightside, to see the Walking Man in action . . . and test your faith against his? Because if he really is what he says he is, a man touched directly by the Supreme Being, then what does that make you?"

"A searcher after truth," said Chandra. "In my travels, I have met many who claimed to hear the Voice of God instructing them to do things, and most of them had to take a lot of medication. Few of them were in any way worthy of the God they claimed to worship. You said it yourself—yours is the way of love and peace. John and I have seen the Walking Man at his work, and it seems to me that if he serves any Lord at all, it is the Lord of Darkness."

"God moves in mysterious way," said Tamsin, implacably.

"So does Walker," I said. "But I've never felt like worshipping him. Save the religious debates for another time. The Walking Man—do you know of any way to stop him, or turn him aside?"

"No," said Tamsin. "No-one can. That's the point."

"We did a lot of reading up on the Walking Man, once we heard he was here, didn't we, sweetie?" said Sharon. "Pretty disturbing stuff, actually. Real Old Testament retribution, eye for an eye and all that. Give him the jawbone of an ass and stand well back."

"We don't know anything for sure about the Walking Man," said Tamsin. "I was hoping he'd come to see me, so I could...reason with him. But I have no authority over him, or any control over his actions. He will do what he will do. He answers to God, not the Church. To be honest, I always thought he was just a myth, a story they tell in seminaries as an example of faith getting out of hand. But myths have a way of coming true in the Nightside, don't they, Lilith's son?"

"If I can't find a way to stop him, he's going to destroy the Nightside and everyone in it," I said, as harshly as I could. "Including you and Sharon and all those poor sinners you were hoping to save. Isn't there any help or advice you can offer?"

Tamsin thought for a long moment. "Only a certain kind of man becomes a Walking Man. Broken men, their lives destroyed by great tragedy and loss. Men with nothing left to lose...seeking redemption, by enforcing justice on a world that seems to have none. Heal them, and they often don't feel the need to be the Walking Man any more. In fact, certain very old texts seem to suggest that the office of the Walking Man only exists to give the most desperate of men a chance to heal themselves and return to a state of grace." She looked at me, not smiling at all. "In another time, and in another place, I think you might have become a Walking Man, John Taylor.

"My only advice...is to go to church. The only real church in the Nightside, St. Jude's. A place where prayers are heard, and answered. If you're really serious about wanting the truth . . . go and talk to the Walking Man's Boss. But remember, John, the only thing worse than asking questions of God . . . is getting them answered."

Chandra leaned forward suddenly. "There is a place here, where a man can talk directly with his God?"

"Yes," said Tamsin. "You should go, Mr. Singh. Ask your questions, and see who answers you."

"Yes," said Chandra. "That should prove most interesting."

Tamsin turned to Sharon. "Mr. Taylor's coat should be clean by now, dear. Go and get it for him, would you?"

"Oh sure, sweetie! Won't be a moment!"

She bounced up off the chair's arm and hurried out the door. It seemed it was time to leave, so I got up. Chandra made a point of finishing his tea first and making appreciative noises, then he got up, too. Sharon came bustling back in with my coat. It was, of course, spotless. I put it back on, and said good-bye politely to the rogue vicar. Chandra was even more polite. Sharon led us back down the cosy hallway to the front door. I glanced covertly at Chandra. Tamsin MacReady had been pushing him pretty strongly about whose god was biggest, but it didn't seem to have ruffled his composure. If there's one thing I've come to be sure of, in all my years of walking up and down in the Nightside, it's that while there are always answers to be found if you know where to look . . . they inevitably only lead to more questions.

Sharon opened the front door for us, and Chandra and I stepped back out into the night. I looked back to say good night, and Sharon smiled at me through the closing gap.

And for a moment I caught a glimpse of her hidden self, the vicar's body-guard—a quick flash of huge teeth and ragged claws and something hideously vile and vicious. Just a glimpse, then it was gone, and Sharon Pilkington-Smythe smiled good-bye as the door closed. I wondered whether Tamsin MacReady knew. I thought she probably did. I looked at Chandra.

"Did you see that?"

"See what?"

"Never mind."

I took a moment to check my trench coat thoroughly, in case Sharon had planted any listening or tracking things, or some other little surprise. You can never be too careful with the truly righteous—their faith allows them to justify all kinds of underhanded behaviour. I found half a dozen small silver crucifixes, scattered through various pockets. They didn't seem to be anything out of the ordinary, but I discarded them anyway, just in case. What is the world coming to, when you can't even trust a rogue vicar and her demon lover?

A movement further down the street caught my attention, and I looked round sharply. Out of the shadows, walking calmly and serenely in the night, came Annie Abattoir, large as life and twice as glamorous. She was wearing a rich purple evening gown, complete with elbow-length gloves, high heels, and enough jewellery to fill a pawnbroker's. Not that anyone would bother her, of course, even here. She was Annie Abattoir. She strode up to me, and I nodded respectfully.

"Hello, Annie. Seduced and killed anyone interesting recently?"

"No-one you'd know," said Annie.

"What is a high-class courtesan, experienced assassin, and truly dangerous individual such as yourself doing in this low-rent area?"

"I'm here to visit the rogue vicar."

I raised an eyebrow, and Annie looked at me witheringly.

"What's the matter?" she said. "Can't a mother visit her own daughter?"

She knocked on the Vicarage door. Sharon opened it and let her in. I looked thoughtfully at the door as it closed. I never knew Annie had any family. I thought she killed them all. So, the most vicious assassin in the Nightside had a vicar for a daughter. Made you wonder which of them was the black sheep...

Chandra Singh and I walked from the Vicarage to St. Jude's. It wasn't far. The church's actual location had become somewhat elusive, ever since the Lilith War, and is seldom to be found in the same place twice. You have to need to find it really badly, then there it is, right in front of you. Or not. It's not supposed to be easy to find. Either way, St. Jude's has always preferred the darkest and most out-of-the-way locations in the Nightside. I must have wanted to find the church really badly, because after only a few minutes walking, it loomed up before me, in a setting I was pretty sure it had never patronised before.

St. Jude's is the one real church in the Nightside, and it wouldn't be seen dead anywhere near the Street of the Gods. A simple cold stone structure that almost certainly predates Christianity itself, it has no trappings, no rituals, and no services. You don't come to St. Jude's for prayer or contemplation or comfort. It's a place to go when you've tried everywhere else. A place where prayers are heard and paid attention to. A church where you can talk to your god directly, and be pretty damned sure of an answer. St. Jude's deals in truth, and justice, which is why most people have the good sense to steer clear of it.

And only the truly desperate would ever use it for sanctuary.

Which is why it really shouldn't have surprised me to find one particular person already there, kneeling before the crude but functional altar, lit by the light of hundreds of candles. I knew him, and stopped just inside the doorway. Chandra stopped beside me, and looked dubiously at the old man in his torn and tattered robe.

"That," I said quietly, "is the Lord of Thorns. Once, and for a long time, the most powerful man in the Nightside. Overseer and Court of Last Resort, very powerful and very scary, he believed God had put him here to be the Nightside's protector. Until Lilith came, and slapped him aside like he was nothing. He's been trying to figure out his true role and purpose ever since. Be warned, Chandra. The Nightside does so love to break a hero."

"It hasn't broken you," said Chandra.

"Exactly," I said.

Even though we'd been talking in low voices, the Lord of Thorns still heard us. He rose slowly and painfully to his feet, as though his many centuries of existence were finally catching up with him, and turned to face us with a certain wounded gravitas. He no longer had his staff of power, supposedly grown from a sliver off the original Tree of Life. Lilith broke it, when she broke him. I could remember when just his presence was enough to make me kneel to him, but he was just a man now. Someone had cut his Old Testament prophet's hair and beard to more manageable proportions, and it looked like someone had been feeding him. People will adopt the strangest pets, in the Nightside.

He came down the aisle to join us, taking his time, and I nodded respectfully.

"Didn't expect to see you still here," I said.

"I look after the church," he said flatly. "Or it looks after me. It's often hard to tell...I keep it clean, keep the candles lit...because someone has to, and I tell myself it's all about learning patience and humility. I'm still waiting for an answer to my prayer, the question I put to God. If I'm not the Nightside's Overseer, then what am I? What is my true nature and purpose?"

"Isn't that what every man would know of his god?" said Chandra.

"Most people haven't lived a lie for as many centuries as I have," said the Lord of Thorns.

"Have you regained any of your power?" I asked.

"No," said the Lord of Thorns, his voice quite matter-of-fact. "I'm just a man. I sometimes wonder if I'm supposed to work out the answer myself, before I can take up my old power and authority again. Right now I'd settle for a sign. Or even a hint." He looked at me thoughtfully. "I could have returned to my old home, in the World Beneath. It has been largely rebuilt and repopulated, since the end of the Lilith War. But it wouldn't feel right. It would feel too much like hiding. So here I stay, in the church named after the Patron Saint of Lost Causes. What are you doing here, John Taylor? Come to talk to God at last, and ask him what you're supposed to be?"

"I already know," I said. "That's my problem."

"A moment, please," said Chandra. "Is this really a place where a man can speak directly with God? And get an answer? There are so many things I would dearly love to ask Him..."

"This is the place," said the Lord of Thorns. "Can't you feel it?"

"Yes..." said Chandra. "There are places such as this in India. Ancient and sacred places that feel like this...But I never considered myself worthy enough, holy enough, to approach them. But then, perhaps this is not a place to find my god."

"God is God," said the Lord of Thorns. "You think he gives a damn what name we choose, just as long as we talk to him and listen for his answers? This is not a Christian place, though it currently uses Christian forms...It's much older than that. This is the real thing, the pure pattern, just a man and his god, and nothing to separate them. Could anything be scarier?"

Chandra looked at me. "You've been here before. Have you ever asked a question?"

"No," I said. "I've got more sense. The last thing any sensible man wants is God taking a keen interest in him. I have no wish to be given a quest, or a duty, or a destiny. I'm not a holy warrior, or any kind of saint. I'm just a man, trying to get through life as best I can. Don't look at me like that, Thorns. You know what I mean."

"Sorry," said the Lord of Thorns. "I thought you were being ironic."

"I decide my life," I said. "No-one else."

"I used to think that," said the Lord of Thorns.

Chandra approached the stone altar, his voice soft and flat with awe. "To speak directly with God, without the intervention of priest or ritual. I am khalsa, a holy warrior. I have dedicated my life to serving my god, and yet still . . . I fear to hear what he might say to me. What does that say about me?"

"That you're still human," I said. "Only a fool or a fanatic never has doubts about himself." I looked at the Lord of Thorns. "What do you know about the Walking Man?"

"I've met a few, in my time," he said easily. "I haven't always been bound to the Nightside. I have met Walking Men, out in the world. Not the happiest of men, usually. Driven, desperate to make the world make sense . . . by making sure the guilty are punished. For supposedly holy men, they seem to have remarkably little faith in the justice of the world to come. They want their justice here and now, where they can see it."

"What if I were to bring him here, to you?" I said suddenly. "Could you stop him from destroying the Nightside?"

"Even if I still had my old power, and my old certainty, I am nothing compared to the Walking Man," said the Lord of Thorns. "He is the wrath of God, you see. And besides...perhaps he's right in what he's doing. Perhaps God has finally decided to do away with the Nightside, for the sinfulness of its inhabitants. There are precedents..."

"There has to be a way to stop him!" I said, almost shouting at the old man. He didn't flinch.

"There might be a way," he said slowly. "Not a very pleasant way, but that's often how these things go...I suppose it would depend on how desperate you are."

"Oh, I am way past desperate," I said. "What is it?"

"To stop a man of God, you need a weapon of God," said the Lord of Thorns. "You need the Speaking Gun."

That stopped me. I turned away. My mouth was suddenly very dry, and there was a chill in my bones.

"What exactly is this Speaking Gun?" said Chandra.

"An ancient, terrible weapon," I said. "It uncreates things. It could destroy everything. So I destroyed it."

"It still exists in the Past," said the Lord of Thorns. "If you could travel back into Time Past...Perhaps if you were to speak with Old Father Time?"

"No," I said. "Not after..."

"Oh yes. Quite. Well then, I suggest you visit the Street of the Gods. Time has never been too strongly nailed down there. And that is where the Walking Man is, right now."

"What?" I said. "Oh shit . . ."

I left St. Jude's at a run, with Chandra pounding along behind me. I had to get to the Street of the Gods. Before the Walking Man brought the wrath of God to things that only thought they were gods.

SEVEN

The Good Man

I'd barely cleared the door of St. Jude's when I found myself charging down the Street of the Gods, with Chandra Singh pounding along behind me. A gift from the Lord of Thorns, or from the church itself? Or maybe even from Someone higher up . . . Some questions you just don't ask, especially in the Nightside. I skidded to a halt and looked quickly around me as I realised the Street of the Gods wasn't in any more of an upset than usual. Gods and worshippers, strange Beings and stranger tourists, all milled about making rather more noise than was necessary, stirring up trouble for themselves and each other, but there was no sign anywhere of the Walking Man. No-one was dead and dying, there were no piled-up bodies, and no-one was screaming . . . so perhaps he hadn't actually got here yet. I made myself take a deep breath and concentrate. I'd spent too long chasing around after the Walking Man. Now I was ahead of him for once, I had to stop and think. Find some way to stop him. The Walking Man already had two massacres to his credit. I couldn't let him get away with a third.

Especially not here.

"It's like a carnival!" Chandra Singh said suddenly. He was staring all around him, beaming widely. "Brightly coloured tents holding wonders within, while hawkers shout their wares, and boast of the glories to be enjoyed by braver and more adventurous souls. The scale may be different, but the spirit's the same. Come in, come in, put your money down, for an experience that will change your life forever! I have seen this before, John Taylor, from the smallest towns to the biggest cities. Religion for sale and faith on special offer. This is just another marketplace!"

"Of course," I said. "Why do you think the Street of the Gods has always been so closely associated with the Nightside?"

"Bit short on taste, though," said Chandra, positively curling his lip at some of the more ostentatious displays.

He was saved from hearing my perhaps overly cynical reply when we were ambushed by a pack of pamphleteers. They seemed to jump up out of nowhere, loud and aggressive and very much in our faces, surrounding us in a moment, forcing their cheaply printed pamphlets into our hands, while keeping up a constant clamour of hard-sell conversion. I glanced reflexively at the pamphlet in my hand.

Better Living Through Urine: Drink Yourself Holy! Worship Baphomet Now—Avoid The Rush When He Finally Manifests In All His Awful Glory! Join The Church Of Smiting: Strike Down The Ones You Hate With A Truly Nasty Act Of God! Suffering And Unfairness Guaranteed Or Your Money Back! Are You Not Sure Of Anything Really? Then Join The Church Of The Undecided. Or Not. See If We Care. We're Only Printing These Things As A Tax Dodge.

Chandra made the mistake of trying to talk kindly to these hyperventilating vultures and was immediately shouted down by a dozen competing voices. Some of them even grabbed at his silk sleeves and tried to drag him off in a dozen different directions at once. So I made a point of throwing all my pamphlets on the ground and stamping on them, and when I had the pamphleteers attention, I fixed them all with a hard stare. They fell back as one, struck suddenly dumb. It's amazing what you can achieve with a good hard stare when you've got a reputation like mine. But by now more pamphleteers had arrived, scenting blood in the water, and filled the silence with their own shouts.

"I saw them first! They're mine!"

"Don't listen to him! Only I can bring you to Enlightenment!"

"You? You couldn't even spell Enlightenment! I offer a tenfold path to true transcendence!"

"Ten? Ten? I can do it in eight!"

"Seven!"

"Four!"

"Dagon shall rise again!"

It got nasty after that. They fell on each other, pamphlets thrown to the winds, fluttering on the air like particularly gaudy autumn leaves. Fists were brandished, shins were kicked, and there was a lot of close grappling and unnecessary biting. I strolled off and left them to it, and Chandra hurried after me.

The Street of the Gods was being its usual strange and unnatural self, with weird shit on every corner and more manifestations than you could shake a crucible at. Chandra enjoyed the sights, like any other tourist on his first grand tour, but every now and again he'd catch himself as he remembered he wasn't supposed to approve of things like this. Organised religions are always jealous of the up-and-comers. But there was a lot to look at and enjoy. Self-appointed saints with neon halos looked disapprovingly on other-dimensional entities playing croquet with the heads of heretics, while rival congregations shouted rap sermons at each other from the safety of their church doors.

And a long line of sad furry animals followed a large scruffy bear as he trudged down the Street, holding up a crucifix to which was nailed a small green frog.

I pointed out some of the more interesting faiths and beliefs to Chandra as they presented themselves, at least partly in the spirit of self-defence. It pays to watch your back in the Street of the Gods. You never knew when some of the more aggressive Ideas will sneak up behind you and mug your subconscious. But there are many sights to be seen in the Street of the Gods, and I enjoyed showing them off to Chandra. It was all so new to him. The glamour rubs off fast after you've cleaned a fallen god's blood off your shoes, as he's viciously ejected from his temple to make way for someone more popular.

I showed him the Church of the Blood Red God—a tall Gothic structure with spiked towers and barbed parapets, a gloomy crimson edifice made entirely out of blood. Blood and nothing but blood, gallons of the stuff shaped and held in place entirely by the will of the Blood Red God. Impressive to look at, though up close it smelled pretty bad. Attracted flies like you wouldn't believe. The God's disciples provide the blood, mostly voluntarily.

"And what, precisely, does the Blood Red God get out of all this?" said Chandra suspiciously. "Apart from a church that smells like a slaughterhouse?"

"Well," I said. "He feeds off his flock, transmutes the blood in his own divine body, then feeds the supercharged blood back to his devotees, a few drops at a time. Their worship makes him a God, and they get to feel divine, for a time. Do I really need to tell you that the process is addictive and that it burns out the human system pretty damn quickly? Not that it matters. There's a believer born every minute."

"But...that means he's nothing more than a glorified leech! Feeding off his followers!"

"I could say something very cynical and cutting here about the nature of most organised religions," I said. "But the Street says it all, really."

Chandra sniffed loudly. "What does he look like, this Blood Red God?"

"Good question," I said. "No-one knows. Like many of

the Beings on the Street, he rarely walks abroad in person. Probably because if their flocks ever got a good look at what they were actually worshipping, they'd go off the whole idea. However, the Blood Red God has been known to send out humanoid figures composed entirely of blood to take care of day-to-day business. Some of the more adventurous vampires like to sneak up behind and stick straws in them."

"Show me something else," said Chandra. "Before I projectile vomit every meal I've eaten in the last three months."

"Well," I said. "If you're looking for something more spiritual . . . over there we have the Hall of Entropy. A dour-looking place for a congregation of real gloomy buggers. They believe that since the whole universe is winding down, and everything that lives is going to die, it's up to us to evolve into a higher order of Being and get the hell out of here in search of a better class of universe. They offer courses in how to become a higher order of Being. Very expensive courses."

"Ah," said Chandra. "And have any of these people ever actually transcended?"

"Funnily enough, no," I said sadly. "According to the people who run the courses, it's because the students aren't trying hard enough. Or because they haven't taken enough courses. There's a pool running on the Street as to how long it will take before the students wise up and rebel, and tear the whole place apart. Probably only to find that the organisation's leaders have already absconded with all the cash. In search of a better universe, presumably."

"Why is everyone staying well away from that one?" said

Chandra, pointing entirely unselfconsciously. "Even the tourists are taking their photos from the other side of the Street."

"Ah," I said. "That is the Church of Sacrifice. Its priests have an unnerving tendency to rush out of their church without warning, grab anyone handy, or anyone who doesn't run away fast enough, and drag them into their church to sacrifice to their god. Usually singing psalms very loudly, to drown out the screams and objections. Their god, who has no name but I think we can all take a pretty good guess at his nature, sucks up the souls and shares the life energy with its followers. No-one on the Street objects, as such. They think he adds colour and character to the Street. And besides, he helps keep the tourists moving. The Church's worshippers wear masks at all times. Because if any of them do get identified, everyone else kills them. Just on general principles."

"This whole Street is a disgrace!" said Chandra, rather more loudly than I was comfortable with. "None of these Beings are gods! Powerful creatures, yes, but not gods! Nothing worthy of worship. In fact," he said, his voice suddenly thoughtful. "Many would seem to me to qualify as monsters..."

"Let us not go there," I said quickly. "We really don't want to start anything. We're here to stop the Walking Man."

"But I'm right, aren't I?" insisted Chandra.

"Well, yes, quite probably," I said. "But it's still not something you want to actually announce out loud unless you like having your testicles expand suddenly and violently, then blow up in slow motion. Some of the gods here have very old-fashioned ideas when it comes to smiting unbelievers."

"You think that will stop the Walking Man?" said Chandra.

"No. But then, his god is bigger than everyone else's god."

"I am a khalsa," said Chandra. "I do not believe . . . that this Walking Man can do anything that I cannot."

"You can believe anything you like, on the Street of the Gods," I said. "But that doesn't necessarily make it true."

There was the sudden sound of loud and angry confrontation, from further down the Street. I started running again, with Chandra pounding along behind me. He was in better shape than I, but he was carrying more weight, so I kept a comfortable lead. I felt a very definite need to encounter situations or Beings before Chandra did. He had a disturbing tendency to say exactly what he was thinking, and that can get you into a whole lot of trouble on the Street of the Gods.

Lots of other people were running right alongside me, including a whole bunch of tourists with their cameras at the ready. We do love our free entertainment in the Nightside, especially if it promises to be dramatic, violent, and quite spectacularly bloody. And given that this involved the Walking Man, it promised to be all three. He was standing quite calmly in the middle of the Street, his long duster hanging open to reveal the guns still holstered on his belt. He was surrounded by proponents of a whole bunch of belief systems, singing the praises of their gods and denouncing the Walking Man as a heretic, an unbeliever, or worse still, a fake prophet. Even more were shouting insults from the safety of their church doors. And yet, nobody wanted to get too close to him. Even the fiercest of believers, the most fanatical wide-eyed extremists, could sense the power and the threat of the Walking Man. Even standing still, he was more frightening and more dangerous than any of the Beings on the Street of the Gods.

You just knew it.

I pushed my way through the crowd surrounding the Walking Man, and most people only gave me a quick glance before getting out of my way. Probably because they were curious to see what I was going to do. My name moved swiftly through the crowd, along with a sense of *Now we're going to see something...* Chandra Singh stuck close behind me. I was huffing and puffing from the run, and he wasn't even out of breath. And then the Walking Man opened his mouth to speak, and everyone fell silent.

"You aren't gods," he said, in a calm but still loud and carrying voice. "You're spiritual con men, confidence tricksters offering false faith and false hope. Is there a greater sin?"

"Even false hope is better than none," I said. "Especially in a place like the Nightside." Everyone around me fell back to what they clearly hoped was a safe distance. The Walking Man looked at me, and I met his gaze firmly. I needed to get him talking, try to reason with him, before the horror I sensed hanging on the air erupted into bloody murder. There had to be a way to reach him. Before all hell broke lose.

The Walking Man did me the politeness of considering my words for a moment, then shook his head. "No. All of... this is just a distraction from the true God, the real God, and a real state of grace. God is God, and none of these pretenders can be allowed to continue in their offences. There's no room for mercy when souls are at stake."

"What are you going to do?" I said bluntly. "Fight your way into all the churches and temples, drag the gods out into the Street, and shoot them all in the head? Even if you could do that, which I rather doubt, there are so many of them, you'd still be at it years from now."

"I have faith," said the Walking Man. "And faith can move mountains, never mind a false Church or two." He stopped and glared across the Street at a grimy stone edifice. "I mean, come on, look at that. The Temple of the Unspeakable Abomination. Who in their right mind would want to worship *that*?"

"Someone looking for an unfair advantage, probably," I said. "It's all about the deals you can make on the Street of the Gods. Faith is currency here, with valuable prizes to be won by the faithful. You can win good fortune, bad cess to your enemies, transformation or immortality, and everything in between, if you make the right kind of deal with the Being of your choice. Though the price will almost certainly be your soul, or someone else's. And I don't see that you're in any position to protest. You made a deal, didn't you? To put your humanity behind you and become the Walking Man?"

He glared at me, all the casual humour gone from his face, and when he spoke his voice was flat and calm and very dangerous. "Don't press me, John Taylor. And don't you dare compare me to the debauched fools and heretics of this corrupt and corrupting place. I serve the real deal, the one true God."

"That's what they all say here," I said easily, refusing to be intimidated.

"But my god has made me strong enough to destroy all their gods," said the Walking Man.

"Is that who you serve?" I said. "A god of blood and murder?"

He smiled suddenly, and I realised I hadn't even touched his faith and conviction. "I am the wrath of God. I punish the guilty. Because someone has to."

Chandra Singh pushed in beside me, positively quivering with eagerness to join the debate. He still thought we were only talking.

"I have no interest or affection for this place, but still, everyone has the right to worship who or what they please, in their own way," he said earnestly. "There are many paths to enlightenment, and none of us are fit to judge them. Do you intend to kill me, for worshipping my god in a way that is different to yours?"

"I don't know," said the Walking Man, with breath-taking casualness. "I haven't decided yet."

"You would kill me?" said Chandra Singh.

The Walking Man shrugged easily. "Only if you get in my way. You're not guilty. Merely deluded. Ah well, time to get to work."

He drew both his pistols and opened fire on the Temple of the Unspeakable Abomination. The crowd scattered to give him room, keeping their heads well down. I stood my ground, and Chandra stood his ground beside me. Under normal circumstances I would have done the sensible thing and run like hell with the rest of them, but somehow I just couldn't while Chandra was with me. Never hang around with heroes; they'll always get you killed. The pistols' bullets hammered away at the front of the temple, punching holes clean through the wall and exploding the ancient stonework. There was a power in those guns and those bullets that the temple was no match for.

Cracks spread jaggedly across the entire front of the temple, then the whole front wall exploded outwards, as the Unspeakable Abomination showed itself for the first time in centuries, to see who was knocking so loudly on its door. Dozens of loathsome tentacles burst out into the street, dozens of feet long and bigger around than the average car, all of them lined with hundreds of vicious suckers packed full of rotating knifelike teeth. The flesh of the tentacles was a sick and leprous grey, as much metallic as organic, an impossibly flexible living metal that dripped corrosive slime. More and more tentacles slammed through the disintegrating front of the temple, as the Unspeakable Abomination rose up from the depths of its night-dark caverns far beneath the Street of the Gods, determined to have its revenge on whoever had dared disturb its sleep of centuries.

The tentacles lashed back and forth, grabbing everything within reach and crushing it to rubble or pulp. People died screaming as the tentacles shot after them faster than they could run. Men and women were snatched and slammed against the ground or the nearest buildings. Razor-packed suckers ate greedily into yielding flesh, and blood and other fluids ran down the Street in thickening streams. The temple was gone now. All that remained was a nest of long, thrashing tentacles killing everyone within reach. And finally, deep in the heart of the tentacles, there rose up a burning three-lobed eye, almost the size of the temple itself, staring unblinkingly on the death and destruction it was causing and finding it good.

Beings of all shapes and sizes and natures came charging out of their churches and temples to face this new threat to the Street of the Gods, for whatever threatened the security and business of the Street was a threat to them all. The Walking Man might have intimidated them, but this was one of their own, and no-one would take you seriously on the Street if you let your neighbour intimidate you. So gods and icons and avatars spilled out on to the Street, and magics and sciences and strange energies spit and crackled on the air. Tentacles writhed and caught fire, exploded and cracked apart, and a choking, noxious smell filled the air as thick black blood spilled. But there were always more tentacles to replace those that were destroyed. Fanatical worshippers rushed in to cut and hack at the tentacles with blessed swords and axes, urged on by their priests, only to see the metal of their weapons break and shatter against the unyielding unearthly flesh of the Unspeakable Abomination.

The three-lobed burning eye looked on god and follower alike and found them all equally hateful in its gaze.

The tentacles churned out from the ruins of the temple,

growing longer and thicker. They snatched up gods and squeezed them till their heads exploded, or pounded them against their own churches like a child having a temper tantrum with its toys. They slammed down on whole congregations, crushing them under their writhing weight until nothing was left but red pulp. The Abomination was awakening from its long sleep and remembering the joys of slaughter and destruction and the sweet taste of blood and suffering.

Chandra Singh strode steadily forward, his long, curved sword glowing almost unbearably bright in the gloom of the Street. Some of the lesser Beings actually flinched away from its light and fell back to give Chandra room to work. He cut savagely at the nearest tentacle, and the shining blade sank deep into the metallic flesh. Steaming black blood spurted, hissing and spitting on the ground, but though the tentacle reached for Chandra, it couldn't touch him. He gripped his sword in both hands, raised it high above his head, and brought it sweeping down in a mighty blow that sheared clean through the tentacle. The severed end flapped and flopped on the Street, curling and uncurling aimlessly. The stump retreated, spurting blood. Chandra went after it, his gaze fixed on the three-lobed eye.

Meanwhile, I had my own problems.

A tentacle came right for me, then hesitated at the last moment, as though it recognised me, or at least something about me. Which was both flattering and worrying. The tentacle humped and coiled before me, as though making up its mind, then suddenly pressed forward. I jumped out of the way, dodging behind a handy stone pillar. The tentacle curled around the massive pillar and wrenched it away with one heave. The roof started to come down, and I was forced back out into the Street. There was nowhere to run; the tentacles were everywhere. I dug through my coat pockets, searching for something I could use, and finally came up with a flat blue packet of salt. I tore the packet apart and spilled the salt on to the tentacle as it reached for me. The metallic flesh shrivelled and blackened and fell apart, the way salt affects a slug.

Never leave home without condiments.

I tried raising my gift, hoping I could use it to find some fatal weakness in the Abomination (seeing as I'd run out of salt), but the aether was jammed with the emanations of all the Beings out on the Street, fighting the Abomination. It was like being blinded by spotlights—I couldn't See a damned thing. I had to screw my inner eye shut to keep from being overwhelmed.

When I could see clearly again, the Walking Man was striding right into the heart of the lashing and roiling tentacles, heading straight for that burning three-lobed eye. It loomed over him, bigger than a house by then. The tentacles couldn't even get close to him, let alone touch him. Something made them pull back in spite of themselves, as though just the touch of him would be more than they could stand. He was protected because he was walking in Heaven's path. He passed by Chandra Singh, still fighting valiantly though surrounded on all sides. The Walking Man didn't even glance at Chandra, all his attention fixed on the three-lobed eye.

He walked right up to the eye, tentacles recoiling from his very proximity, and when he was standing right before it...he raised one of his long-barrelled pistols and shot the eye three times; one bullet for each lobe. The eye exploded in a blast of incandescent fire, and a wave of almost unbearable heat rushed down the Street, but none of it touched the Walking Man. The tentacles collapsed and lay still, slowly melting away, disappearing into long blue streams of decaying ectoplasm. The Unspeakable Abomination was gone. I'd like to think it was dead, but such creatures are notoriously hard to kill.

All around, Beings and men alike stared at the Walking Man, and a whisper went down the Street; *Godkiller*...

I started towards him, and Chandra Singh came forward to join me. He looked like he'd been in a fight, his silks torn and steaming from black blood-stains, but he still held his long sword, and his back was straight and stiff. He only had eyes for the Walking Man, and he looked mad as hell.

"You!" he said, when he was close enough. "Walking Man! You did this! How many dead and injured, simply because they happened to be here when you chose to pick a fight with the Abomination? How many innocents dead today, because of you?"

"There are no innocents here," the Walking Man said calmly. "Not on the Street of the Gods, or in the whole damned Nightside. Isn't that right, John?"

"Not everyone here needs killing," I said stubbornly. "Sometimes, a place like this can be a haven for the damaged and the broken...a place to go when no-one else will have you. You can't just kill everyone."

"No?" said the Walking Man. "Watch me."

He didn't even bother with his guns this time. He walked unhurriedly down the Street, turning his terrible implacable gaze this way and that, and buildings and structures on all sides began to shudder and shake and fall apart under the impact of his deadly faith. Centuries-old stone and marble cracked and splintered, while construction materials from a hundred worlds and dimensions collapsed, or shattered like glass, or melted away like mist. For what use was antiquity and mystery in the face of his brutal faith? He was the Walking Man. He had God on his side, and he wasn't afraid to use Him. Beings and creatures and things beyond reason stumbled horrified out on to the Street, driven from their places of worship. Some came out howling and screaming, some sobbing bitterly, and some came out fighting.

The Robot God, the Deus in Machina, demon construct from the forty-first century, all strangeness and charm and vicious quarks, came stamping down the Street on its solid steel legs, its divine metal workings exposed, clanking and scraping against each other. Its eyes were multi-coloured diodes, and its slit mouth roared static. All kinds of energy weapons emerged from secret recesses, and the Robot God unleashed all its terror arsenal on the Walking Man, seeking to blast him right down to the quantum level.

The Walking Man swaggered down the Street to meet it, flashing his old insolent smile, and when he got close enough, he jumped lightly up to grab a handhold on the massive metal body and tore the Robot God apart, piece by piece, with his bare hands. Future energies howled and sputtered around the pair of them as the Robot God lurched back and forth, screaming bursts of static. In a matter of moments, all that remained was a scattered pile of metal parts and a few dispersing energies.

The Inscrutable Enigma appeared out of nowhere, forming itself around the Walking Man in spiralling circles of coruscating intensities. Its living energies had burned up through the material world to reach the Street, and its very presence set fire to the ground and ignited the air. Unearthly flames burned all around the Walking Man, but could not consume him. The Inscrutable Enigma might have been as much idea as matter, an alien concept manifesting in the material world, but it was still no match for the power that burned within the Walking Man. And all too soon the Enigma exhausted its energies and faded away, its base idea consumed by a bigger one.

Pretty Kitty God gave it her best shot. She was an utterly artificial god, cold-bloodedly designed and created by marketing groups to appeal to the biggest possible audience. But they did their job too well, and Pretty Kitty God became real, or real enough. She escaped the confines of her planned Christmas Special, broke the shackles of her trade-mark, and took up residence on the Street of the Gods, where she belonged. She was vast and powerful and almost unbearably cute. All fluffy pink fur and enormous eyes, ten feet tall and wondrously soft, she advanced on the Walking Man with her padded arms outstretched for a hug, to overwhelm as she always had, through sheer, unnatural cuteness. The God of Lost Toys, designed to appeal to all those who never got over finding out Father Christmas wasn't real, or having their favourite teddy bear thrown out by their mother because *they were too old for it now*, though they weren't and never would be. I'd seen Pretty Kitty God subdue and smother old-school horned demons within a deluge of sheer niceness.

She always gave me the shudders. Toys should know their places. They certainly shouldn't want you to worship them.

The Walking Man gave Pretty Kitty God a hard look, and she burst into flames. She waddled away sadly, her leaping flames lighting up the gloom of the Street. The Walking Man, still smiling his mocking smile, looked unhurriedly about him, and all the gods of the Nightside stood there and stared back, not knowing what to do.

Then Razor Eddie appeared, and everything on the Street of the Gods went really quiet. He didn't come walking down the Street, he didn't make an entrance. He was suddenly there, the Punk God of the Straight Razor, a terrible thin presence in a filthy old coat, more than a man but less than a god. Or just possibly the other way round. Thin to the point of emaciation, his eyes dark and feverish in his sunken grey face, Razor Eddie was one of the more disturbing agents of the Good in the Nightside. He slept in doorways, lived on hand-outs, and killed people who needed killing, all in penance for the sins of his youth. He did awful things with his straight razor, in the name of justice, and didn't give a damn.

I suppose he's my friend. It's hard to tell, sometimes.

He wandered down the Street towards the Walking Man, who turned and considered him thoughtfully. Like two gunfighters in a Western town who'd always known that some day they'd have to meet, and sort out once and for all which of them was fastest on the draw. The wrath of God and the Punk God of the Straight Razor finally stood facing each other, maintaining a respectful distance, and it felt like the whole Street was holding its breath. God's holy warrior and the most distressing agent the Good had ever had. The Walking Man's nose twitched. Eddie lived among the homeless, and up close his smell could get pretty rank. But when the Walking Man finally spoke, his voice was calm and measured and even respectful.

"Hi, Eddie," he said. "I wondered when you'd get here. I've heard a lot about you."

"Nothing good, I hope," said Razor Eddie, in his pale ghostly voice.

"You should approve of what I'm doing here. Striking down the false gods, punishing those who prey on the weak."

"I don't give a damn for most of the scum who infest this place," said Razor Eddie. "And yes, I've killed a few gods in my time. But Dagon... is my friend. You don't touch him."

"Sorry," said the Walking Man. "But I really can't make exceptions. Bad for the reputation. People would think I was going soft."

"Bloody hell," I said, stepping forward. "The testosterone's getting so thick around here you could carve your initials in it. Both of you, take a step back and calm the hell down."

The Walking Man looked at me. "Or?" he said politely.

I met his gaze steadily. "You really want to find out?"

"Oh you're good," said the Walking Man. "You really are, John."

I looked at Razor Eddie. "You've got a friend here, on the Street of the Gods? You've been holding out on me."

He shrugged briefly, the merest lifting of his shoulders. "Do you tell me all your secrets, John?"

"Can we at least give reason and common sense a try?" I said. "Before the shit hits the straight razor, and I have to get seriously peeved with both of you?"

"All right," said the Walking Man. "I'm game. Try me."

"The Street of the Gods serves a purpose," I said, trying hard to sound both firm and reasonable. "Not everyone who comes to the Nightside is ready for the real thing, for true faith. You could say this whole place is a repository and a haven for the spiritually walking wounded. They have to work their way up, in easy steps, one step at a time, out of the dark and back into the light."

"There is only one way," the Walking Man said patiently. "There is good, and there is evil. No shades of grey. You've been living here too long, John. Made too many compromises along the way. You've got soft."

"I haven't," said Razor Eddie. "You're not so different from me, Walking Man. We both gave up our old lives, and all human comforts, to serve God in violent ways, to do the dirty work no-one else wants to know about."

"If you understand, then step aside and let me do my work," said the Walking Man. "You don't have to die here today, Eddie."

"Can't do that," said Razor Eddie. "Hard as it may be to believe, there are some good people here. And some good gods. One of them is my friend. And what kind of . . . good man would I be, to step aside and let my friend be killed? Sometimes this Street can be a place for second chances, one last opportunity to make something better of one's life. I found new hope here. You have to believe that."

"No I don't," said the Walking Man. And he shot Razor Eddie in the head.

Or at least, he tried to. Razor Eddie's hand came up and round impossibly fast, his straight razor blazing like the sun, and cut the bullet out of mid air before it could reach him. The two separated halves fell to the ground, and the two small sounds seemed to echo on forever in the hushed quiet of the Street of the Gods. The Walking Man stood still, openly stunned, defied and defeated for the first time in his life since he'd left his simple humanity behind to become God's hit-man. Things like this weren't supposed to happen any more. And while he was standing there, trying to make sense of what was happening, Razor Eddie brought his straight razor round in a blindingly swift arc and cut the Walking Man's throat.

Or at least, he tried to. The supernaturally sharp blade, which had been known to cut through Time and Space, sliced across the Walking Man's throat but couldn't touch it. The blade just swept past, held back the merest fraction of an inch from the bare skin, by the power and the force operating within the Walking Man. The two men just stood there, shocked silent, looking first at each other, then down at the weapons that had betrayed them. And from the crowd that had gathered all round, there came the busy murmurs of many bets being made.

The Walking Man's hands were suddenly full of his guns. He blazed away with both pistols, firing over and over again, but somehow Razor Eddie was never there to be hit. He surged back and forth, dancing through the fusillade of bullets, here there and everywhere at once, like the grey god he was. The Walking Man swept his guns back and forth, raking the Street with bullets, and everyone watching fell to their knees or flattened themselves on the ground, as bullets flew overhead. I had to pull Chandra Singh down beside me. He was so caught up in the spectacle of two earthly gods going at it right in front of him that he forgot all about self-preservation.

Both guns kept firing long after they should have run out of bullets, but for all the deafening thunder of the gunfire, Razor Eddie was drawing closer, step by step. Now and again he cut another bullet out of mid air, just to prove the first time hadn't been a fluke, slicing clean through the flashing bullet with his shining blade. And finally, inevitably, he drew close enough to go head to head with the Walking Man. He cut and sliced and slashed, moving almost too fast to be followed by mortal eye; and still he couldn't touch the man touched by God.

And finally, inevitably, they duelled each other to a standstill. They stood facing each other, both breathless from their exertions, close enough to feel each other's panting breath on their faces, eyes staring into eyes. Neither of them beaten, neither willing to admit defeat. And then, quite unexpectedly, the Walking Man took a step back. He put his guns back in their holsters and showed Razor Eddie his empty hands. And as Eddie looked, and hesitated, the Walking Man snatched the straight razor out of Razor Eddie's hand. Eddie cried out, as though he'd lost a part of himself. The Walking Man threw the straight razor the length of the Street. It tumbled end over end through the air, the blade flashing brightly, until it vanished into the distance. And then the Walking Man clubbed Razor Eddie to the ground with his bare hands, beating him unmercifully again and again until Eddie crashed bloodily to the ground and stopped moving. The Walking Man stood over him, breathing harshly, blood dripping from his fists. And then he drew back his foot to kick the fallen god in the head.

"No!" said Chandra Singh. "Don't you dare!"

I was back on my feet again, and so was he. And if he hadn't spoken out, I would have. But when Chandra advanced steadily on the Walking Man, I stayed right where I was and let him do it. I was still observing the Walking Man, seeing what he could do, and making up my mind as to what I was going to have to do. So I let Chandra Singh take his shot, to see what would happen. I can be a real cold-blooded bastard when I have to.

Chandra stood protectively over the fallen Razor Eddie, and stuck his face right into the Walking Man's. Chandra was clearly steaming mad, but his face and his gaze had never looked so cold. The Walking Man met Chandra's gaze calmly and didn't budge an inch. One holy warrior facing off against another. This was what Chandra had wanted all along, whether he'd admitted it to himself or not. Why he insisted on sticking with me. To end up here, in this place and at this moment, for a chance to test his faith and his god and his standing, against the legendary Walking Man.

He stepped quite deliberately over the unconscious Razor Eddie, putting himself between the fallen god and further violence, openly defying the Walking Man to do anything about it. He didn't draw his sword, made no move to attack or defend; but stood there, confident in his faith and the righteousness of his cause.

"Go ahead," he said steadily to the Walking Man. "Shoot me. Kill a good man. Just because you can."

"A good man?" said the Walking Man, raising an eyebrow. "Is that what you are, Chandra Singh? After all those creatures you killed, merely for the sin of being...different?"

"You'll have to do better than that," said Chandra, entirely unmoved. "I have only ever acted to save lives. Can you say the same?"

"Yes," said the Walking Man.

"Too much faith can blind a man," said Chandra. "Especially to his own faults. I admit, I came here for selfish reasons. I wanted to test myself, my skills, my faith, against yours. To prove once and for all that I was your equal, if not more, in everything that mattered. But now that I have seen you at your bloody work, your murderous function...I see I have a duty here. You have to be stopped. You're out-of-control. What you are doing...is not God's work. He may have his wrath, but He tempers it with mercy and compassion."

"Mercy," said the Walking Man. "Compassion. Sorry, not my department."

"Then I must represent it," said Chandra. "Even with the

blood of so many unfortunate creatures on my hands. Because someone has to. John Taylor was right. There is still some hope left in the Nightside, and not everyone here deserves to die."

"If you stand against me," said the Walking Man, quite casually, "you stand against God's plan. God's will."

"This is your will," said Chandra. "Your need to punish the guilty and avenge your lost family. How many deaths will it take, Mr. Saint, how many murders, to put your soul at rest?"

"Only one way to find out," said the Walking Man.

They didn't just throw themselves at each other. They were both professionals, after all, with many years of experience in what they did, and they knew enough about each other to respect each other's skills. So the Walking Man didn't go for his guns, and Chandra Singh didn't draw his sword. Not just yet.

"I am the wrath of God," the Walking Man said finally.

"No," said Chandra. "You're only another monster."

He drew his sword with inhuman speed, and thrust the blade straight for the Walking Man's heart. It all happened in the space of a single breath, all of Chandra's strength and speed compressed into a single deadly strike, planned and launched while he was still speaking, to catch the Walking Man off-balance. But that was never going to happen. The Walking Man hardly seemed to move, but one hand came out of nowhere to grab the long, shining blade and stop it dead in its track. The two men stood face-to-face for a long moment, straining almost imperceptibly, Chandra to push the blade forward, the Walking Man to hold it where it was. Until finally the sword blade snapped, broken clean in half by the two immovable forces working upon it. Chandra staggered and almost fell. The Walking Man opened his hand, and the broken half of the blade fall to the ground. His hand wasn't even bleeding. Chandra breathed harshly, swaying as though he'd been hit, but he didn't drop his broken sword, and he still stood before Razor Eddie, protecting him. The Walking Man smiled on Chandra, almost kindly.

"Nice try. But you're only a khalsa, a holy warrior, whereas I am so much more. I made a deal with God Himself." He looked at me for the first time. "Always get it in writing, eh, John?"

"You'll have to kill me to get to Eddie," said Chandra.

"Kill you, Chandra?" said the Walking Man. "I'm not here to kill men like you. You're a good man. Unfortunately for you, and everyone else here, I've gone far beyond that." He looked at me again. "Are you going to try and stop me, John Taylor?"

"You really think you're ready to throw down with me?" I said. "I may not be holy, but I'm sneaky as hell. I move in really mysterious ways, and I guarantee you'll never see it coming."

I met his gaze easily, holding my breath . . . and he shrugged abruptly and turned away from Chandra and Eddie.

"I'm wasting my time here," he said. "I've allowed myself to become distracted. I came to this godforsaken place to kill your precious new upstart Authorities before they can organise the Nightside into a real threat to the outside world. I can always come back here, after I've killed them. So, stop me if you can, John."

He turned his back and strolled away. I let him go. I was thinking furiously. He hadn't realised I was bluffing. And that...was interesting. Chandra Singh knelt beside the unconscious Razor Eddie, hugging his broken sword to his chest. He was crying.

EIGHT

There Is Always a Price to Be Paid

The crowd was already dispersing. Money was reluctantly changing hands, as many bets were settled. I was frankly amazed that anyone had been ready to bet on Chandra Singh and me against the legendary Walking Man. But then, the Nightside has always had a weakness for the long odds. Chandra was still on his knees, still hugging what was left of his broken sword to his chest, still sobbing quietly. And I stood there and did some hard thinking.

I'd seen the Walking Man in action, seen how implacable and relentless he could be. I'd tried reasoning with him. I hadn't expected that to work, but I had to try. And I'd stood back and let Chandra have his run at it, just in case one man of faith could bring down another. Now it was up to me to take the detestable, necessary, and maybe even evil step that was all that was left.

When all else fails, you can always damn yourself with a necessary evil, for the greater good.

Meanwhile, all around us the shot-up, blasted, and downright-ruined churches and temples were already starting to rebuild themselves. Cracked stonework came together again, splintered marble smoothed itself over, and vast edifices rose unmarked from their own graves, given shape and substance again by the unrelenting faith of their congregations. Those faithful whose certainties had taken a severe kicking from seeing the Walking Man in action were already looking for Something new to follow, leaving their smashed-up churches to rot in the rubble. And people passing on the Street only paused to spit on the remains of the Temple of the Unspeakable Abomination. Some of the more up-and-coming Beings were already squaring off to see who would take over the more valuable positions on the Street. There'd be lightning strikes and plagues of boils and general massed smiting going on soon, and I planned to be somewhere else when it happened.

Razor Eddie sat up suddenly. His eyes snapped back into focus as his injured face repaired itself, then he shook himself sharply, like a dog emerging from a cold river. Chandra Singh, to his credit, immediately put aside his grief and his bruised pride and helped Eddie to his feet. Which made him a braver man than I. I wouldn't have touched Razor Eddie's filth-encrusted coat for all the gold in Walker's teeth. Razor

Eddie nodded brusquely to Chandra and raised his right hand. His straight razor was immediately there again, shining as brightly and as wickedly as ever. The Punk God and his straight razor were never separated for long. I don't think they can be any more. They belong to each other.

"Well," said Razor Eddie, in his grey and ghostly voice. "That was . . . unexpected. It's been a long time since anyone was able to put me down so thoroughly. It would appear the Walking Man actually is the real deal, after all. Which is kind of scary, if you think about it. So I don't think I will." He smiled slowly, showing rotten yellow teeth. "I suppose it is possible I've been getting a little cocky, of late. The occasional humbling can be good for the soul. Though you mustn't overdo it, of course."

I took advantage of Razor Eddie's unexpected chattiness to recover the broken half of Chandra's sword and offer it to him. The metal wasn't glowing any more. It looked like just another broken sword. Chandra nodded his thanks and accepted the blade as though I were handing him the body of his dead child. I felt like slapping him. It's always a mistake to get too attached to things. Chandra carefully slid both halves of the broken sword back into the scabbard at his side.

"It cannot be repaired or remade," he said, his voice surprisingly steady. "Or at least, not by any human hand. It was a most ancient weapon, entrusted to me to protect the innocent and punish the guilty, and I have brought about its destruction through my own stubborn pride."

"You had the right idea," I said, touched despite myself.

"But the wrong weapon." I turned to Razor Eddie. "To stop a man of God you need a weapon of God. One particular and very nasty weapon."

Eddie looked at me thoughtfully. "You want a weapon, John? I thought you were above such things."

"You know what weapon I'm talking about," I said.

He nodded slowly, reluctantly. "No good will come of this, John."

"I need the Speaking Gun," I said, and the Punk God of the Straight Razor shuddered briefly.

"Nasty thing," he said. "I thought you destroyed it."

"I did," I said. "But as with so many other awful things in the Nightside, it's only ever one step away from a comeback. Any idea where I might find it?"

"You know I know where it is," said Razor Eddie. "How is it you always know things like that?"

"Because it's my job," I said. "Now stop stalling."

"You'll find it at the Gun Shop," said Razor Eddie. "At the place where all weapons are worshipped."

"Is that where you got your straight razor?" said Chandra.

Razor Eddie looked down at the steel blade shining so brightly in his hand and smiled briefly. "Oh no," he said. "I went to a far worse place for this."

"Then the Gun Shop it is," I said, trying hard to sound like I knew what I was doing.

"Wait," said Chandra, moving forward to stare me in the eye. "You think you can stop the Walking Man, John Taylor? After I failed so miserably? After seeing him throw down all these false temples and churches? After he beat down the Punk

God of the Straight Razor and shot the Unspeakable Abomination in the head? After he broke my blessed sword, a thing not achieved in centuries of trials against evil? What makes a man like you believe he can defeat the Walking Man?"

"You have to have faith," I said. "And I believe I'm a bigger bastard than the Walking Man will ever be. I'll find a way to stop him. Because I have to."

Chandra nodded slowly. "Are you ready to die to protect your friends, John?"

"Not if I can help it," I said. "I was rather more planning on making him die. That's why I'm going to the Gun Shop."

"Want me to come with you?" said Razor Eddie. The straight razor flashed briefly, eagerly, in his hand.

"No," I said. "They see you coming, they'll probably lock the doors, slam home the bolts, and hide under the bed until you've gone away again. I would."

"They couldn't keep me out," said Razor Eddie.

"True," I said. "But I think I'm going to need them on my side, for this."

"Fair enough," said Razor Eddie. He looked about him. "I think I need to spend a little quality time here, walking up and down the Street of the Gods, carving up the minor Beings and doing terrible things to their gullible followers, just to prove I've still got it. Reputations have to be carefully maintained and nurtured, or people will start thinking they can take advantage. Besides, I'm in the mood for a little carnage and mayhem."

"Never knew you when you weren't," I said generously.

"I will go with you to the Gun Shop," said Chandra Singh.

He was standing straight and tall again, his eyes dry and his voice firm. "The game isn't over yet, and I am not beaten till I say I'm beaten."

Heroes and holy warriors. They always bounce back faster than you'd think.

So we nodded our good-byes to Razor Eddie and watched him stride off down the Street. People and Beings took one look at what was coming their way and suddenly remembered they were urgently needed somewhere else. I looked at Chandra.

"Are you all right? The Walking Man really did a number on you."

"I am fine," he said. "Or at least, I will be. I failed to understand what was really going on here, you see. I thought this was a conflict between the god I serve and that of the Walking Man, to see which was the greater. To determine which was the one true God, and therefore which of us was the true holy warrior. But instead . . . it was a conflict between two men. And in the end, it was my faith that proved to be lacking. I doubted I could beat him, and in that moment, I was lost."

"You really believe that?" I said.

"I have to believe that," said Chandra. He looked around him, taking in the ruins and the rubble, the dead and the dying. And the tourists, taking photos of it all. "No true God would approve of this . . . this indiscriminate slaughter. No, everything that happened here is down to the pride and needs of one stubborn man. And if there is one thing in this world you can be sure of, John Taylor, it is that the proud shall always be humbled."

"Yeah," I said. "And the Nightside does so love to break a good man."

I was looking right at him when I said that, but he still didn't get the point. "So," he said briskly, "where is this Gun Shop?"

"Right here on the Street of the Gods," I said. "It isn't just a Gun Shop, you see."

"Of course," said Chandra Singh. "I should have known."

"The Gun Shop . . . is the Church of the Gun," I said. "It exists because of all the people who worship weapons. Everything that is worshipped strongly enough and long enough has a place here. People do have an awful lot of faith in weapons, and the more people believe in them, the more power and influence they have in the world. You can find anything in the Gun Shop, anything that kills, from swords to nukes to energy weapons from future time-lines. The Speaking Gun will be there. Because even a terrible thing like that needs somewhere to go that feels like home."

We walked down the Street of the Gods, and people and other things hurried to get out of our way. Chandra Singh, because so many people had just seen him go head to head with the Walking Man and survive, and me . . . because I was John Taylor, and had done far worse things in my time. And might again. Meanwhile, I did my best to explain to Chandra exactly what the Speaking Gun was and what it could do. He needed to be prepared.

"The Speaking Gun is an old horror," I said. "And I mean really old. So ancient it was created before the days of History, from the time of Myth and Legend. A gun fashioned from flesh and bone, that breathes and sweats and hates everything that lives. Its power comes from God, indirectly."

"And that's why you think it will work against the Walking Man," said Chandra.

"Exactly. You see . . . in the beginning was the Word, and the universe burst into existence. Or so they say I wasn't there. But anyway, as a result, the echoes of that Word live on in everything that exists. In their true, secret, descriptive Name. The Speaking Gun can see that Name and say it backwards. Thus . . . Uncreating them. I destroyed the Speaking Gun by forcing it to speak its own true Name backwards, and making it Uncreate itself. Seemed to work well enough, at the time. But the bloody thing still exists in the Past, and in certain future time-lines. And so the Gun Shop will always be able to reach out to it because its very nature links it to every weapon that ever was, is, or will be."

Chandra Singh shook his head. "Words fail me."

"Well, quite," I said.

It didn't take us long to track down the Gun Shop. I didn't need to use my gift. Like so many places on the Street of the Gods, the Gun Shop lies in wait for those who need it. Never far, always ready to be of service, always ready to slap a gun in your hand and encourage you to use it. Death And Destruction "R" Us, but don't come back crying when it all goes horribly wrong.

It wasn't much to look at, when it finally hove into sight before us. More like a corner shop than a church, which I suppose was only to be expected. A simple wooden door next to a single glass window, showing off all the wonders to be found inside. I stopped, and looked. I couldn't help myself. Chandra stood beside me. And in the window of the Gun Shop, weapons showed themselves off like whores. Swords and axes, guns and rifles, energy weapons and shifting shapes that made no sense at all. All of them utterly glamorous and sweetly tempting.

Come inside, find something you like. You know you want to.

I pulled my gaze away from the display and looked at Chandra. "Those aren't just weapons," I said. "They're icons, archetypes, avatars of their kind. The Onlie True Originals, of which everything else are but pale reflections."

"Yes," said Chandra, turning his head abruptly to look at me. "Not just guns, but the Spirits of Guns. Every gun, every sword, maybe every bomb, too. You don't come here looking for something to protect the innocent or punish the guilty. These are simply instruments of death. Means to murder."

"Got it in one," I said. "Once we get in there, watch yourself. Murder is a sacrament in the Gun Shop, and temptation comes as standard."

I headed for the door, and it opened silently before me, without my even having to touch it. The Gun Shop was expecting me. I strode in as though I'd come to condemn the place on Moral Health grounds, and Chandra was right there with me, giving the place his best snotty and entirely unimpressed look. Sharp fluorescent lighting blazed up, revealing a huge emporium containing every killing tool known to man, and a few that wandered in from adjoining dimensions. Like so many churches in the Street of the Gods, the Gun Shop's interior was much bigger than its exterior. It's the only way they can fit everything in. The Shop fell away before us, retreating endlessly into the uncomfortably bright light, with lines and lines of simple wooden shelves, stretching away into the distance for further than the merely mortal eye could follow. I never knew there were so many types of weapon.

And then I blinked, and almost fell back a step, as the Gun Shop's owner, or manager, or high priest was suddenly right there before me. A respectable-looking middle-aged man in a respectable suit, with a broad square face, retreating hair, and rimless eyeglasses, he looked more like an undertaker than anything else. Which was only appropriate, I suppose. He had that quiet, remorseless calm that comes from dealing with death on a regular basis, and his warm, professional smile didn't touch his calm dead eyes at all. He nodded briskly to me, then to Chandra. My skin crawled. It was like being noticed by some poisonous snake or spider that might strike at any moment. He was an icon of suffering and slaughter; cold-eyed, cold-hearted, always ready to cut a deal, everything for sale but nothing on credit. And why not? You didn't come to the Gun Shop for a gun. You came to get yourself an unfair advantage, a weapon so powerful no-one could stand against it.

"Good to see you at last, Mr. Taylor," said the storekeeper, in a voice like every salesman you've ever heard. The ones who don't have to try too hard, because everyone wants what they've got. "Always knew you'd drop in, eventually. Everyone

JUST ANOTHER JUDGEMENT DAY

does, eventually. And Mr. Chandra Singh, renowned monster hunter. How nice. You may call me Mr. Usher, if you wish. What can I do for you?"

"Are you a god?" said Chandra, honestly curious.

"Bless you, no, sir," said Mr. Usher. "Nothing so limited. Gods may come and beings may go, but the Gun Shop goes on forever. I am the human face of this establishment. An extension of the Gun Shop, if you will. Because people find it easier to discuss business with something that looks like people. I am the Gun Shop."

"So...you're not really real, then?" Chandra persisted.

"I'm as real as the Shop is, sir. And the Gun Shop is very real and very old. Many names, but one nature. Ah, sir, the old jokes are still the best. I always find a little humour helps the medicine go down more easily, as it were. I see you have a broken weapon about your person, sir. A most excellent and powerful sword, sadly now in two pieces, its very nature abused and shattered. Such a shame. Would you like me to repair it for you, sir?"

"No he wouldn't," I said quickly. "Tell him, Chandra. He could do it, but the sword would never be the same afterwards. And you really wouldn't want to pay the price he'd ask."

"I am quite capable of making my own decisions," Chandra said stiffly. "The sword was entrusted to me, and I allowed it to be broken. I have a duty to see it repaired. If it can be repaired."

"Oh it can, sir, it really can," said Mr. Usher. "I know all there is to know about swords."

"Including restoring its true nature?" I said.

"Ah," said Mr. Usher, reluctantly. "Well, no. You have me there, sir. I deal strictly with the material, not the spiritual."

"Then I cannot let you touch this sword," said Chandra. "I will take it home, to be remade again."

"As you wish, sir." Mr. Usher turned his attention away from Chandra to concentrate on me. "Mr. Taylor, what brings you at long last to the Gun Shop?"

"You know why I'm here," I said, keeping my voice cold and unmoved. "It's your business to know things like that. I'm here for the Speaking Gun."

"Oh yes, sir," said Mr. Usher, reverently. "Of course. A most remarkable weapon. Older than the Nightside, they say. Certainly older than I am. A gun that is so feared and worshipped it's practically a god in itself."

"I destroyed it, not long ago," I said.

"Why bless you, sir, I don't think so. Oh, you may have put an end to its story in the here and now, but it still persists, in other times and places. It will always exist somewhere, in the Past or some Future time-line."

"How can that be?" said Chandra, frowning.

"Because it's fished for," I said. "It's always being looked for, stalked, and possessed by various talented individuals with more ambition than sense. Like the Collector. You have heard of the Collector, Chandra?"

"I am not a rube," said Chandra, with some dignity.

"Can you locate the Speaking Gun, either in the Past or some accessible Future time-line?" I asked Mr. Usher, and he gave me a polite but pitying smile.

"Of course, sir. Wherever or whenever the Speaking Gun may be, it is still always on a shelf here somewhere. I am in constant contact with every weapon ever made or believed in. I have them all here, from Excalibur to the Despicable Word. Though, of course, you'd have to be particularly gifted, or cursed, to be able to use either of those two items. I can provide anyone with anything, but getting it to work is up to the client." He smiled his mirthless smile. "Ah, many the customer I've known, with eyes bigger than his stomach, if you follow me, sir."

"I want the Speaking Gun," I said. "I can make it work."

"Of course you can, sir."

He turned and started unhurriedly down his endless hall of weapons, leaving us to follow after. I stuck close behind him. It would be only too easy to get lost in a place like this. Chandra stared about him, almost hypnotised by the endless shelves of endless weapons. I could hear them calling out to me. Singing swords of legend, rings of power, future guns with AI interfaces, pieces of armour still haunted by their previous owners. All of them asking, pleading, demanding to be taken up and used.

"You see," said Mr. Usher, "I have it all. Everything from the first club, fashioned from a thigh-bone by some forgotten man-ape, right up to the Darkvoid Device, which wiped out a thousand star systems in a moment. I can provide you with anything your heart desires. All you have to do is ask."

"And pay the price," I said.

"Well, of course, Mr. Taylor. There is always a price to be paid."

I was beginning to have second thoughts. I had no doubt that if anything could stop the Walking Man in his tracks, it would be the Speaking Gun, but...I still remembered how the Gun had made me feel, still remembered what using it even briefly had done to me. Just to touch it was to dirty your soul, to burden yourself with almost unbearable temptation. And even more than that, I remembered seeing the Speaking Gun grafted on to the maimed arm of a future incarnation of Suzie Shooter, by my future Enemies. Sent back in time to kill me, to prevent the awful future world they lived in. The same people I was trying to save, now. Sometimes I swear the Nightside runs on irony.

I had thought that by destroying the Speaking Gun, I'd saved my Suzie from that horrid destiny. Would bringing it back into the Present make that particular Future possible again?

"What is the price?" I said abruptly to Mr. Usher. "What do you want for the Speaking Gun?"

"Oh, no price for you, Mr. Taylor," he said, not even looking round. "No price, as such, for a renowned and important gentleman such as yourself. No, just...a favour. Kill the Walking Man. He really is terribly bad for business, with his limited and inflexible morality. Even though both his wonderful guns came from here, if he only knew..."

I decided not to pursue that. I didn't think I really wanted to know. But still...kill the Walking Man? He had to be stopped, and stopped hard, but who was I to remove such a vital agent of the Good from this world? He did kill people who needed killing. Mostly. He was wrong about the new Authorities, but I still thought I could talk him out of that if I could just make him stop long enough to listen. And even the Walking Man would stop and pay attention with the Speaking Gun aimed right at him. Anyone would. But if he wouldn't, couldn't, listen . . . Then I would kill him if I had to. His view of the world, of the Nightside, of people . . . was too limited. I had to think of the greater good.

And no, the irony of that wasn't lost on me.

Mr. Usher came to a sudden halt and stepped aside, indicating a particular spot on a particular shelf with a theatrical wave of the hand. I recognised the small black case immediately. I looked at it for a long moment as my breathing speeded up and small beads of sweat popped out on my brow. My hands had clenched into fists. I knew how the box would feel if I picked it up—eerily light and strangely delicate, though nothing in this world could break or damage it. The case was about a foot long, maybe eight inches wide, its surface a strangely dull matte black, a darkness so complete that light seemed to fall into it.

Seeing that I had made no move to touch it, Mr. Usher took the case off the shelf and offered it to me. Holding it didn't seem to affect him at all. I still didn't want to touch it. I leaned forward and pretended to examine the only marking on the lid of the case, a large letter C with a stylised crown inside it. The mark of the Collector, the only man ever to own the Speaking Gun and not use it. Because for him, ownership was everything.

"Open it," I said, and Mr. Usher smiled broadly.

He lifted the lid of the black case, and there it was, nestling in its bed of black velvet. The smell hit me first, of mad dogs in heat and the sweat of horses being dragged screaming to the abattoir. The stench of spilled blood and guts. The Speaking Gun looked just as I remembered. It was made of meat, of flesh and skin and bone, of dark-veined gristle and shards of cartilage, all held together with long strips of pale skin. Slabs of bone made up the handle, surrounded by freckled skin, that had a hot and sweaty look. The trigger was a canine tooth, and the red meat of the barrel glistened wetly. It was a thing, the ultimate killing tool, and it was alive.

Chandra Singh leaned in close beside me for a better look, and I could sense his revulsion.

"Is that really it?" he said finally, his voice hushed and strangely respectful.

"Yes," I said. "The gun created specifically to kill angels, from Above and Below."

"Who would want such a thing?" said Chandra. "Who ordered it made?"

"I don't think anyone really knows," I said. I looked at Mr. Usher, but he had nothing to say. I looked back at the Gun, in its case. "I've heard Merlin Satanspawn's name mentioned, but he gets the blame for most bad things, on general principles. Then there's the Engineer, or the Howling Thing...There is a name marked on the Gun somewhere—of its original manufacturers, Abraxus Artificers."

"Ah yes," said Mr. Usher. "The old firm. The sons of Cain,

solving problems since the Beginning. They're responsible for many of the more impressive items on my shelves."

"You know them?" I said.

"Not . . . as such, sir. I know my place."

The Speaking Gun stirred in its black velvet. I could feel its rage and hate. It remembered me, and how I fought to use it rather than have it use me. I hoped it didn't know that someday in its future, I would be the one to finally put an end to it.

"Close the lid," I said, and Mr. Usher did so with an elegant flourish. I made myself take hold of the case and slipped it quickly into a pocket inside my coat, next to my heart. I could still hear it breathing. I looked at Chandra.

"Time to go," I said.

"Quite definitely," he said, sounding distinctly relieved. "This is no place for a holy man."

"You're not the first," said Mr. Usher equitably. "And you won't be the last." He looked at me. "See you again, sir?"

"Maybe," I said. "Suzie would love this place. Perhaps I'll bring her here for her Christmas treat."

We'd only just left the Gun Shop when my cell phone rang. It still plays the theme from the *Twilight Zone*. When I find a joke I like, I tend to stick with it. Walker's voice sounded urgently in my ear.

"The Walking Man is on his way to the Adventurers Club. He's coming for the new Authorities, and even my best people are barely slowing him down. Tell me you have something that will put him in his place."

"I have something," I said. "But I don't think you're going to like it."

"How very typical of you, John," said Walker.

He opened up a doorway with his Portable Timeslip and brought Chandra and me right to the Adventurers Club.

NINE

Last Man Standing

At the Adventurers Club, they'd done everything but drain the moat and pull up the drawbridge. Chandra and I arrived in a lobby packed full of heroes, adventurers, border-line rogues, and even a few quite definite villains. Someone had put out the call, and everyone had come running. Either to defend the Club, or the new Authorities, or because they just couldn't resist testing themselves against the legendary Walking Man. It was the last stand of the Adventurers Club, and no-one wanted to miss it.

I'd never seen the place so full. They'd already pretty much drained the bar dry, and the barman had been reduced to pulling dubiously dusty bottles off the back of shelves he'd forgotten were even there. There were figures out of Myth and

Legend that I'd never thought to see in the flesh, and some faces I knew for a fact had even less business being in the Adventurers Club than I did. Augusta Moon and Janissary Jane were there, of course, the spinster-aunt monster hunter and the veteran demon killer, right at the front of the crowd and spoiling for a fight. I saw Mistress Mayhem and Jacqueline Hyde, Bishop Beastly and Sister Igor, Dead Boy and the Mad Monk. Colourful figures all, in every sense of the word. Common cause can bring about the strangest of allies, especially in the Nightside.

And yet for all the size of the crowd, containing some of the most powerful people in the Nightside, it was still surprisingly quiet in the lobby. The atmosphere was tense but focussed, waiting for the true star to arrive. There was none of the usual boasting, or showing off of powers, no rousing speeches or pep talks. Everyone knew about the Walking Man—who he was, and what he represented, and what he could do. Beyond the usual cold professional preparedness, I could tell they were all, quietly and very secretly, scared out of their minds. Just like me.

But still, credit where credit was due, here they all were...the good and the bad and the rogues, ready to stand shoulder to shoulder and lay it all on the line, to defend the new Authorities. Impressed as I was, I had to wonder why.

"Why are all these people prepared to risk their lives and reputations for the sake of the new Authorities?" Chandra asked Walker, beating me to it. "I have been a member in good standing of this Club for many years, and I don't think I've ever heard anyone here say one good word about the

Nightside, or the Authorities. We only come here to challenge our courage and our skills against it."

"They believe in the new Authorities," Walker said calmly. "Julien Advent has been doing the rounds, talking to people; and you know how persuasive he can be. Especially when you know he's right. He is the greatest adventurer of all time, after all, and people respect that. And it does help that people want to believe what he's saying. That the Nightside, and everyone in it, can be redeemed, with the new Authorities leading the way."

I looked at him curiously. "Do you believe that?"

"I believe in duty and responsibility," said Walker. "I leave hope and faith to people like Julien Advent."

"You didn't answer the question," I said.

"No," said Walker. "I didn't."

He led us through the crush of the crowd, through the lobby and the bar, to the stairs at the back of the room, and people fell back and gave way for him, where they wouldn't have budged an inch for me, or even Chandra Singh. No-one messes with Walker. Familiar faces bowed briefly to him, nodded and smiled to Chandra, and gave me long, thoughtful looks.

"So, John, what did you find to set against the unstoppable Walking Man?" said Walker, as we made our way up the stairs to the back room where the new Authorities were waiting. "Something truly dangerous and appallingly destructive, I trust?"

"Yes," I said. "I think that's a fair description."

"Then why are you so sure I'm not going to approve of it?"

"Because it's the Speaking Gun."

Walker stopped dead on the stairs, then turned and looked back at me. I'd never seen his face so cold, or his gaze so utterly bleak.

"Oh John," he said. "What have you done?"

"What I had to," I said. "Revived an old terror to stop a new one."

"I was under the impression you had destroyed the vile thing."

"I did," I said. "But some things just won't stay gone. You should know that."

"I was there when a Shotgun Suzie appeared out of a possible future, with the Speaking Gun grated on to her mutilated arm," said Walker.

"I know," I said. "I was there, too."

"Are you really prepared to put Suzie at such awful risk to preserve the new Authorities?"

"Yes," I said. "Because you're not the only one who understands about duty and responsibility."

"And Suzie?" said Walker.

"She'd want me to take the risk," I said.

"Yes," said Walker. "She would, wouldn't she?"

Upstairs, in the barely furnished back room, the new Authorities were preparing themselves for war. Julien Advent, the great Victorian Adventurer, sat at his ease in a chair tilted back against the far wall, polishing the slender steel blade that usually lay concealed in his sword-stick. His handsome, almost saturnine, features were completely without fear or concern. Julien had never cared whether he lived or died, as long as he was fighting on the side of the right. He had a certainty in his cause to match that of the Walking Man.

Jessica Sorrow, that gaunt and still scary presence who used to be the Unbeliever, was striding up and down in her flapping black leather jacket, scowling at anything and everything. She'd only recently found faith in the everyday world and the people around her, and she was clearly furious at the prospect of having it all taken away from her again. Everyone else was keeping a cautious eye on her, and giving her plenty of room, just in case things started disappearing around her.

Annie Abattoir, in a fabulous off-the-shoulder emerald green evening gown, was mixing something potent and noxious with an old-fashioned pestle and mortar, then using the resultant heaving mixture to daub disturbing symbols on to an Aboriginal pointing bone that looked big and mean enough to take out a blue whale. Her face was fixed and intent, but not altogether concerned. Annie had killed many men in her career, and to her the Walking Man was only another man.

Shifting plasma lights sparked and sputtered on the air around Count Video, as he hovered in mid air in the middle of the room, concentrating on his weird binary magics. I always knew he could be a Major Player, if he could just grow a pair. I suppose there's nothing like imminent death and the destruction of everything you believe in and care about to bring out the true nature of a man.

King of Skin was crouching in one corner of the room,

surrounded by dark and nasty images that could only be glimpsed out of the corner of the eye. I still couldn't believe he was on the side of the Good, if only because the Good usually wouldn't have him on a bet. But still, here he was, preparing to stand and fight with the others, when I would have bet good money he'd have been legging it for the horizon by now.

Larry Oblivion sat alone, not looking at anyone, frowning heavily, caught up in whatever dead men think about. Of us all, he had the least to lose.

The new Authorities, who had been and might yet be again my future Enemies. I could walk away and let them die. Except then, I would be the kind of man the Enemies always said I was. And I hate to be predictable.

They all looked up with some kind of hope as I walked in, ignoring Walker and Chandra. I smiled and nodded to all concerned, doing my best to look relaxed and confident. Julien Advent got up from his chair, slipped his blade back into the stick, and strode forward to shake my hand in his usual hale and hearty way.

"I knew we could rely on you, John. What have you found that will stop the Walking Man?"

"He's found something," said Walker. "But you're really not going to like it."

"Oh bloody hell," said Larry Oblivion. "He hasn't got Merlin up and walking around again, has he?"

"Worse than that," I said, savouring the moment despite myself. "I bring the Speaking Gun, and all that goes with it."

It went very quiet in the room. They all knew of the Speaking Gun, what it was and what it could do. I watched them considering the possibilities of whether it might actually be the one thing that would slap down the Walking Man, against whether just using it would go against everything they were trying to achieve. And damn all their souls in the process.

"Maybe we should have asked Chandra Singh to find something," said Annie Abattoir.

"No," Chandra said simply. "I have tested myself against this Walking Man and failed. John Taylor is your only hope."

"Then we are in deep trouble," said Count Video.

"You have got to be kidding!" said Larry Oblivion, striding forward on his silent feet so he could glare right into my face with his dead blue eyes. "We can't risk using the Speaking Gun! It's . . . evil! More dangerous than the Walking Man himself!"

"Yes," said King of Skin, giggling suddenly. "It is. And that's why it will work."

"Oh, it'll work all right!" said Count Video, shifting uneasily from foot to foot. "It'll kill him, then kill everyone else! That's what it does!"

"I remember the Speaking Gun," said Jessica Sorrow, and everyone stopped to listen. She knew more about the unseen world than we ever would. "I can hear it, drawing closer. It moans and sings and hates. It is a hunger that can never be satisfied, a rage that can never be eased. Because that is how it was made. It has murdered angels and delighted in the destruction of God's work."

"But can it stop the Walking Man?" said Annie Abattoir, and we all waited to hear what Jessica would say.

"The Walking Man is both more and less than an angel," she said finally. "He was designed to perform a function, just like the Speaking Gun. Who can say what will happen when the divine and the infernal come face-to-face?"

"Well, that was about as helpful as we had any right to expect," said Count Video.

"No-one's ever killed a Walking Man," said King of Skin. "But they can be broken. It seems to me that a gun constructed to kill God's messengers should be just what we need to do the job." He sniggered suddenly, his sleazy glamour beating on the air like musty wings. "I can't wait to see . . ."

"You disgust me," said Larry Oblivion.

King of Skin smiled. "It's what I do best."

"Going head to head with the Walking Man is our last resort," Julien Advent said firmly. "I don't want any killing unless it's absolutely necessary. There's still a chance we can reason with the man, make him understand that we're not what he thinks we are. Make him understand what it is we're trying to achieve."

"I think he already knows," I said. "And I don't think he gives a damn."

"We can't allow ourselves to be destroyed," said Larry. "We are the last hope of the Nightside."

"Whether we want to be or not," said Count Video.

"I knew your father," said Julien. "This is what he wanted for you. He would be so proud of what you're doing."

"You always did know how to fight dirty, Julien," said Count Video. But he smiled a little as he said it.

"I just want to see a Walking Man go down," said Annie. "To do what no-one else has ever done."

"It doesn't have to come to that," Julien insisted. "I refuse to believe that God would allow His servant to wage war against the Good once its nature had been made clear to the Walking Man."

"I've met the man," I said. "And I think the God he serves is strictly Old Testament. Eye for an eye, tooth for a tooth, and to hell with repentance. Mercy and compassion, and just possibly reason, too, are not in him any more. He gave all that up long ago, for a chance to punish the guilty."

"We have to make a stand," said Julien. "We're all of us powerful people, in our own way. Perhaps together we can do what no-one else has . . ."

"Right," said Larry. "And hey, I'm dead. What else can he do to me, after all?"

"You really don't want to know," said Annie.

"We have to make a stand," Julien said doggedly. "To prove we are worthy to be the new Authorities."

"And all those adventurers and rogues gathered down below?" I said. "Are you ready to let them fight and die, sacrificing themselves to defend you?"

"No-one asked them to do this," said Julien. "They are volunteers, every last one of them. It's about faith, John."

"Right," said Larry. "They wanted to do this. You couldn't drive them out of here with sticks."

"Of course," said Chandra. "We are adventurers. Heroes and warriors and defenders of the Light. It is what we are here for."

"At least half the people I saw down there wouldn't fit that description if you used a tire iron to squeeze them in," I said. "In fact, some of them are exactly the kind of people you and your kind formed this Club to fight."

Chandra smiled. "What is it you people say—needs must when the Devil drives?"

"You've grown cynical," I said. "It doesn't suit you."

"That's what comes of hanging around with you," said Chandra, and we both smiled.

"I still have hope that seeing so many men and women of good faith come together will shock the Walking Man back to sanity," said Julien.

"Yeah, well," I said. "Good luck with that."

"He's here," said Jessica Sorrow, and we all stopped and looked at her. Her gaunt face was blank, her eyes empty and far away. "He is at the door. And the rage that burns within him is cold . . . so very cold."

"Stay here!" I snapped at Julien. "Let us test the waters first, see if he can be talked down. Or stopped. Having you people there would only concentrate him on his mission."

"Give it your best shot, John," said Julien Advent. "But preferably not with the Speaking Gun."

"We're relying on John Taylor to reason with the Walking Man," said Larry Oblivion. "We're doomed."

Walker and Chandra and I scrambled back down the stairs at speed and charged through the bar into the lobby. All the heroes and the rogues and the morally undecided were standing together, tense and silent, their eyes fixed on the closed front door of the Club. Walker gestured for Chandra and me to stay with him at the back of the crowd and observe how things went before we committed ourselves, and I was happy to go along with that. I really didn't want to do what I was there to do. The tension in the air was almost unbearable, like waiting for the bullet to come your way, knowing your name is on it. The front door shook suddenly in its frame, as some massive force slammed against it. Like God himself knocking on the door and demanding entry. There was another great impact, and the huge door flew inwards, blasted right off its hinges. It slammed flat against the floor, and in came Adrien Saint, the Walking Man.

Just a man in a long coat, with worn-down heels on his shoes from walking up and down in the world, doing good the hard way. He hadn't even drawn his guns. But still he was the most dangerous, the most frightening man in the Club, and we all knew it. He walked in Heaven's way, and Death walked with him. He was as inevitable as an earthquake or a flood, as implacable as cancer or heart failure. He was smiling his insolent smile, his gaze openly mocking as he contemplated the rows of adventurers gathered against him. He had come here to do a thing, and he was going to do it, no matter what we might set against him.

He walked forward, and all the Club's built-in security defences went to work. Force shields sprang into being before him, fierce energy screens generated by salvaged alien machines down in the Club basement. The Walking Man strode through the force shields, and they popped like soap bubbles. Protective magics and potent sorceries snapped and crackled on the air, bending the very laws of reality to get at him, and none of them could touch him. Even the mechanical booby-traps failed to slow him down. Trap-doors opened beneath him, and he just kept walking. Spikes protruded from the wall, only to break in half against his long duster as though it was armour. Man-traps snapped together around his ankles, and he kicked them away.

The Walking Man headed straight for the packed crowd of waiting adventurers, who tensed, ready for action; and then he stopped before them and smiled easily. He looked back and forth, nodding briefly to familiar faces, and all the time his smile said *I can do any damned thing I want, and none of you can stop me.*

"Stand aside," he said finally, and his voice was quite cheerful and relaxed, as though he couldn't imagine not being obeyed. Augusta Moon sniffed loudly and stepped out of the crowd to ostentatiously block his way. She scowled fiercely at him, her monocle screwed firmly into one eye, and brandished her staff of blessed wood tipped with silver.

"And if we don't? Eh? What will you do then?"

"Then, I will kill as many of you as I have to, to get past you," said the Walking Man, his voice as calm as though he was discussing the weather. "I walk in straight lines, to get to where I have to be, to do what I have to do. To carry out God's will in this sinful world."

"This isn't His will," I said, from the safety of the back of the crowd. "This is your will."

"Ah, hello, John," he said happily, and actually waved at

me. "I was wondering what had happened to you. But you're quite wrong, you know. When I take my aspect upon me, His will and my will are one and the same. To protect the innocent, by punishing the guilty."

"You'd really kill us?" said Janissary Jane, her voice cold and measured. "All these good people?"

"If they're standing against me," said the Walking Man, his voice the very epitome of reason and patience, "then they're standing against God's will. Which means, by definition, they're no longer good people. It's really up to all of you what happens next. I'm not here for you. I want the Authorities."

"Well you can't have them!" snapped Augusta. "Never heard such arrogance in all my life! Now get out of here or I'll stick this staff in one end and out the other!"

The Walking Man sighed. "There's always one..."

Augusta Moon roared with rage and lashed out at him with her staff, her tweeds flying bravely as she launched herself at him. But the staff that had struck down so many monsters in its time slammed to a halt a few inches short of the Walking Man's head, then snapped in two as it finally met an immovable force. Augusta cried out in shock and pain as the unexpected impact tore her half of the staff right out of her hands, and she watched in horror as the two pieces fell to the floor. The Walking Man looked at her sadly, then struck her down with a single blow. And since Augusta was really just a middle-aged woman, she hit the floor hard and lay there groaning.

Janissary Jane drew two automatic pistols out of nowhere

and opened fire on the Walking Man. Veteran of a hundred demon wars, her guns were always loaded with blessed and cursed ammunition, but still none of them could find their target. Janissary Jane might be prepared, but the Walking Man was protected. She fired and fired, until both guns were empty, and the Walking Man stood there and let her do it. In the end, Jane looked down at her empty guns, put them away, and knelt to comfort Augusta.

Next up was Zhang the Mystic, Asian master of the unknown arts. A hero and a sorcerer since the nineteen thirties, Zhang wore a sweeping gown of gold, his long fingernails were pure silver, and his eyes burned with eldritch fires. He'd duelled demons from the Inferno, and faced down Elder Gods in his day, and founded most of the combat sorcery schools in the Nightside, and no-one knew more magic than he did. But all his spells and sorceries detonated harmlessly, savage destructive energies reduced to nothing more than fireworks. The Walking Man waited patiently until Zhang had exhausted himself, and then did Zhang the final insult of ignoring him.

Walker made his way forward through the crowd, and everyone fell back to let him pass, and see what he could do. Chandra and I stuck close behind him. The Walking Man's smile widened as he recognised Walker, becoming insolent and taunting almost beyond bearing. Walker stopped right before him and studied him sadly, like a teacher disappointed by a promising pupil.

"Hello, Henry," said the Walking Man. "It's been a while, hasn't it?"

"Hold everything," I said. "You two know each other?"

"Oh, he knows everyone, don't you, Henry?" said the Walking Man. "Especially when they can be useful to him, to do those dirty and dangerous jobs that no-one else wants to know about. Henry doesn't just deal with problems in the Nightside, you know. Especially after he lost his famous Voice and had to go out into the world to find a replacement."

"That's all right, Adrien," said Walker, entirely unmoved. "I got it back. *Now stand down, Adrien, and surrender yourself to me.*"

And there it was, Walker's Voice that could not be denied, hammering on the air like the Voice of God. This close, even I could feel the power of it, like the thunderstorm that breaks right over your head. I looked at the Walking Man, to see how he was taking it.

He laughed at Walker. "I know that Voice," he said cheerfully. "I hear it every day. Only rather more clearly than that. I have to say, Henry, I'm very disappointed in you. That you of all people should be prepared to defend these upstart new Authorities. A mixture of old heroes and worse villains, and even two authentic monsters? What were you thinking?"

"I know my duty," said Walker.

"So do I," said the Walking Man. And he struck Walker down. The punch came out of nowhere, and Walker crashed to the floor and lay still. I was actually shocked. No-one touches Walker. And on the few occasions they had, he'd always bounced right back. But instead he lay there on the floor, barely moving, blood flowing from his mouth and nose. The Walking Man regarded the fallen man thoughtfully, then drew one of his guns. I reached inside my coat.

"Leave that man alone!"

The voice crackled on the air with natural authority, and we all, including the Walking Man, turned to look as Julien Advent led his new Authorities through the crowd. Julien looked very fine and every inch the hero, in his traditional Victorian clothes, including a sweeping black opera-cloak. The others gathered defensively around him, each with their own deadly glamour and gravitas. Even in such august company, surrounded by heroes and adventurers on all sides, there was still something noble and impressive about the new Authorities. Good and bad, determined to be better, not just for their own sakes but for all the Nightside. I moved in on one side of Julien, and Chandra took the other.

"We are the new Authorities," Julien said flatly to the Walking Man. "We are the hope of the Nightside. For the first time in its long existence, the Nightside is being run by its own kind. The good, the bad and the unnatural, working together for the greater good. For a better future. We will remake the Nightside..."

"Don't be naïve," said the Walking Man, cutting right across him. "This place corrupts everyone. Look at you, the great Victorian Adventurer, reduced to running a cheap news rag. Look at who you associate with—the infamous John Taylor, who could have been so much more but settled for being just another sleazy enquiry agent. And Chandra Singh, standing up for the kind of monster he used to hunt. I had such hopes for you two... I thought, if I showed you... but you wouldn't listen. The Nightside grinds everyone down, dragging them down to its own level, just because it can. There is no hope here, no future. Only filth and evil and corruption of the body and the soul. I will kill you, all of you presumptive Authorities, and that will send a message that cannot be ignored. Leave the Nightside, or die."

"We can redeem the Nightside!" said Julien Advent.

"I don't care," said the Walking Man.

And then everything stopped, as I drew the flat black case from inside my coat and took out the Speaking Gun. People cried out all around me, shrinking back from the sudden dark presence in the room. It felt like standing over the corpse of your best friend or looking down at the hilt of the knife protruding from your guts. The Speaking Gun was death and horror and the end of all things, and just to be near it was to feel your heart stutter and taste bad blood in your mouth.

Julien Advent turned his head away, unable to look at it. The Walking Man curled his lip in disgust.

The Speaking Gun was right there in my head with me. A vicious, spiteful presence, almost overpowering in its ancient and awful power. It crashed against my mental shields, trying to force its way in and take control. Wanting, needing, demanding to be used, because for all its power, it couldn't fire itself. It lived to kill, but it needed me for that, and so its voice howled in my head, telling me to pull the trigger and kill someone. Anyone. It didn't care who. It never had. It just ached to say the words that would uncreate. The red raw meat of the Gun was heavy in my hand, a weight on my soul, dragging me down. But slowly, steadily, I set my will against it. And won. Because bad as it was, I had faced far worse in my time.

Somehow I kept the struggle out of my face, and when I finally pointed the Speaking Gun at the Walking Man, my hand was entirely steady. He looked at the Gun, then at me, and for the first time I heard uncertainty in his voice.

"Well," he said, trying for a light touch and not quite bringing it off. "Look at that. The Speaking Gun; almost as infamous as you, John. I should have known it would show up here. It belongs in a place like this. I thought I destroyed it in Istanbul, five years ago, when the Silent Brotherhood were fighting their endless feud against the Drood Family . . . but it always comes back. Would you really use such a vile thing, John? Would you use such an evil thing, to stop a good man in his work? To use that Gun, in that way, would damn your soul forever."

"Yes," I said. "It would."

And I slowly lowered the Speaking Gun, even as it hissed and squirmed in my hand. Because that was the real price the Gun Shop owner had wanted me to pay—for me to damn my own soul. And I wouldn't do that, not even to save my friends. If only because I knew they would never have wanted me to do that.

"What are you doing?" Chandra Singh asked. "After all we went through to get that thing, now you're not going to use it?"

"No," I said.

"Then give it to me. I am not afraid to use it!"

"Chandra . . ."

"I have to do something! *He broke my sword!*"

And he grabbed the Speaking Gun and wrestled it from

my hand. He aimed it at the Walking Man, but already his hand was shaking, and his eyes were very wide as he heard the Gun's awful voice in his head, the terrible temptation—to use the Gun and keep on using it, for the sheer joy of slaughter. Julien reached out to Chandra, seeing the horror in his face, but I stopped him with a sharp gesture. This was Chandra's fight, he had to do it for himself. For the sake of his own soul. Or he'd always wonder what he would have done.

I had faith in him.

And slowly, inch by inch, he lowered the Speaking Gun, fighting it all the way, refusing to be tempted or mastered. Because he was, at heart, a good man.

The Walking Man waited until the Speaking Gun was pointing at the floor, then he reached out and gently eased the Gun out of Chandra's hand. The Indian monster hunter swayed, and almost fell, but Julien and I were there to support him. He was clearly shaken, and there was cold sweat on his grey face. The Walking Man hefted the Speaking Gun in his hand, turning it back and forth as though he'd never seen anything so ugly before. If he heard anything in his head, he hid it well. And having examined the thing thoroughly, and found not a trace of good in it, he crushed the Speaking Gun in his hand.

The bone and cartilage cracked and shattered, the red meat pulped, and the Speaking Gun cried out in agony in all our heads as it died. The Walking Man slowly opened his hand, and the already decaying pieces of the Speaking Gun fell from his hand to spatter on the floor. The Walking Man lifted his foot to crush what remained; but it had already disappeared, every last bit of it. Gone, back to the Gun Shop perhaps, or to wherever else in the world it could do the most harm.

I didn't need to check inside my coat to know the black case was gone, too.

"Well," said the Walking Man. "That's that. Now, back to work."

"No," I said, and stepped forward to put myself directly before him, placing my body between him and the new Authorities. I was thinking hard on what the rogue vicar had said—*To stop a broken man, heal the man.* Julien had been right, too. There had to be a way to reach Adrien Saint. Even after everything he'd done, he was still a man. I had to try reason because I'd run right out of weapons.

"So much justice," I said, holding his gaze with mine. "So many dead, for the sake of those taken from you. So much blood, and suffering, in payment for the loss of your family. You killed the joy-riders responsible. Did that make you feel any better?"

"Yes," he said. "Oh yes."

"Really?" I said. "Then why are you still walking back and forth in the world, punishing the guilty? How many deaths will it take, before you can say *enough*? How much more of this . . . before you become as bad as they are?"

"I'm not like them. I don't kill for the pleasure of it, or the profit in it. I only kill those who need killing. When law fails, and justice has become a joke, there is always the Walking Man."

"You see any justice in this?" I said. "This isn't about justice, and you know it. You kill because that's all you can do. Because there's nothing else left in you. I've done my share of killing, in my time—to protect others, and yes, sometimes, to avenge injustice. But every killing, every death, eats away at you a little. Until there's nothing left but the gun and how good it feels when you use it. How long, Adrien, before you start to seek out your victims, like any other addict eager for his fix?

"Look at the people you're planning to kill here! Julien Advent, the greatest adventurer of his time, and this. Jessica Sorrow, who fought her way back from Unbelief to sanity. Larry Oblivion, who wouldn't let Death itself keep him from fighting the good fight. The others . . . are trying. Determined to put aside their past and make something better of themselves. And not just for themselves, but for everyone in the Nightside. Not by killing off everything that's bad, but by helping bring about real change, one step at a time."

The Walking Man nodded slowly. "I'm still going to kill them. Because it's all I can do."

I moved in even closer, and suddenly both his long-barrelled pistols were in his hands. I was so close now they pressed against my chest. I could feel both barrels, quite distinctly, through the cloth of my coat. I stood very still, my hands open and empty at my sides.

"I'm not going to fight you, Adrien. But I will stand here, weaponless and defenceless, blocking your way. If you strike me down, I'll just get up again. As many times as it takes. You're going to have to kill me, to get to my friends. To the people who matter more to the Nightside than I ever will."

"You're ready to die for them?" said the Walking Man. He sounded honestly curious.

"No-one's ever really ready to die," I said steadily. My mouth was dry, and my heart was hammering in my chest. "But I'm still going to do this. Because it's necessary. Because it matters. Are you ready to kill an unarmed man in cold blood, just because he's in your way? A man who's only trying to do the right thing?"

"Sure," said the Walking Man.

He raised one gun, and placed the barrel square against my forehead.

"One last chance, John."

"No," I said.

He pulled the trigger.

The sound of the hammer falling was the loudest thing I've ever heard, but the gun didn't fire. There were bullets in the chambers, I could see them, but the gun didn't fire. The Walking Man frowned and pulled the trigger again, and again, but still the pistol wouldn't fire. He tried the one pressed against my chest, and still nothing. I took a deep breath, stepped back a pace, and slapped both pistols out of the Walking Man's hands and punched him right in the mouth. He cried out and stumbled backwards, and sat down suddenly. He put his hand to his smashed mouth, and looked in shock at the blood on his fingers.

"You're only untouchable as long as you walk in Heaven's path, Adrien," I said, a bit breathlessly. "And you left that behind when you were ready to murder an innocent man."

"Innocent?" he said. "You?"

"For once, yes," I said. "Give it up, Adrien. It's over."

I offered him my hand, and after a moment he reached up to take it. I pulled him back up on to his feet, and steadied him as he got his balance. It had been a long time since he'd felt pain, and shock. He shook his head slowly.

"I've been doing this for so long," he said. "I just got tired. It was easier to act, than to think. Maybe . . . the world needs a new Walking Man. If I could be so wrong about this, I'm no longer fit for the job."

"Hey," I said. "No-one ever said you had to do this forever."

He nodded again, his eyes lost and far-away, and he turned and walked out of the Adventurers Club. No-one felt like going after him. Chandra Singh moved in beside me.

"That . . . was something to see, John Taylor. Did you know he wouldn't be able to kill you?"

"Of course," I lied.

EPILOGUE

Sometime later, upstairs at the Adventurers Club:

The Club's kitchens had put together a superb buffet at short notice, and the new Authorities were all making healthy inroads into the piles of food and drink, in celebration of the fact that they weren't going to die, after all. Julien Advent was already on his second bottle of pink champagne and was rattling the rafters with an enthusiastic rendition of an old Victorian drinking song, "Dr. Jekyll's Locum." An altogether filthy song, but then the Victorians did like their filth, on the quiet. Jessica Sorrow had discovered a wholly splendid dessert, made up of white chocolate mousse layered over milk chocolate mousse layered over a dark chocolate truffle base.

With cream. Every now and again, when she thought no-one was looking, Jessica would allow herself a small mouthful.

Count Video and Annie Abattoir had made complete fools of themselves over the cooked meats, and were now performing a tango up and down the middle of the room, complete with twirls and dips. King of Skin had put together a surprisingly healthy salad for himself, while drinking messily from a tall glass of snake-bite. (A terrible drink made up of vodka, brandy, cider, and cranberries. And other things. Drink enough of it and you can puke fruit and piss petrol.) Larry Oblivion, being dead, didn't need to eat or drink, but the Club's chef had prepared a special delicacy for him that he swore always went down well with the Club's other mortally challenged members. I don't know what it was, but it smelled *awful*, and it moved about on the plate. Larry seemed to enjoy it.

Walker and I were there, too, probably because neither of us have ever been able to refuse an offer of free food and drink. Chandra Singh declined. He said he had a duty to return home to India, to see what could be done for his broken sword, but I think he'd simply had enough of the Nightside.

I made a point of sampling a little bit of everything, just in the name of research and broadening my horizons. The Club's chef had a spectacular reputation. Walker, on the other hand, didn't touch a thing. Which was unlike him. I studied him thoughtfully as he stood alone on the other side of the room, peering out the only window, lost in his own thoughts. He was holding a folded handkerchief to his nose, which still hadn't stopped bleeding. I found that worrying. The Walking Man hadn't hit him that hard.

Julien Advent wandered over to join me, biting great chunks out of a huge steak and stilton pasty with his perfect Victorian teeth. He clapped me on the shoulder with more than usual good fellowship.

"You did well, John. I'm really quite proud of you. Imagine my surprise."

"You're welcome," I said dryly. "You will remember to put your name and address on the back of the cheque, won't you?"

"You're not fooling me, John. This wasn't only for the money."

I decided to change the subject and nodded at Walker. "What's up there? Walker's always had the constitution of an ox, and the stubbornness to go with it."

A lot of the good humour went out of Julian. I could actually see it slipping away. He looked at Walker, then at me.

"He hasn't told you, has he?"

"What?" I said. "Told me what?"

"It isn't public knowledge yet," said Julien. "And won't be, for some time. Not until things are ... settled."

"Tell me," I said. "You know I need to know things like this."

"I'm sure he would have got round to telling you. When he thought the time was right."

"Julien!"

"He's dying," said Julien.

It was like being hit in the guts. I actually felt a chill in my heart. I looked across at Walker, still dabbing carefully at his blood-caked nostrils with his blood-stained handkerchief. He looked healthy enough. He couldn't be dying. Not

Walker. But it never once occurred to me to doubt Julien's word. He was never wrong about things like that.

I couldn't imagine the Nightside without Walker. Couldn't imagine my life without Walker. He'd always been there, for as long as I could remember. Usually in the background, pulling strings and moving people around on his own private chessboard. Sometimes my enemy and sometimes my friend...When I was young, and my father was too busy drinking himself to death to have any time for me, it was Uncle Henry and Uncle Mark who were there to take care of things. Walker and the Collector. Perhaps the greatest authority figure and the greatest rogue the Nightside ever produced.

Walker. Who ran the Nightside, inasmuch as anyone did, or could. I'd worked for him, and against him, defied and defended him, according to which case I was working on. He'd threatened my life and saved it, for his own reasons. It seemed to me then that much of the time, I defined my life by how much it would affect his.

What would I do, when he was gone?

"How can he be dying?" I said. "He's...protected. Everyone knows that. Did somebody finally get to him?"

"No," said Julien. "There's no villain to pursue here, no crime to avenge. It isn't a voodoo curse, or an alien weapon, or some old case come back to haunt him. Just a rare and very severe blood disorder. Runs in the family, apparently. He lost his grandfather, his father, and an uncle to it, at much the same age he is now."

"But...this is the Nightside!" I said. "There must be something someone can do."

"He's tried most of them," said Julien. "But some things...must run their course. I suppose there is still hope. Miracles do happen in the Nightside. But you shouldn't put too much hope in that, John. He doesn't. We all die from something."

"But...if he isn't going to represent the new Authorities, who is? Who else is there, who can hold things together the way he has?"

"Ah," said Julien. "That's the question, isn't it?"

He clapped me on the shoulder again and moved away to talk with Jessica. Who was actually almost half-way through her dessert. People can change. I looked over at Walker again. Much had suddenly become clear. I knew now why Walker had found it necessary to visit my house for the first time and call me son. When a man is facing his end, the first thing he thinks of is family, and who will carry on the family business. Walker turned suddenly, and caught me staring at him. He regarded me thoughtfully, dabbed at his nose one last time, folded the blood-stained handkerchief into a neat square, and tucked it back into his top pocket, then nodded for me to come over and join him.

I did so, carefully not allowing myself to be hurried, and stood beside him at the window. He stuck out his hand to me. I went to shake it, and he shook his head.

"The rings, John," he said, firmly.

"Rings?" I said, innocently. "What rings?"

"The alien power rings you took off Bulldog Hammond earlier tonight, here at the Club. You know I can't allow you to keep them."

I dug into my coat pockets and handed them over. He counted the rings carefully, then made them vanish somewhere about his person. I wasn't too upset. It wasn't like I had a clue how to work the damned things.

"I was rather hoping you'd forgotten about them," I said.

"I never forget anything that matters," said Walker. "Julien . . . told you, didn't he?"

"Yes."

"I swear, that man never could keep a secret."

"I don't think he believes in them," I said. "That's why he runs a newspaper, so he can tell people things he thinks they ought to know. When were you going to tell me?"

"Eventually," he said. "I was working up to it. I didn't want to muddy the waters, not when there were still so many things we needed to work out between us."

"This is why you're not a part of the new Authorities," I said, the penny suddenly dropping.

"They don't need me," said Walker. "In fact, as a new force in the Nightside, they're better off operating without an outsider like me. They need to start with a completely clean slate, not having to be committed or supportive of any decision or action I might have taken in the past. They need to be their own people now. Of course, I still have a lot to do, while I'm still able to do it."

"And when you're not?" I said.

He looked at me steadily, then smiled unexpectedly. "I thought you might like to take over, John."

"Me?" I was honestly shocked. "You know how much I've always hated authority figures!"

"The best man for my job is the man who doesn't want it," Walker said easily. "The man least likely to be corrupted by power is the man who never wanted it in the first place. And besides, doesn't every father want his son to follow in his footsteps?"

"Don't start that again," I said. "Look, there has to be someone in the Nightside better qualified than me..."

"Almost certainly," said Walker. "But who else do I know as well as I know you, John? Who else could I trust as much as I have learned to trust you?"

"Give me a minute, and I'll make you a list," I said. "Walker... Henry, there must be somebody who can help you."

"No," said Walker. "There isn't. I've looked. In all the places you can think of, and a few that would never even occur to you."

"What about the Street of the Gods? There are Beings there who raise the dead and heal the sick every day of the week, and run special matinees for the tourists!"

"Not in any useful way," said Walker. "There are... possibilities, I admit, but they all involve paying a price I find unacceptable." He looked at me thoughtfully. "You did well today, John. The Walking Man really might have killed you."

"Yes," I said. "He might have."

"I wonder," said Walker. "Would he really have been able to kill the new Authorities if he had been able to get to them? Or would his God's power have failed him at the last moment, as it did with you?"

"We'll never know now," I said. "And I have to wonder just who was being tested here today?"

"All of us, probably," said Walker. He paused for a moment, looking around the room at nothing in particular. "I enjoyed meeting your father again, during the Lilith War, even if only for a short while. Helped me to remember who he and I used to be, all the things we meant to do, before life got in the way . . . I don't think he would have approved of the man I've become. But I know he was proud of you."

He turned abruptly and walked away, heading for the buffet. I didn't go after him. I had a lot to think about. The trouble with Walker . . . was that anything could be one of his schemes. He wasn't above using even a truth like this to manipulate me for his own ends. Julien came over to join me.

"I'm pretty sure I know what that was about," he said.

"Pretty sure you don't," I said.

"He wants you to take over his role in the Nightside. Not a bad idea, actually. I may not always have approved of the way you do things, but I've never doubted your heart is in the right place. But consider this, instead. What if I were to offer you a place in the new Authorities?"

"People are lining up today to offer me things I don't want," I said. "Thank you, Julien, but no. My job is to look out for the people the Authorities can't or won't help. To be there for people the system has failed. But I will . . . hang around. Work with you, when I can. Be your conscience, when necessary."

Julien sighed. "You always have to do it your own way, don't you?"

"Of course."

"I'll talk to the others."

"You do that," I said. "Preferably when I'm a safe distance away."

We shook hands, very solemnly, and he walked off again.

The door slammed open, and Suzie Shooter strode into the room. Everybody stopped what they were doing to look, holding themselves very still. Suzie glared at them all impartially, then dismissed them all with a sniff, to join me. Everyone else went back to their food and drink with a certain amount of relief, like a group of animals who'd just been joined at the watering hole by a well-known predator. Suzie nodded calmly to me, and her bandoliers of bullets clinked softly.

I've always liked the soft, creaking sounds her leathers make.

"You've missed all the excitement, Suzie," I said. "Not like you."

"I've been busy," she said, in her usual cold, measured tones. "Looking after the abused children we rescued from Precious Memories. Making sure they got all the help they needed, arranging for them to get safely home again. Or seeing they had somewhere safe to go, if that wasn't going to be possible. And then . . . I stayed on anyway. Just being with the children, comforting them. They wouldn't let anyone else touch them, at first. They'd learned not to trust anyone. But . . . they could accept it, from me. I suppose we can always recognise our own kind." She smiled, briefly. "I held them, and they held me. And I wonder . . . who was comforting who?"

"Suzie . . ."

"Hush," she said. "Hush, John. My love."

She put her arms around me and hugged me close. It was a careful, gentle hug, but unmistakably the real thing. For the first time since I'd known her, Suzie didn't have to force herself to touch me. I held her back, carefully, gently, and her breathing in my ear was slow and easy and content.

Miracles do happen, in the Nightside.